# SLEEPING WITH THE BEAST

## CONNER KRESSLEY
## REBECCA HAMILTON

EVERSCORCH

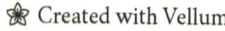

# CHAPTER 1

*I*t wasn't supposed to be like this. When Abram offered to take me to Grimoult—an island off the coast of Greece—it was supposed be a vacation. But after that first body jumped from a cliff and fell dead at our feet, Satina told us our vacation had turned into some sort of mission.

We had been through so much already, what with magic monsters and undead Conduits to deal with, and the idea of soaking up the sun with my brand new boyfriend seemed like just the balm I needed to feel like myself again.

Whatever that meant.

After all, I'd only recently learned I was a Supplicant and that my body was the key to unlocking magic throughout the world. Sometimes magic that would be used for nefarious purpose, but still. This was supposed to be our time. Time to connect with each other without the threat of almost dying constantly looming over us.

Too bad the dead bodies falling from the sky had to go and ruin that.

Abram banged against the castle's old wooden door. Its

knocker—a steel dragon with its mouth open menacingly—swung back and forth as Abram's fist collided with the wood.

"Are you sure this is the right place?" I asked, settling next to him and shaking my head. "We've been at this for several minutes now. I think it's safe to say no one's home."

Which wouldn't have surprised me. This wasn't some restaurant or gift shop. It wasn't even a house. It was a giant freaking castle. Old, hulking, and sitting atop a plateau of sorts. We had just watched some poor sap throw himself off the cliff opposite this one, with the words 'She Sleeps' carved into his forehead, and now we'd hiked up this twin cliff in hopes of finding...what, exactly?

Not the best start to a vacation by anyone's definition.

Naturally, I assumed the castle was empty—a forgotten relic of a time long past, like Blockbuster Video or hoop earrings. But when Satina gave us this address and told us to come here to find answers, Abram informed me Grimoult not only still had a royal family, but it was one of the last countries in the world to actually give power to the inbred idiots.

Backward thinking was always so charming.

"Someone is here." Abram huffed, still pounding. "I've been to enough castles to know that you never leave one completely empty. My guess is that they're watching us, trying to figure out what it is we're doing here."

"And what *are* we doing here, besides wasting prime sunbathing time? I bought a skimpy little two-piece that's getting awful lonely in my suitcase," I said, batting my eyelashes.

He stopped pounding on the door, no doubt to ponder the mental image I had just given him...which, you know, was the whole point.

"As tempting as that sounds, you heard Satina. We have work to do."

"All work and no play makes Jack a dull boy."

2

Abram turned toward me, his face twisting up. "Your friend's son Jack?"

"What?" I asked, then I remembered Abram was older than sand and probably hadn't seen or read The Shining, as modern as he liked to pretend he was. "Never mind. I just meant all we do is work. We never have any fun."

"That's not how I remember it," he said, his voice dropping seductively. "But I'm afraid you'll need to learn some patience, Ms. Bellamy."

A blush ran up my cheeks, remembering all the 'fun' we'd had back in New Haven. It had been something to write home about, assuming your home was Penthouse magazine. I had hoped for an encore of that here.

Okay, so maybe I had hoped for *ten* encores interrupted only long enough to reapply sunscreen and down what Travel Magazine called "the most sinfully delicious piña coladas in the world."

Though, looking around, it seemed unlikely anything could grow here, let alone the ingredients for fresh tropical concoctions.

"Everything's dead around here," I said, looking at the scorched earth and brown grass. "It's depressing."

"They've had a monumental drought," Abram said, his knocking back in full swing. "I read about it on that thing you showed me."

"The internet?"

He turned to me. "Yes, that. And I won three MVP players, and a member of the Nigerian royal family would like to send me ten million dollars in exchange for my socialite number, but I couldn't find one on your device."

"Just stick to Google, Slick," I answered, smiling. *MVP players. Socialite number.* I giggled inwardly, but the amusement was replaced by a strange thought worming its way into my mind. "Wait. Why would you take me somewhere that you knew was going through a drought?"

Before he could answer, the large wooden door creaked as the handle turned. We both stepped back instinctively.

"Oh, God," I murmured, realizing I was about to be met with royalty and we didn't have even the smallest glimmer of a plan. "What are you gonna tell them?" I whispered. "That people are falling from the sky and we're here to investigate? You'd need a Mystery Machine and a bright orange ascot if you wanted to make that plausible."

"I'm going to assume that's one of your pop culture references. In the future, you should be aware that I sort of pulled out of public life after the 1920s and didn't reemerge until right before I met your father." He raked his fingers through his hair before adding, "And of course I'm going to say something much more believable."

"Such as?" I asked as the door swung the rest of the way open.

Abram straightened his stance. "I have no idea."

# CHAPTER 2

*I* wasn't sure why I expected to see an old-timey knight, complete with a suit of armor and glistening sword, standing on the other side of the door. Maybe all the movies my mother force-fed me in my formative years were finally catching up to me. But, when the door finally did part, the person I saw didn't fit that bill at all.

He was tall and sleek, dressed in a black suit with a gun on his hip. He looked more like Secret Service than someone you would expect to find roaming the halls of a castle.

"State your business," he said in an accent that landed on the rough end of German and Russian.

"We're here to see the king," Abram answered, standing as straight and broad as a statue.

"Tourists," the man at the door muttered disgustedly. "The king has matters of great importance to attend to. He hasn't time to greet every person who visits our island." He started to close the door. "Though rest assured, he appreciates your patronage."

Abram's hand slammed against the wood, stopping the door in its tracks. The guard's eyes went wide enough that I could imagine he was thinking of going for his gun.

"Would that change if His Majesty knew that royalty was at his gates?"

The guard leaned forward, inspecting us. The door moved back open, though just a little.

"You?" he asked, eyeing our flip flops and beachwear. "You are royalty?"

"I'm Prince Anton Serval of the island nation of Backus," Abram answered, taking on an accent that sounded almost identical to that of the guard.

When I giggled, Abram shot me a look that said I needed to take this more seriously. But royalty? And an entire island nation? Since he was undoubtedly pulling all of this out of that wonderfully sculpted ass of his, part of me was more than a little impressed with the improv skills.

"I'm afraid we'll need a little more than an announcement," the guard said, narrowing his eyes.

"I would be happy to accommodate. However, I think your king will be rather cross with you if he learns this is how you have greeted his royal guests," Abram said, suddenly looking as regal as man in beachwear could as he crossed his arms over his chest. "I'm sure he'll be anxious to give us a proper greeting."

"Very well," the guard said, and then the door slammed shut.

I spun toward Abram, my head so hot I thought my ears might be on fire. "How the hell are you going to get us out of this?"

"Careful. That's no way to speak to your king," he answered, a devilish grin flickering across his face.

"Now who needs to be more serious?" I asked him, jutting my hip to my side as I crossed my arms. "Honestly, Abram, how are you going to convince some backwater king that you own an island you just made up?"

"I didn't make it up." He broke eye contact and pinned his attention straight ahead. "Backus exists, or at least it used to. Historically, Backus feuded with Grimoult for centuries, fighting over lands and trade routes—the kind of thing that hardly seems to matter anymore. It was absorbed into Greece over a hundred years ago. But my guess is that the prospect of its return will be enough to at least get us an audience with...what did he say the king's name was?"

"Dumbass?" I muttered, turning away from him to stare at the door.

"Not a fan of royalty?" he asked, brushing his hand across my cheekbone to sweep away a loose tendril of hair. I wasn't going to let him charm his way out of this one, though.

"It all seems very outdated to me. One group of people thinking they have the right to tell everyone else how to live just because they happened to be born with a silver spoon up their butt. This isn't the dark ages."

"It is a bit old fashioned," Abram conceded. "But then again, so am I."

"Well, there's good-old and bad-old," I answered, looking him up and down.

I loved the sight of him, of the way everything he wore seemed custom made to fit around his biceps, the curve of his smile so beautiful that it had to be rare. And his heart, the one I knew beat in tandem with my own.

He was definitely good-old. Even if he didn't know who Scooby Doo was.

The door opened once more. This time, the guard had company—two more similarly dressed men, each with guns at their hips.

"Follow me, Your Highness," he said to Abram. "The king eagerly awaits to...take you in."

Abram extended his arm, and I took it as we proceeded into the castle like the beach bum rulers we were pretending to be.

The interior of the castle didn't do much to sate the seven-year-old Disney princess enthusiast I used to be. The castles in those movies were bright, vibrant, and colorful. This place was dark. The walls were dingy gray stone, and the windows were shrouded with black curtains. The only light, which was few and far between, came from single bulbs that sat in lantern-like holders on either wall.

"God, it's like a vampire lives here," I whispered to Abram, noticing the lack of sun.

"Let's hope not," he answered.

"Shut up." I jabbed him in the stomach. "I know there's no such thing as vampires."

"Right, of course, because magic does not exist."

"Be serious."

He raised his eyebrows at me.

"Abram, tell me there's no such thing as vampires right this instant!"

"Whatever you say," he answered quietly, grinning.

I rolled my eyes. "You're such a dick."

There was definitely no such thing as vampires. How completely ridiculous. Now was not the time for his goading. I refused to think about it for even a second longer.

We moved out of a long hallway into a huge foyer that housed a lit fireplace, a blood-red couch with matching chair, and an old painting of a bald man with a beard and a wine glass and not much else.

The guards gathered at the far end as we settled into the room.

"Make yourselves at home," the first guard said. "The king will be in to see you shortly."

Shooting us a less-than-stellar look, the three exited the room, closing a mammoth black door behind them.

"And this is where we die," I said as the door slammed closed.

"Hardly," Abram answered absentmindedly, already pacing the room. "We should use this time to look around. Whatever clue Satina alluded to might be here. For all we know, it could be in plain sight."

Although in some ways Satina had helped us, the truth was, she really pissed me off, even when she wasn't around. Knowing her, she was probably ecstatic for the chance to barge in on our 'us' time.

But as much as I hated to admit it, her intrusion hadn't been without good cause. I could still see it every time I closed my eyes —the way that poor man crashed into the ground and the strange words that were etched in his forehead.

*She Sleeps.*

Yes, she'd interrupted our vacation, and yes, she had a good reason to do so. But was it really my responsibility to solve this mystery? Selfish as it might sound, I didn't want this. I didn't ask to be followed halfway around the world by whatever magical bad luck seemed intent on drilling its way into me. All I wanted was a vacation with my boyfriend. And dammit, why shouldn't I have that?

"I don't like this," I said flatly.

"Neither do I. It feels a little rushed," Abram said, picking up the end of the couch with one hand to look underneath. "But if we can manage to gain the king's trust, then we'll have more time to investigate."

I sighed. "Not that. This was supposed to be *our* time, Abram," I said, hating how whiny I sounded but determined for my feelings to be heard. "We've already been through hell. Or have you forgotten that? All I wanted was a few days to unwind before we decided what our life together was going to look like." I raised my hands as if to surrender. "Is this it? Is this what our life is going to be? People falling out of the sky? A dead Conduit telling us what to do? This isn't what I want my life to look like, Abram. This isn't what I want *us* to look like."

He set down the couch carefully and moved toward me. His dark eyes bore into me the way they always did, drawing out the deepest of my emotions and laying them plain on my face.

Once at me, he swept the hair out of my face with his thumb and forefinger. My skin lit at his touch, and sparks flittered across my face. If life could just be this—he and I and this touch always and forever—that would be glorious. That was what it should be. That was what we had earned.

"I'm sorry this happened. I'm sorry all of it happened. I know what we went through was difficult, and I don't blame you if you need time to heal."

I pulled away from him. "This isn't about what happened in the past. This is about our future. And I don't want our future to revolve around some makeshift magical detective agency. We deserve more than that."

The look on his face darkened. "One of us does."

"Don't do that. You're not the person you used to be," I said, taking his hand.

"But those sins still exist," he said. "And they must be made right. I have so much to atone for, Charisse, and like it or not, Satina was channeling something when she told you that your story wasn't finished. You obviously play an important role in something that's bigger than either of us, and I think the reason I'm here is to help you do it."

"I thought you were here to love me," I said softly, my eyes filling up.

"Always and forever," he said, brushing my cheek with his lips. "But we have work to do, you and I. And this is where it has to happen."

"Fine." I sighed, half because I knew he was right and half because the sensation of his lips against my skin was enough to give me a pleasant shudder. "But after this, we're going to Cozumel."

He smiled against my neck. "Yes, ma'am."

A trumpet—a literal trumpet—blared. Abram pulled away from me as the far door opened.

Two dozen or more Guards funneled in. They made a pair of perfect lines leading up to our feet and, between them—striding toward us—was a short stocky man who bore more than a passing resemblance to the wine-guzzling buffoon in the painting.

A sickly grin split his pudgy face as he approached. When he reached us, he held his hand out and shook Abram's hand. I held mine out, too. The king ignored me. I scoffed, but Abram's glare told me now wasn't the time to rip into the royal bastard.

"It's a pleasure to meet you," the king said. "But unfortunately, there's a bit of a problem."

"What might that be?" Abram asked evenly, but I could feel his energy shift from confident to concerned.

The king tilted up his chin, but he would have a hard time looking down his nose at either of us. I had been a model for Christ's sake, and Abram was even taller than me.

"The problem," the king cut out, glaring at the both of us, "is that I have an extremely low tolerance for liars."

# CHAPTER 3

*A*bram gave a small bow to the king. "It seems, then, that we already have something in common," he said lightly. "I cannot tolerate lies myself."

The king sighed and signaled with his hand. One of the guards pulled up a throne-like chair behind him. It was large, golden, and as ostentatious as one would expect from a pint-sized man who fancied himself a king.

He sat and indicated the sofa for us to join him. "Well, then, why don't you tell me what truths you have come here for."

"To be honest, Your Majesty, I was rather stunned by the reception. My family gave the impression you were expecting my arrival." Abram's tone remained even, and his fake accent never wavered. I was a bit unnerved by how gracefully he lied. "Did you not receive word from them?"

If this formality kept up much longer, I was going to puke.

The king rubbed the side of his face, frowning. "I received no such notice. And if I had, I would have written them back and told them not to bother sending you."

I placed my hand on Abram's forearm and leveled my gaze at the pudgy royal person. "I'm sure if you would hear him out—"

The king slapped the arm of his chair, and his eyes bulged as he looked from me to Abram. Abram glared at me, and I closed my mouth, too weirded out by everyone's reaction to be angry.

"I most certainly will *not* hear him out," the king said, his face growing redder with each word. "Backus!" He shook his head. "The nerve!"

Abram steeled his gaze, and I could feel the undercurrent of angry energy buzzing beneath his skin. He was growing more than a little irritated with the king's tantrum. If this didn't end quickly, I was afraid my monster man was going to start growling.

"Backus," Abram said with a forced calm, "is reinstating. And we were hoping," he ground out, "to form an alliance with you."

The king laughed bitterly. Then he stopped suddenly and scowled at Abram. "Last I checked, your kingdom folded out of hope we wouldn't take you out ourselves. Perhaps your family has hoped for enough."

Abram held steady. "I meant no disrespect, Your Highness. You have my deepest apologies. I shall inform my parents you are not interested in accepting our gift in exchange for an alliance with your kingdom."

As he rose, he pulled me to my feet by my arm to stand beside him and started to guide me toward the exit. I wanted to ask him what he was doing, but no one had listened to a word I had to say since I got here. And I wouldn't dare let them hear what I wanted to say to Abram right now anyway. Namely, "Why the hell did you waste my morning just to give up halfway through your glorious yarn of shit?"

If being here was so important, how were we going to get back in once we left? Abram had already played the most outlandish card in his deck.

He pulled hard, not even looking at me as we passed the guards and neared the exit.

But before we made it to the door, the king stopped us. Or rather one of his guards stopped us, which I could only assume meant the king made another wave of his arm or something, as that seemed to make up for about half the guy's communication skills.

"Prince Anton," the king said in a sing-song voice. "Before you go—I would love to hear about this gift. Assuming you really did have something to offer."

Abram froze, his gaze sliding over to me and lingering for a long and almost worrisome moment before he turned around. He smiled brightly. "My parents have set aside a large sum of money as a peace offering, and in exchange for our welcome to keep a summer home on your island."

The king gestured to the great room around him. "Do I look as though I need your money, boy?"

I held back a laugh. This "boy" was over a century old.

"I'll thank you not to call me 'boy,' your Majesty," Abram said through clenched teeth. "Regardless of whether or not you've come to believe my statements, I am of royal blood. Just like you. And I'm afraid my father would have me strung up if I allowed anyone, the king of Grimoult included, to speak to me in such a manner."

They stared at each other like two men getting ready to pull pistols in one of those spaghetti Westerns. But which one would crack first?

"The gift is meaningless. I have all the riches any man could need," the king said finally, leaning forward in his throne.

"I wasn't finished," Abram said quickly. Too quickly, though, because it made the pause that followed more noticeable. Finally, he continued with, "They would also like to offer you unadulterated access to the finest women of our land."

I choked on the air, but Abram squeezed my arm tighter, his sudden firm grasp a clear warning.

The king rubbed his tongue along his teeth. His gaze shifted from Abram to me, then back again. "How about her?"

Oh great. *Now* they took notice of me.

Abram gave a hearty laugh, as though the two had shared some fantastic joke with a punch line I wasn't privy to. "Oh, come now, Your Majesty. She was a gift to me, and surely you would like to have your choice from a wider selection."

The king nodded slowly, and his fingertips tapped the arm of his chair. "You know, that was the only thing your Godforsaken kingdom was ever good for," he said, though he sounded a little less hateful now than he had minutes ago. "Our island is small, and unfortunately, so are the women it births. This one," he said, waving his hand toward me, "is full and vibrant. She's got life in her bones, along with a titillating amount of meat. Besides, we aren't the tourist trap we used to be, and in today's age, it's rare we get the gift of a human life."

*There's a reason for that, jackass.* I had to bite my lip to keep that sentiment a thought instead of a spoken reprimand.

"But I still think I would like to sample the spoils of your country," he said, his gaze crawling over my body like a thousand tiny spiders.

I elbowed Abram, but all that earned me was another glare.

Abram patted my arm as though he was pacifying a child, then addressed the king again. "Your Majesty, I insist you allow me to arrange for a proper selection for you. I would hate for you to judge the women of our country based on *her*. She was only gifted to me recently, and I'm afraid her manners are rather...unforgivable."

The king narrowed his eyes at Abram, then cleared his throat. "I see that."

Silence stretched between the two men for longer than I thought I could handle. I just wanted to get out of here. Away from that man. Away from this screwy situation.

"Well," the king continued, "I'm sure we can make some sort of arrangement while we sort out the details."

"Wonderful," Abram said with a bow. "We'll stop by again

tomorrow morning, after you've had the evening to think about our offer."

The king pushed up out of his chair and shook his head. "No, no, that won't do. We can't have our royal guests shacked up in some tourist hotel on the island."

Oh, no. That was where I drew the line. We were not going to stay here with this creep!

"That really won't be necessary," I said as sweetly as possible.

The king's face split with a grin that reminded me of the Cheshire Cat. "Oh, you delicious little trumpet, I insist."

"Thank you," Abram said, before I could get another word out.

I couldn't be sure, but I think he was more agitated with me than with King Jerkface.

A short few moments later, we were being escorted through a new set of doors and down another dungeon-like hallway. The guard who had greeted us at the door led the way, and two more guards followed behind, though thankfully they allowed us a little breathing room.

"*What the hell was that about?*" I hissed.

"I should ask you the same thing," Abram muttered.

"*Me?* You're the one selling off women as barter for allegiance with another kingdom."

One of the guards cleared his throat. "Is there a problem?"

"No," Abram said quickly. "I'll take care of it."

"*Take care of what?*" I demanded.

"You," he growled, and it didn't sound like he meant it in a good way. "Just please, stop talking until we get to the room."

Leave it to Abram to find a nice way to tell me to shut up.

Of course, that didn't mean I was going to listen.

"Sure, tell the woman to shut up. Who cares what she thinks?"

"Charisse, *please!*" he whispered, and I decided to entertain his request for now, but only because the last thing I wanted to do was draw the king's attention again.

We reached the end of the hall, and the first guard swung open

17

a large wooden door leading into a bedroom that was at least six times the size of our hotel room.

"This will be your living quarters for the duration of your stay," the guard said, ushering us inside. I was beginning to wonder if the other guards were mute. "Please ring if you need anything."

He tugged on a string that hung just inside in the doorway, and a bell near the top of the doorframe jingled.

"I'll return later to collect you for dinner," he said, and with that, he closed the door.

"Collect us?" I asked. Then I scoffed. "Yeah, that sounds about right for this place."

Abram grabbed me firmly by either shoulder. "You need to stop playing around, Charisse. This is not New Haven, and it's certainly not New York. Their values are completely different from ours. Please follow my lead."

But I wasn't following anything—not at the moment. Because as I looked past Abram to the room beyond, I noticed this bedroom was meant for a little more than just sleeping in. Opposite the bed, in place of where one might normally find a TV, was a dresser with…well, I wouldn't even begin to know how to classify the things I saw on that dresser.

There was a paddle, a strap, and a riding crop I sensed wasn't for the horses out in their stables. On the other side of the dresser was rope, a glass object that a proper girl wouldn't even take a guess at, and a few things I assumed must be torture devices of some kind.

"Charisse?" Abram said, giving me a little shake. "I mean it. Everything I do is to protect you. I need you to trust me."

"Huh?" I said, shaking my head. I returned my attention to Abram and pointed to the table. "What the hell kind of room is this?"

Abram spun slowly, and his shoulders sank. "I was hoping for more of a chance to explain."

"Well, here's your chance," I said, narrowing my eyes. "You told me we were coming to ask a few questions...not to spend the evening in a room full of torture devices!"

Abram made a passing glance at the items on the table and shrugged. "You call them torture devices, but some may say they are more for pleasure."

I pointed at him. "Don't even start."

He raised both of his hands. "Calm down. Being invited to stay here is a good thing. It will give us the chance to—"

The door behind us made a loud clicking sound, and my heart crashed in my chest.

*Please, no.*

I ran to the door, praying the sound didn't mean what I thought it did and knowing my prayer would go unanswered.

I grabbed the knob and tried to turn it, but it didn't budge.

We were locked in.

I spun back toward Abram, a new fury lighting in my gut.

"Abram, I don't think we're guests," I said, gritting my teeth. "I think we're prisoners."

# CHAPTER 4

*W*hen I woke the next morning, I found Abram sitting up in the bed next to me. He wasn't under the covers, and he hadn't even removed his shoes, much less anything else.

"You've been up all night?" I asked, rubbing the sleep from my eyes.

"The door is still locked," he said, staring at it intently.

We had tried half the night to open that stupid thing, but it was no use. It was obvious the king didn't trust us and, judging from Abram's insomnia, he hadn't found much to trust about the king himself.

My stomach growled, reminding me of the guard's broken promise to collect for us dinner. *Asshat.*

"You could just, you know, break it down," I suggested, lying my head against his shoulder.

My eyes were tired and sore, and I didn't feel rested, which had nothing to do with the mattress in this room, as that was absolutely the most comfortable thing I had ever slept on.

Abram shook his head. "We don't know what they're up to. This could be more about their own safety than anything to do with us. Besides, in addition to outing ourselves as having something to be nervous about, breaking that door down would let them know how powerful we are. We don't need to tip our hand like that, not yet."

"You're using the term *we* loosely," I said, stretching.

I threw my blanket off and grabbed the shirt I came here in. As I threw it back on, I caught sight of those ridiculous contraptions on the nightstand, the stuff Abram suggested might not be for torture at all.

Fighting the urge to roll my eyes, I turned back to Abram and said, "I could try every minute for a month and never even put a dent in that door. You're the powerful one."

He ran a hand through his dark hair. "I don't have even a hundredth of the potential that you do. The fact that we're here— that Satina saw fit to send us to this place—is a testament to that."

"Really?" I asked, moving away from him. "So this is *my* fault? Is that what you're saying?"

He looked more than a little confused. His cheeks, dusted in a five o'clock shadow even though it was, at latest, ten in the morning, sunk in more than usual.

"Of course that's not what I'm saying. There is no fault in this. This is something that happened, that is happening." He stood, as if to get a bit of distance before he made the next statement. "Don't say it like this is a bad thing."

"We're trapped in a strange man's castle."

"Only because we choose to be," he countered.

His muscles, flexing in the mid-morning sun that streamed through the open drapes, seemed to make his point for him. Abram could rip through those guards like a warm knife through butter. If he so chose, we could be out of here and back on the beach in ten minutes.

"Great," I said. "Then why don't you do me a favor and go beast-mode on that door so we can get out of here?"

"I can't."

"Of course you can, Big Boy. Now hurry up before we miss all the good sunning hours."

"No," he said more slowly this time. "You don't understand, Charisse. There is no 'beast-mode' right now."

"I'm in no mood for games, Abram. You just said we're only here because we choose to be. Well, I choose not to be anymore, okay?"

"I meant that we chose to get ourselves here," he said, "but as it turns out...we can't choose to leave."

"Yes, we can," I said firmly, my heart-rate picking up in fear that Abram wasn't kidding. "Abram, please tell me we can leave."

"I didn't foresee this situation when we came here, but it seems there is some sort of enchantment on the castle. One that blocks magic. I didn't resist turning last night...I was unable to."

I rubbed my hands down the sides of my face. We'd been up half the night, but I thought he was just fighting off his true nature to keep me safe. Then I'd fallen asleep. Was it really possible?

"No. No, you have to be wrong," I said, but deep down, I knew Abram, and that meant this was neither a joke nor a lie. I dropped my hands to my sides. "This is terrible. What if they never let us leave?"

He slipped over to where I was sitting and moved my hands from my face. "Don't worry, my love. I don't think the enchantment was meant for us. Just something general to protect their estate."

"Not helping," I said, stepping away from him. "I really don't care who it's meant for. I don't like that we're stuck here!"

"Don't look at it that way," he said, pulling on his shirt that had been strewn over an ornate chair beside the bed. "We wouldn't be leaving now even if the door *could* open, right?"

I raised my eyebrows at him.

"We could do some real good here, Charisse. We just have to be patient."

I rose to meet him, bridging the gap between us to challenge him, despite being dressed in only my shirt and panties. "That's easy for you to say."

Abram stared down at me with that infuriating steady calm of his. "I'm not sure what you mean."

"You know damn well what it means," I said bitingly. "You're old, not stupid." I could feel all the blood rushing to my face as I thought about what happened yesterday. "That pig of a king, the way he looked at me, the stuff he said. And you just agreed. Hell, you basically offered me up on a silver platter!"

"I did no such thing," he growled. "This place has antiquated values, Charisse, and I assure you they aren't all bad. Second, I offered up women who don't even exist. This is a charade. You know that."

I scoffed. "First of all, antique is a word I reserve for furniture and clothing, not to excuse people who treat other people like objects. And second of all, there is nothing imaginary about me!"

Abram's nostril's flared. "I specifically told him that you weren't on the menu, that you belonged to me!"

I felt my eyes grow wider than those ugly mega earrings that were in fashion for about a week last year.

"Listen," Abram said, raising his hands slowly, clearly realizing he had misspoke.

"No!" I said. "Just stop. Do you hear yourself right now? Off the menu? I belong to you? Are you serious?" My teeth ground together. "*Please* tell me that isn't the way you really think of me."

"Of course it isn't," he said. But there was less atonement in his voice than I would have cared for. "I told you that I'm doing this because I have to."

"You *have* to?" I was angrier than I cared to admit, and I wasn't in the mood to try and shut myself down, not while I stood in the castle this macho bullshit mentality had built. "You *have* to treat me like piece of meat? You *have* to treat me like I don't matter? Like I'm some two dollar whore who jumped on your cock because I thought you were gonna make it worth my while? You *have* to do that?"

"I have to fit in," he said, and he sounded about as angry with me as I felt with him. "These people live in a different world, Charisse. Women aren't their equals here. And, though it might churn my stomach to think of it, they wouldn't respect a man who looked at a woman with anything more substantial than lust in his eyes." He moved closer to me, a sign of his intention to put an end to this disagreement. "This is a part that I'm playing, nothing more. I promise I won't let anyone lay a finger on you. And, if I'm being honest, I expected you would understand that. I had hoped you would know me better than this."

"Don't," I said, but my voice was softer than it had been before. "Don't pretend like this was something we discussed. And don't pretend I'm supposed to know everything about you. You lived for nearly two hundred years before we met. The world has changed a lot since you were a kid. How am I supposed to know what your values are? Maybe you think the same way King Archibald does. Maybe, deep in your heart, you don't see me as an equal, either."

He was at me now, his fingers grazing my palm.

"You know better than that," he said quietly. "You're hurt, and you're lashing out. But you know me, all of me. And you know better than that."

I exhaled loudly. "I do." He was right. Of course he was. I knew him, the true Abram that existed beneath the guise, beneath the beast. He loved me. He valued me. Not only did he see me as an equal, he saw me as his match. "It still hurts to hear you say those things."

"I know," he answered, brushing my lip with his thumb. "But I'm afraid you're going to have to bear with me. Not for much longer, and I'll do my best to keep the nonsense in check, but if we're going to stand a chance of putting a stop to this, I need us to remain where we are."

"All this because of one guy." I sighed. Of course it couldn't be a normal suicide. Oh, no. It just *had* to be something supernatural going on. Something to send Satina hurtling back into our lives and giving our vacation a new "purpose." I bet she was tickled by the whole thing.

"No," Abram said, pulling the phone I'd bought him from his pocket. "Not one."

He handed it to me, the screen displaying a web page that featured a news story with the headline: "Strange Happenings on Quaint Island."

"Fifteen people have died in the last two months," he said. "Every one of them have thrown themselves off the same cliff. Every one of them had the same strange words carved into their foreheads."

"She sleeps," I murmured.

"Seems fitting, doesn't it?"

I ripped my gaze away from the news article to look at him. "What do you mean?"

Abram cocked his head. "I told you last night." He sighed. "Were you mm-hmming me while falling asleep again?"

I couldn't help but roll my eyes. "If I was mm-hmming you, I was already asleep. So spit it out. What makes it fitting?"

"This castle." He shook his head, as though mesmerized by whatever he was about to say. "This is where it all happened, Charisse. The king you detest so much—he's the father of Sleeping Beauty."

# CHAPTER 5

"I think I just had a mini stroke or something," I said, shaking my head. "Because I could have sworn I just heard you say this douchebag king's daughter was actually—"

"Sleeping Beauty," Abram finished, nodding curtly as though he had just told me my chicken salad sandwich was ready or that there was a cardholder's sale at Saks Fifth Avenue.

Actually the last one would have required more oomph.

"Sleeping Beauty?" I asked, leaning forward. "Like the mythical princess Sleeping Beauty? You're not serious."

"When am I ever not serious?" he asked, arching his eyebrows.

The man had a point.

"But that's not possible. Sleeping Beauty is a fairytale." I didn't even realize I had stood until I was already pacing the room.

"So what?" he asked. "So am I."

The morning sun glinted off Abram's dark eyes, making them shine like discs of black water. Somewhere in the back of my mind, it occurred to me that I had wasted an entire night—maybe the only one I would ever get—when the man I loved would be a human.

He had his arms, his legs, his heart, and several other parts that

I had taken quite a liking to. He was himself all night long, and instead of savoring that—instead of pressing myself against him and relishing his form for the Renaissance masterpiece that it was —I had just slept there beside him, probably dreaming about shoes.

But I couldn't think about that now. Like it or not (and I absolutely did not like it) Abram had a point. Against my own personal objections, Satina sent us to the castle for a reason. Fifteen people had died, and we needed to figure out why. Even if that meant missing out on what was supposed to be the sexiest vacation of my life.

Abram moved toward the window, pulling open the drapes and letting the sun invade the room. "The fact is, most fairytales— most mythologies, really—have a kernel of truth to them. They originate from actual events and, because people have a tendency to either exaggerate or play down the truth, depending on the needs of the age, those stories are changed and twisted into what you now know as fairytales."

The view outside would have been spectacular if everything wasn't brown and dying, no doubt a side effect of the drought. Still, the ocean was crisp and blue, and the island was full of gorgeous hills, valleys, and plains. Abram cleared his throat as he pointed to a cliff in the distance.

"That's the original site of the Grimoult Royal family stronghold. For two centuries, the Navaars ruled from a stone castle that had once been on that cliff—that cliff people are now jumping to their death from."

"How do you know that?" I asked, settling beside him and looking out the window to where he was pointing. "Have you been to it?"

"No." He leaned on the windowsill, resting his forehead against the glass. "That castle has been gone for over five hundred years, long before my time. But I've met people who have been to it, people I trust, people whose word I take as fact. This island is where the story originated, and that castle is where the final battle took place."

"This is insane," I muttered, mostly to myself, watching the way the waves crested and fell against the rocks that made up the base of the former castle's cliff.

"You haven't heard the half of it, at least not half of the truth." Abram moved away from the window and, as always, my gaze followed him. No landscape could compete with him, no matter how beautiful it might be. "Jacob Navaar was king then. He's the man you saw in the painting yesterday, the balding one with wine in his hand." Abram's eyes glazed over. "There was peace then. He was a good king and a good ruler. He was also a good father. His daughter—her name has been butchered by history, so we'll call her Rose—was a beauty by any man's standard. She was the only child of a king, so even if she'd been a troll with bad breath and a penchant for breaking wind in bed, she would have still been a catch. But fate saw fit to give her beauty, brains, and a heart of gold. At least, that's what I'm told."

He ran a hand through his hair and sighed, as though he might be remembering someone or something. He did that a lot. Though, when you had lived for as long as Abram had, it only made sense that you would rack up connections.

I didn't press him on it.

"Her mother died suddenly after being thrown from a horse. King Jacob, wanting to give his daughter as normal and healthy a life as possible, decided to remarry. But it wasn't as commonplace back then for people to just move on."

A chill ran up me, as though there might have been more to that statement.

Abram continued, "King Jacob met a merchant's daughter from a far off land. The name also has been lost. To make a rather predictable story shorter, he fell in love with the woman and made her his wife, his queen. But the woman was a Conduit."

My entire body tensed up. God, I hated that word. Conduit.

"And Rose, to her detriment, was a Supplicant."

I might have actually hated that word more.

"The Conduit placed a powerful sleeping curse on Rose and, while she was deep in her slumber, the Conduit siphoned all the magic she could from the poor girl." Abram shook his head. "It went on like that for years. Day in and day out, the king would sit by his daughter's bedside, never knowing that it was his own wife who had perpetrated this against him. Stories began to pop up." He swallowed hard. "And the drought worsened every day Rose remained asleep."

"A drought?" I asked, moving forward. "There was drought here then, too?" My mind spun feverishly. My eyes narrowed as the realization laid itself in front of me. "You knew," I said. "You knew about the drought. You knew about the suicides. You knew about the words and the history. That's why you suggested this place, because you knew there was something going on here."

"Charisse," he started. "I didn't—"

I shook my head. "I'm not mad. I get it. We have to do what we have to do."

"But Charisse—"

"Just finish the story," I said softly. "People thought true love would break the curse." I took Abram in with my eyes, the look on his face and the solidness of his stance. "But something tells me you don't agree with that."

"Love doesn't solve everything, Ms. Bellamy. It's beautiful and vital and it makes life worth living. But it doesn't fix problems, not even in fairytales."

"So what did fix it?" I asked, a bit peeved by his statement. "I mean, we know she woke up. How?"

"I don't know," Abram admitted. "But if you consider the real Sleeping Beauty never married, I don't think the fairytale has that part right. My guess is Jacob found out what his wife was up to and made some sort of deal in exchange for his daughter's life... given his current state."

"Current?" I asked, brushing stray hair out of my eyes. "You mean the king here—"

"Archibald." Abram nodded. "Archibald Navaar, the current king of Grimoult, is thirty seven years old. At least that's what he tells the world. I found it in one of Grimoult's online newspaper archives."

"Kudos for cracking the internet." I stared at our hands as his fingers grazed my palm. "But I thought you said this king was Sleeping Beauty's father. That doesn't line up."

"When we were in the foyer, I studied that painting as closely as I studied the king. There was a purple, star-shaped mark on Jacob's right hand. I saw the same one on Archibald's hand."

"So?" I asked. "Birthmarks can run in families. Surely he's just an ancestor of Sleeping Beauty's father."

"That's not a birthmark." Abram let out a slow breath. "It's a branding, a Conduit's mark sometimes left on their victims to stake their claim. And my guess is that it's cursing him to a life without end."

"You think King Douchebag is five hundred years old?" I asked.

"At least," he answered.

"And you think he has a hand in what's going on here?"

"He either has something to do with what's going on, or he knows something more about it than we do," he said. "He has to. And it's probably why he's suspicious of us."

Abram's gaze moved past me, and his eyes widened. He rushed toward the window.

"Charisse," he said, pressed against the window.

"I see it," I said breathlessly.

In the distance, a dot stood on the cliff where the original castle used to sit. Whether it was a man or a woman, we were too far away to tell.

"Don't look," Abram said as the dot neared the edge.

"I have to," I said. "I need to see why we're doing this."

CONNER KRESSLEY & REBECCA HAMILTON

Abram took my hand and squeezed it. "We can't stop this one."

"But we'll stop the next one, right?" I asked, flinching as the person ran toward the edge and threw themselves off. I didn't take my eyes away. I watched that poor soul the whole way down. I needed to see. I needed to get the beach and vacations out of my mind. I needed to have no doubt that we were doing the right thing by being here. "Tell me we'll stop this, Abram."

"We will," he answered. "We'll stop it."

I looked over at him, fire and moisture burning through my eyes. "Then let's get to work."

# CHAPTER 6

*A*fter my declaration, the hours seemed to drag on endlessly. I wanted nothing more than to get this over with, to find whatever it was that Satina sent us here to find and put a stop to whatever King Archibald (or whoever was ultimately responsible) was up to before anyone else got hurt.

But the door was still locked and, as strange as it was to think, the magic surrounding this castle had rendered Abram completely human. As such, he was powerless to either free us from this makeshift prison or defend us from whatever might come.

What if the castle was having the same effect on me? Had my blood been neutralized, too? And, if so, was there any way I might be able to take this castle's curse with me when (or if) we left?

I sat by the window, watching that horrible cliff and praying no one else would hurl themselves off of it before we could get out of here. The sun hung low in the sky when the door finally swung open.

Abram stood, his body tensing as two guards entered. They were dressed in white, so that the pistols on their hips stood out even more brilliantly. Anywhere else on Earth, those pistols might as well have been water guns for Abram. But within these walls, they could spell his end.

I tried to shake off that thought as the taller of the guards spoke.

"The king has requested your company for dinner."

A third guard entered with a three piece suit in his hand.

"You are to wear this," the taller guard said, holding it out toward Abram. "And the king has asked what you would prefer your woman to be dressed in."

*Your woman?* He made it sound like I was a dog.

I balled my fists but, as if sensing my hostility, Abram placed a hand on my arm.

"She'll wear whatever is customary," he said flatly.

For a long moment, the guard looked at me, as if he had noticed more to my reaction than I had intended to share.

"I see," he said. And then he took his leave.

A few moments later, a short woman who seemed intent on not making eye contact with anyone came and handed me a lengthy blue dress that, while covering every inch of my body below the neck, hugged me like wet paint. Every curve was accentuated and put on display. I might as well have been naked for all it left to the imagination.

The sun had almost set outside now, stretching our shadows along the floor, and my heart bobbed in my stomach. I frowned at myself in the mirror and spoke to Abram over my shoulder.

"I suppose this is what is what is expected of 'your' woman," I said.

"Don't start," he said, struggling with his tie.

"How old are you? And you still can't work a bow tie." I shook my head, making my way to him.

I took the fabric and slung it over his neck. He smelled masculine, like pine and musk. But there was something else there—a sweetness that, even now, I couldn't put my finger on. It had been his scent that had driven me crazy the first time we hooked up.

Crashing together against the walls of the nightclub, I had breathed him in and could hardly hold myself together. It was that scent that made me want him then, and that same scent making me want him now.

"I tend to steer clear of this particular fashion choice," he said as I moved across the stubble that dotted his Adam's apple. "It always seemed juvenile to me."

I tied the bow and took a step back. "It's a classic."

"I suppose that depends on your perspective."

He was a vision, an Adonis who had no business looking twice at someone like me, much less being in love with her. But he was. He loved me, and knowing that somehow made my annoyance with our situation fade. Everything was better with him. I would do good to keep that in mind.

"And how is your perspective, Abram?" I asked coyly.

He gave me a long look, drinking me in with his gaze. "At the moment, it is unparalleled, Ms. Bellamy."

"You haven't called me that since we've arrived here." I smiled, taking his hand. "I've missed it."

The door flew open again. The taller guard was alone this time. Apparently they didn't see us as much of a threat anymore.

He gave Abram a curt nod. "You are to be seated for dinner immediately."

Without hesitation, Abram moved toward the doorway, though he dropped my hand as he did. I followed, reminding myself about the poor bastard now lying at the bottom of that cliff. Abram had to pretend to be some royal womanizer in order for us to ensure that sort of thing didn't happen again.

And I had to go along with it.

We swept through the hallway, and I didn't look around much this time. Whatever magical illusion this place held before had quickly vanished in the time I had been objectified, held captive, and treated like a second class citizen. When I was a little girl, I used to dream of meeting a prince and spending the night in a castle. Now that I had done both, I had no desire to repeat the process.

I would hold it together, but only because I had to.

Abram and the guard were a few feet in front of me when I heard the noise. It was a moan, as if a woman was in pain, coming from an open door on the left. Though a piece of me said it was a bad idea, I just couldn't walk by. If someone was being hurt, I needed to stop it.

I hesitated toward the open door as the moaning grew louder. The room I found myself looking in was large and carpeted in lush reds. A bed, huge and circular, sat in the middle. And on that bed, displayed like a trophy in a case, was a woman.

The breath caught in my throat. The woman lay flat on her back. Her hands were tied together and bound to the headboard. She was blonde and bare chested. Some kind of small metal... jeweled bobby-pin type things...clamped her nipples, and her breasts bounced as she arched her back, moaning again.

What I had once thought of as a painful exclamation, I now saw as an expression of ecstasy. Her body language suggested she was in fact writhing in pleasure, and much to my dismay, I couldn't take my eyes off of her.

This was disgusting. Certainly, it should be. This was chauvinism at its finest. Binding up a woman and leaving her there to writhe, sweaty and half-satisfied, door thrown wide open for anyone to see... It was insane.

But the look on her face left no doubt: She enjoyed this. She wanted this.

And something about that piqued my curiosity.

Her eyes met with mine, and I flinched away.

She laughed loudly, her body jiggling with the movement. "Don't be so shy," she said in a thick accent. "You should join us. We only bite if you're very bad. Have you been bad, girlie?"

A blush crept up my cheeks, and I turned tail, nearly stumbling as I raced after Abram and the guard. I thought I was going to trip on this damn dress, but I caught up with them before they even realized I had been gone. Apparently they hadn't noticed my short absence, much the way you might not notice an old lipstick you haven't worn in months was missing from you spare make-up case.

"The king will join you shortly," the guard said.

Tapping his heels together, he motioned for us to enter a large room with a giant oblong table. Then he left.

Abram moved forward, and I followed. I wanted to tell him about the woman, about the ties and the clamps, about the look on her face. But something stopped me. What would I say even? The fact I was still thinking about her was ludicrous. I had no ties to this woman and, no matter what that tingling in my stomach might imply, the whole thing left a bad taste in my mouth.

"Maybe we should look around," I said, my voice shaky. "You know, while we have the chance."

"Haven't seen enough?" he whispered huskily, turning to me and raising an eyebrow.

Heat flared in my cheeks, and I couldn't even look at him. "You saw?"

His hand snuck to mine just long enough to graze his finger along my pinky. "I saw your reaction," he whispered, then he dropped his hand away. "It was very *telling*."

I bristled, part of me wanting to deny whatever he thought he saw in my reaction, and part of me knowing Abram probably knew me better than I knew myself.

"What would you know?" I whispered back anyway.

Before he could reply, King Archibald's voice drifted into the room. "And what would you suggest I do about that?"

Abram shot me a look and then moved toward an air duct, the origin of the noise.

"Old castles don't hold many secrets," he whispered to me.

"Tell that to Sleeping Beauty," I muttered.

"Of course it's an issue, and of course I'm looking into it." King

Archibald stopped short. He must have been on the phone, because there were a few seconds of silence followed by a more fierce nature in his voice. "Months!" he yelled. "It has been months since it rained! Of course I know what that means!"

Another lull. Then: "I thought this was a done deal." ... "Yeah, well, it didn't work. Do you think I would still be here if it worked?" ... "Who do you think you're talking to? The crops are the least of our worries. Do you have any idea how long this could stretch?"

The following silence was dotted with furious huffs from the king. "Blame hardly matters at this point. Lay it at whoever's feet you wish. I paid you, and I certainly didn't make that agreement for fun. Fix it!"

Silence filled the air again and, as soon as we realized that signaled the king's call was done and he was on his way to his next arrangement—dinner with us—Abram and I darted back to the center of the room.

We settled there and acted nonchalant as King Douchebag entered the room. He looked equal parts angry and constipated as he took us in.

"I would apologize for your containment, but we would all see through that, wouldn't we?" He circled the table toward us. "It was a necessary precaution while my men took the time to verify your story."

Verify our story? The words sent chills down my overdressed spine. A quick Google search probably would have verified Abram wasn't Prince Made-up Name and that the island nation he claimed to come from hadn't sent us at all.

My body went rigid. King Archibald was about to accuse us of lying to him, of sneaking into his castle under false pretenses. Which, of course, we had done. What would be the "antiquated" punishment for that?

So long as we were trapped here, this castle's enchantment made Abram about as fierce as Snoopy on Sunday morning. We had no defense and, should they attack us, no chance of survival. They could throw us in a dungeon or, worse, slice off our heads. At least I wouldn't put it past them. This place seemed adequately mired in the Dark Ages to make that seem plausible.

My eyes slid to the dinner table. There were knives and forks sitting there, slightly out of reach. Sure, they wouldn't do much when the guards started pouring in, but nobody would be able to say Charisse Bellamy went down without a fight. And hell, maybe I would even get to show them what women were capable of while I was at it.

"And I take it everything checked out?" Abram asked from my side. His voice was steady and betrayed none of the nervousness he was likely feeling.

"You wouldn't believe how many people lie to us, try to pass themselves off as someone they aren't to gain access to our home and our lives. I don't have to tell you what becomes of people like that," King Archibald said. He was close to us now. My fingers were itching, and just as I was about to reach for the steak knife, he added, "It's a good thing you were telling the truth."

My entire face dropped.

"What's that now?" I mumbled.

The king shot me a look, as if to shut me up, then turned to Abram. "I apologize for whatever discomfort you might have felt last night. I'm sure you understand."

"Of course." Abram nodded, again free of emotion. He was good at this. Better than me, obviously. I needed to work on my poker face.

"As an act of contrition, I would be pleased to offer you another companion. Variety is, as they say, the spice of life." He gave me another look. "And I'm sure I can find some way to keep your current traveling partner occupied."

Bile rose into my throat, and my whole body tensed as I braced myself for Abram's reaction, my mind racing with thoughts so quickly I couldn't pick one from the next. This couldn't be happening.

"A generous offer," Abram said, "but it won't be necessary. At least, not tonight. I have my mind set on being the one to mold her into what I wish, and until she's properly trained, she won't be leaving my sight. She is, after all, my first gift. I'm sure you know how that goes."

The king grinned widely. "Ah, indeed I do. I was a young prince once, too, and I remember the days of my first as well. They are always the most challenging, but often the most rewarding. I'm sure you will teach her to serve well."

"Of course," Abram replied curtly. "And I've too much pride to share that challenge. Now, shall we eat? The business of contrition can certainly wait until our bellies have been filled."

King Archibald nodded. "Let us eat then."

Abram pulled out my chair, and I sat, my head spinning. How was this possible? What twist of fate had just saved us? Abram had pulled this alibi out of his ass. I watched him do it. How on Earth had King Archibald actually found confirmation of that ridiculous story?

My eye caught a shimmer in the far off drape. A woman's face —no, Satina's face—glittered in one of the folds. She winked, then faded into nothing.

"Of course," I mumbled.

There might have been a time where I would question why she couldn't find some other way to help us out—some way that didn't involve us being trapped here—but knowing Satina, our situation to her was some afterlife reality show. She probably only helped us to make things more interesting for her.

I turned to Abram to see if he had noticed what I had, but instead, I was met with the chest of a servant who was attending to the dinner.

"Your hands, Princess," the servant said.

I looked up at him, a bit stunned by the title, and he looked back at me equally stunned, but by what I didn't know.

"Place them behind your back, please," he said, then quickly he added in a low voice, "Mind your attention. No eye contact during dinner."

"Is there a problem?" King Archibald asked, pulling out of small talk with Abram to look at me.

The servant smiled thinly. "The Princess is nearly settled."

The King glared at me, and I was too confused to ask any questions. I placed my hands behind my back, and the servant deftly tied them together with what felt like a piece of silk or a satin ribbon of sorts.

What the hell kind of dinner custom was this? How was I supposed to eat?

I looked over to Abram, horrified, hoping for some kind of unspoken explanation.

But he didn't even look at me.

# CHAPTER 7

"Y ou'll have to excuse her," Abram said to the King. "To be honest, our kingdom no longer follows the dinner custom, and I have failed to prepare her on how to attend one as a guest."

He damn well better have failed to prepare me because he didn't know himself, or we were going to have it out later.

The king tilted up his chin ever-so-slightly. "This should be a good learning experience for her, then." He leaned a little over the table. "A word of advice, if I may. I find it best not to go easy on them in the beginning. They tend to spend the rest of their time in service trying to get that soft side out of you again."

Abram gave me a sideways glance. "I can see how that might happen," he said, sliding his attention back to the king. "I certainly appreciate the guidance of my elders, and will keep that in mind."

My stomach was doing flip flops, and not the kind I should be wearing on the beach right now. Abram was so convincing that I was starting to question if there was any truth to some of the things he was saying. Did he really feel this way, even if only a little?

As the servants carted in elegant trays of food, the king's attention was pulled from us to a woman who was presenting a bottle of wine. Abram pinched my thigh through my dress.

I spun my attention to him to give him a scowl, but his glare stopped me in my tracks. "The servant said no eye contact. You need to obey their rules."

I opened my mouth to speak, but he cut me off.

"No arguments. *Please*, Charisse." That last part sounded pleading, and for some reason, it was like a shot of fear had been injected into my veins. "Only speak when spoken to. If you aren't sure what to do, don't do anything."

I dropped my gaze to the table, noticing for the first time there was no plate in front of me. Desperately I wanted to look up again, to take in more details of my surrounding, but I could feel the king staring at me, and I sensed it best to take Abram's warning.

*He's on my side,* I reminded myself.

I could see out of the corner of my eye that Abram did have a plate, and one of the servants were, at present, ladling some kind of dingy gray soup into his bowl.

After a few bites, Abram placed a finger under my chin to lift my face. I kept my eyes toward the ground on the chairs between us.

"Good," he whispered, and I felt like a child being praised for coloring inside the lines. This was horrifying.

"Here, eat," he said gently. He fed me a small bite, and I immediately wished he hadn't.

Had the soup been made with old potatoes and something one might find at the bottom of a washing machine? I would have expected more from royalty. But I forced myself to swallow the bite and sent up a mental prayer that I wouldn't be offered anymore, or at least not of this dish.

I must have made a face after tasting it, because King Douchebag grumbled something.

"Is it not to your liking?" he asked coldly.

I almost didn't respond, thinking surely the question was rhetorical since the man almost never spoke to me, but then I remembered Abram's warning to speak when spoken to. Then and only then. But this was one of those times.

"It's wonderful," I lied.

"Typical," the king hissed, shaking his head. "A woman's palette is such a primitive thing. Wouldn't you agree, young prince?"

Abram shuffled in his seat. At least he seemed to be as uncomfortable by this situation as I was. Still, from under my eyelashes, I could see he smiled politely at the king.

"I have found that to be the case, unfortunately."

The king set his spoon down on the table beside his plate very neatly. Too neatly. It made my skin crawl how deliberately he did it, though I couldn't pinpoint why that bothered me so much until he spoke.

"Perhaps we'll just have to give her something that her mouth is more accustomed to receiving."

I felt myself tense and, though I knew I shouldn't, I began to raise from my chair.

Abram's hand found my bound wrists and grasped the satiny ribbon to keep me in place. Besides, what was I going to do? Walk away with my hands tied behind my back?

I took a long slow breath and reminded myself what we were doing here and how important it was for me to keep the charade going.

"She's a feisty little thing," King Archibald noted. "And my guard tells me she was less than receptive about the clothing she was provided." He stared at me again. "I must admit, I don't see why. It hugs her in all the right places. Please tell me she isn't the type of female who shies away from her natural attributes. Those types bore me so quickly, and I find they tend to overcompensate with strong opinions and overzealous values." He scoffed. "Who has the time for that?"

My blood started to boil. Sure, I had never been the type to carry picket signs and boycott establishments. Heck, most other women passed plenty enough judgment on me solely in regard to my career as a model. But I always believed a woman was every bit the equal of a man. In fact, one of the reasons I loved modeling was because I found it empowering, not because—as some believed—it was objectifying.

Women could do anything they set their minds to. We had proven so over and over again. And the fact that this dipshit had his head so far up his own ass that all he could see were tits and ass shouldn't have been my problem.

Besides which, if Abram was right—if this was the man in the painting—then he had a daughter once. A daughter he loved and valued enough to change his life entirely. But how could that man be the same one who now sat before me? It didn't make any sense.

"Leave my traveling companion to me, good king. She won't be an annoyance, I assure you." He rose a glass of dark red wine and, I assume, took a swig.

"I would hope," he said, raising his own glass. "I'd hate to think that the newly reinstated royal family of Backus couldn't do so much as keep their women in line." He laughed heartily like the drunken slob he was, slapping his knee.

"I think you'll find the future of Backus to be quite secure," Abram answered coolly.

This sobered King Archibald, which was likely Abram's intention. Sure, Abram didn't give a damn about the connected politics of two shoebox-sized islands off the coast of nowhere. But if he began that conversation, the king would drop the current tirade he seemed intent on. And, given my short fuse on the matter, that was probably a good thing.

The second and third courses—a split chicken with a stripe of sauce and a roast that lacked any vegetables whatsoever (probably thanks to the drought)—followed as Abram and the king went back and forth about trade routes, ancient disagreements, and which country housed the better vineyards. Meanwhile, Abram shared bites of his food as was apparently their "custom" while not paying any attention to me beyond that the entire time.

I was as bored as a fashion major at Harvard when Abram finally said something that grabbed my attention.

"Your country has a rich heritage. It's home to a very popular fable, is it not?"

King Archibald leaned forward in his chair. "And what fable might that be?"

"Sleeping Beauty," I answered as quickly as the words left his mouth.

He was obviously playing coy and, given that at any moment another person might throw themselves off a cliff because of what was going on, we didn't have time for that. But no sooner had I spoken the words than I remembered I was supposed to just be sitting here as a piece of eye candy.

*Only speak when spoken to.*

But I'd spent decades speaking freely, and this was not an easy habit to change over dinner. The king, unfortunately, did not miss my blunder.

"Silence," he growled. "Men are talking."

And suddenly it was no longer about habit. I just didn't give a fuck anymore. "You—"

"Quiet, Charisse!" Abram shouted.

Though part of me knew this was an act, the tone of his voice took me aback.

Every fiber of my being begged me not to, but I leaned back in my chair and stayed silent anyway.

"I apologize," Abram said to the king. "Though she was horribly out of line, my traveling companion was correct. Sleeping Beauty *was* the fable I was speaking of. Legend has it the entire thing took place in the island's original castle."

The room got quiet. Too quiet. And I wasn't about to volunteer to change that again. Instead, I peeked up at the king, who was definitely too intent on Abram to notice me now.

King Archibald's face remained as empty as a closet on "What Not To Wear" pre-shopping spree. Finally, a smile spread across the man's face.

"The whole thing?" He raised his eyebrows. "You mean with magic and dragons and sleeping curses. Surely you jest. You're a grown man, and soon to be a ruler, no less. Certainly you don't believe in childish things like spells, and witches, and Suppli—"

He cleared his throat and drowned the rest of the word in a swig of wine. And that was about when I lost my cool completely. I was *done* with this. Either he was going to give us answers, or we were going to have to get them another way.

"What were you about to say?" I asked, standing up.

I knew the answer, of course. And he knew that I knew. Supplicants weren't in the fable. If anyone outside of the "know" was even aware of what the word meant, then I would salt this horrifically uncomfortable dress and eat it. King Archibald had tipped his hand, and I wasn't about to let him get away with it.

I unfastened the satiny tie from my wrists, which hadn't been tied on very well to begin with, and threw it on the table.

"Go on," I goaded him, crossing my arms and cocking my hip. "Continue, please. We're all *dying* to hear what you have to say."

He stood to meet me. "Silence yourself!"

"I will not!" I answered with equal fervor. I'd had enough of this, of his lies *and* his attitude. We were too far along to turn back. He had given us an opening, and I was about to tear it in half. "Tell me what you were saying!"

King Archibald slammed his hand against the table. Looking to Abram, his eyes went wide and his nostrils flared. "I will not be addressed in this manner! Not by a woman or anyone else!" His hand slammed flush against the table again. "You will control her, or I will control you both!"

I opened my mouth to speak again, but Abram stood, pulled me toward him, and sat back down. My head was spinning as he bent me over his knee. My body tensed, and my eyes met the floor. I was about to ask him what on Earth he was doing when his hand met flush with my rear end. The sting of it vibrated through me. It wasn't hard, and God knew it didn't hurt. But he was spanking me.

Abram was spanking me.

He pinned my hands against the small of my back and tapped me again, his hand cupping my ass with each stinging smack. It sounded like he was hitting me harder than he was. I felt his hand against my body, firm and in control. Suddenly, I thought about the woman in the other room—tied up, clamped, and loving it.

Something lit up inside of me as he swatted me again. Something hot and confusing that I desperately wanted to deny. With each slap, by body rocked forward in his lap, and a rush ran through me...through to places that made my face burn hot with a blush I hoped no one else could see. I felt like the woman in that room...but unlike her, I found it embarrassing.

The following slaps came a little harder and faster, perhaps under the scrutiny of the king, or perhaps because Abram could feel the heat radiating off my body into his lap.

My breaths came quick and shallow. My hands tightened, still pinned, leaving me feeling helpless. But helpless to Abram was a glorious, arousing thing. And apparently not just for me. I could feel his shaft stiffen beneath me. Against my will, a moan —much like the one I heard in the room down the hall—escaped my lips.

Abram pulled me up. His face was red and his mouth was set.

Looking at him, much of the rush that had washed over me began to fade. It was replaced by shame and anger and confusion. My expression probably spoke of every question, every fear, every sense of betrayal. But I couldn't speak. I was too hurt.

"Just go, Charisse," he said breathlessly and through clenched teeth. "Go to our chambers at once. I will finish with you when I'm done here."

My whole self shut down at the thought of leaving the

emotional safety of his presence. I needed him right then. I couldn't be alone, not now. Not feeling like this.

"Abram, please," I started, but his mouth pressed into a firm line.

"*Now*, Charisse," he said. "Don't make me say it again."

# CHAPTER 8

*B*efore I could fully process what had happened, I was escorted back to our sleeping quarters. My whole body was on fire in more ways than one. Hurt, anger, embarrassment—each emotion coursed through me. Abram had betrayed me. And worse, my body had betrayed me, too, sending currents of arousal I could not understand through every nerve cell in my body.

I paced the room, my heart thundering in my chest, my hands shaking, my mind swimming—or maybe more like drowning—in the swirl of confusion. I couldn't think straight. I couldn't bear the thought of facing him after that, and yet I burned for him to walk through that door. For more reasons than one.

When finally he did arrive , all I could do was stand frozen, staring at his back as he closed the door and rested his forehead against the old wood.

He sighed, shaking his head. "Charisse—"

"*How could you?*" The words left me like a whisper. Tears stung my eyes.

Abram turned toward me, and the look on his face made me take a step back. I couldn't tell if he was sorry or angry.

"How could *I*?" he asked. "How could you make me? How could you not control yourself with everything at stake?"

"I thought—"

"I know what you thought. But I asked you to trust me, and clearly you don't."

"So you hit me?"

"I spanked you," he said evenly. "Because if I didn't, *he* would have."

"And what? You would be powerless to stop him?"

He crossed the room and cupped his hands firmly on the sides of my shoulders. "Is that what you think?" he asked, searching my eyes. "That because I am not a beast right now, that I am weak?"

I opened my mouth, but no words came out. There were no words. No words that would be right for me to say.

"Charisse, if I felt for a second you were in any real danger, we would leave. Forget this island and anyone who jumps from that damned cliff."

"You can't say that," I said, shaking my head. "We have to be here."

"We *should* be here, but we don't *have* to be here. There's always a choice. Tonight, you were in no real danger. Not across my lap nor across his. But the idea of him…laying a hand on you at all…I would not have been able to control myself. I did what I had to do."

I attempted to steel myself before I spoke again, but I trembled instead. "You enjoyed it, Abram. I felt you."

His nostrils flared. "I felt you, too," he said, his voice thicker than before. "And had we not had such an audience, I would have given you a satisfying ending."

I raised an eyebrow, my mind rapid-firing through images of all the ways Abram could satisfy me. I was trying to hold onto that anger, that repulsion at his actions. But with him standing there, the moonlight casting shadows on his face that made him all at once intimidating and exotic, I could not stay mad.

"Now what?" I whispered.

His grip on my shoulders lightened, and his hands slipped a little down my arms. "You're either going to love it, or you're going to hate it."

I narrowed my eyes. "Love or hate what?"

"The king thought I was too easy on you."

I could not stop the horror from pulling on my face. "You can't be serious. What business is it of his?"

"It's not," he said, "but we can't have him thinking I am weak. He will never create an allegiance with my kingdom if he believes we are soft."

"You do realize you aren't really a prince and no kingdom is reinstating, right?"

Abram gave me a flat look. "Of course I know that, Charisse. But *he* doesn't know that, and we need to keep up the charade if we don't want him to grow suspicious. Again. We didn't exactly start off on the best foot."

I nodded. "Right. So what do we do? You want me to be on my best behavior?"

"I wanted that before," he said, glaring at me. "For right now, we're going to have to put on a show."

"A show?"

"Do you hear that?" Abram pressed his lips together, and I held my breath. Footsteps shuffled down the hallway. "That's him coming to have a listen. He's looking for part two of your punishment, Charisse. You'll have to help me orchestrate something to appease him."

The idea of that was all at once terrifying and disgusting. The king listening in on us? Gross! But somewhere deeper inside, I didn't care. He would be a creep no matter what Abram and I did. And now that my anger had subsided, there was only one feeling left to contend with—the burning arousal sending shocks of need through my body.

"How do we pull it off, then?"

"You'll have to pretend I'm punishing you. Cry out, or something."

I placed my hand on Abram's chest and pressed in closer to his body. "I'm afraid I can't do that, my prince," I said. "I'm a terrible actress."

I peered up at him through my eyelashes, and his fiery gaze lingered hungrily on my own. "You don't know what you're asking me to do, Ms. Bellamy."

My heart skipped a beat the way it always did when he called me that, and I tilted my head to the side. "Isn't that half the fun?"

"You're a terribly bad girl," he said, and he leaned down to brush his lips against mine. That kiss traveled through my body like wildfire. He leaned over and whispered in my ear. "You need to let me know if I hurt you, *really* hurt you."

"But he'll be listening," I whispered. "I think he's there now."

"I know," Abram said just as quietly. "Call out *'my prince'* and I will stop. That shouldn't sound too out of line here."

A small rush spread through me, and I nodded. My body was trembling again. Part of me knew we had to do this, and a bigger part of me wanted to, but I was so nervous. I'd never done any kind of role-play in the bedroom before, and certainly not anything like *this*.

Abram slid my dress first from my shoulders, then peeled the sleeves down my arms. My breasts broke free, and he paused to graze his palm over them and kiss me.

"You'll do fine," he said. "Relax. It's easier if you aren't tense."

He took my dress the rest of the way off but left on my underwear. He turned me to face the bed.

"Put your hands on the mattress, Princess."

His voice was more commanding now, and loud enough to be overheard, but there was an ease to it. It didn't seem forced, and I think that was the part about this that kept getting to me. Every time he was "acting," it seemed so natural.

I did as I was told. I had a feeling I shouldn't do any talking since that was what I was in "trouble" for in the first place.

Abram came around to my side and fastened a strap to one of the posts at the foot of the bed. Then he passed the strap under my hips and fastened it to the other side. I had to use my hands to balance, as the height of the strap now stretched between the two bedposts had lifted me onto my toes.

"What are you doing?" I whispered. My stomach fluttered, and my body would not stop trembling.

He leaned forward to whisper back in my ear. "Keeping it interesting, Ms. Bellamy," he said. "Need I remind you you're not supposed to talk?"

I tried to suppress a giggle, but it didn't work.

"You won't be laughing in a few minutes," Abram said sternly.

For some reason this made me giggle more.

As he tied a ribbon around one of my wrists, he added, "Unfortunately for you, I'm much better at this than the servant who tied you at dinner."

He fastened the other end of the ribbon to the bedpost, closer to the mattress. He repeated the same on my other wrist, leaving me so that I was nearly folded in half, with my head resting on its side on the soft pillowtop. Then he slipped off my underwear and did the same to my feet, tying them to the bedposts, but closer to the floor. He left just enough length in the ties to keep me comfortable but short enough to spread my legs wide apart.

Abram stood behind me and traced a finger down my spine. "You're beautiful," he muttered."

His finger slowed at the small of my back and stopped when he reached the cleft between my cheeks. Being naked and on display like this made me hyper-aware and hyper-aroused all at once. Abram and I had had our fair share of sexcapades since getting together, but there were still parts of me he hadn't seen. Until now.

I still wasn't sure how I felt about being tied up, but there was something about not being in control of the moment that was oddly freeing. I didn't have to worry about being a "strong woman" or proving myself as an equal. What was going to happen was going to happen, and all the pressure was off of me to fight it. Having a code phrase to let him know when it was too much didn't hurt, though. Abram always knew how to make me feel safe.

While I was busy pondering how red my ass was from the earlier spanking, Abram replaced his finger with something cool and smooth. It shocked me out of my thoughts, and my heart raced as the small object slipped a little lower, trailing dangerously close to the part of my body I didn't think I would ever share with anyone. I thought for sure he would stop, but he didn't. He just kept going until he reached his target.

I hadn't ever used one before, but I could guess what it was—a butt plug. One of the least sexy names for a sex toy ever. He couldn't actually be trying to use one on me!

He nudged me with the object, and I was horrified to discover that it aroused me just as much as it made me uncomfortable. This was not the over-the-knee spanking I was expecting, and I was starting to get nervous. Nervous and *hot*. My body squirmed, and my cheeks flared with embarrassment, but some small part of me anticipated what he might do next, hoped for it, yearned for it.

He leaned down to whisper in my ear again. "If you trust me, Ms. Bellamy, you might find my protection and devotion to you are only a small part of what I have to offer."

I knew he was right. Whatever tonight held—whatever the future held—Abram only ever wanted to please me. And this wasn't the first time he'd proven he knew my body better than I knew it myself.

He pulled the object away and let out a small sigh. "Unfortunately, I think this could be more of a reward for you...and I'm trying to teach you a lesson." Then he whispered low-enough to evade the king's ears, "I'm trying to teach you to trust me. Do you trust me?"

If I didn't before, I did now. It'd only taken him a few minutes of me tied up for him to prove that even the things I feared could make me feel amazing. So it was with that in mind I nodded, letting him know I did, in fact, trust him. Oddly enough, he'd managed to prove that with a butt plug. Perhaps I should've been questioning my sanity more so than my trust in him.

Abram left my side and returned a few moments later to set some items on the bed. A paddle, a belt-like strap, and what looked like a long stick.

Yikes.

My throat went dry, but the rest of my body seemed to be having the opposite reaction.

# CHAPTER 9

"Now that we have that out of the way, which do you fear the most?" he asked. This was loud enough that anyone outside the room would have heard, and I wanted to tell him I hadn't signed up for *this* game, but there was no way to tell him that with him standing so far away. At least I still had our code word.

I assessed the items. I figured the paddle wouldn't be so bad. Didn't they used to hit school kids with those? The stick looked flimsy. In the end, I figured the belt would probably be the worst. That's what they used in most movies when trying to make someone look like they were abusing their wife or kids.

"I asked you a question, Princess," he said sternly. "Which do you fear the most?"

"The belt," I mumbled.

He leaned over me to take it and whispered in my ear, "You shouldn't."

After he stepped back again, he snapped the belt, and I flinched at the sound. "Your behavior at dinner tonight was unforgivable. You will learn to serve in the manner in which you were promised to me."

With those words, the belt slapped at my buttocks, loud enough to make a cracking sound and painful enough to lift me even farther onto my toes. The belt stung hot and sent vibrations through my body that created an unexplainable aching between my legs.

I braced myself as another blow came, the smooth leather cupping around my bottom as it hit. The belt wasn't as bad as I expected, but the second blow hurt more than the first. Instinctively, I pulled against my binds. It was no use. I could call out at any time—I knew the words to make him stop—but now would be too soon. The king would think he went easy on me.

And, deeper down, if I was behind honest, I wanted to see what Abram would do next.

The third time the belt cracked against my skin, it hit the underside of my butt, and a small cry escaped my lips. But despite the pain, the heat that had begun to radiate from every impact point was stirring a fire in my belly. Each blow sent little shock waves through to my pleasure zones, and my cries had nearly turned to moans.

A sudden need radiated through my body, every inch of me humming with desire. I wanted to beg him to fuck me—even if that hadn't worked when I'd tried the same thing back in New Haven. But at this moment, I didn't care. It was only my attempt to keep the charade going that stopped me. My body, however, begged in her own way, my hips bucking as much as the strange constraints would allow.

My face burned hotter, thinking of how desperate I must look to Abram right now. The way I writhed, the way I moaned, the way I was most certainly glistening—Abram surely knew right then how badly I needed him inside of me.

I wasn't sure if it was that or the charade that kept him going, but each blow came a little harder than the last. Each crack of belt thrust my body slightly forward against the bed, the comforter rubbing roughly against my nipples. Tears began to slide down my cheeks, and I couldn't be sure if it was a hormonal rush of emotions causing them, or if my body was starting to register Abram's blows as actually painful. But none hard enough to illicit anything I couldn't handle.

Until the next one.

That following crack made me shudder, and the words flew from my lips before I could stop them.

"My prince!"

At once, the belt fell to the floor, and Abram rushed to my side, hastily untying my binds and gathering me into his arms. He sat on the edge of the bed, cradling me against his chest and kissing away the tears on my cheeks.

Footsteps shuffled down the hallway in the other direction, and when they faded, I looked up at Abram. "Is he gone?"

Abram nodded. "Are you okay?"

I shook my head.

"You're hurt. You should have stopped me sooner."

I shook my head again. "I just need you."

His brow furrowed, and I tipped my head up to kiss his lips. He didn't resist as I turned out of his lap and pulled his body on top of mine, never letting his mouth deviate from my own.

The comforter on the bed was a little rough against my bottom, but the tenderness only heightened my arousal. As his body hovered over mine, my mind played through the ways our little "scene" could have played out differently. What if the king hadn't been there? What if Abram had dropped the belt sooner and taken me while I was still tied up? Would I have liked that sort of thing?

It seemed impossible, given how much I loved to have my hands all over Abram's body. And yet, at the same time, the thought of it skyrocketed my arousal.

"I want you," I whispered.

"I want you, too," he said. "*All* of you."

My mind was swimming again, but this time not with confusion. Instead, my thoughts swelled with images of everything that had just happened between us, of every touch, of all of his power —even when he wasn't being the beast—of the way he managed to use even my discomfort to enhance my sexuality.

I would never tire of this man.

He pulled his clothes off and returned to me with the same fervor I felt for him. He kneeled between my legs, leaning over me, and moaned as he pressed his shaft into me, stretching my walls to accommodate him. He thrust in a little faster than usual, as if unable to contain his need, and I bit down on his shoulder.

He growled at me. "Better watch it, Ms. Bellamy," he warned, pausing. "If you remember, I know more than one way to punish you."

I whimpered, squirming beneath him. I could not handle Abram withholding an orgasm from me like he had back in New Haven. He needed to give the goods. And as hard as he was right now, something told me he couldn't hold back if he tried, but I wasn't about to test that theory.

I slid my hands up his chest and kissed him hard, silently daring him to resist fucking me senseless. It worked. He grasped my wrists and pinned them over my head, then swayed forward, his cock filling me completely and his pelvis rubbing against my clit. I gasped as each thrust sent a quiver through me, and whenever he would pause, my hips bucked uncontrollably, trying to get more of him.

His hands kept their powerful grip on my wrists the whole time, and he kissed my lips hard as he rammed into me. My bottom beneath me felt tender, even a little inflamed, and that feeling seemed to intensify with each forceful stroke of his cock.

Abram had never fucked me like this before. It was as though something had come over him—over *both* of us. A raw hunger, a pounding desire, a thundering need. I could taste it on his lips every time he kissed me, as though with each kiss he was feeding some part of him I had never seen before. And maybe there was a time that would have scared me, but I trusted him. *Really* trusted him. And I wanted him. Wanted *this*.

He moved his mouth to my nipples and bit down hard, eliciting a sharp cry from me and sending me to the brink. Between the friction and the penetration and the aftereffects of my "punishment," I felt every atom of exposed flesh buzzing, and I became hyper-aware of every throb of his shaft inside of me. Everything was just...*more*. I wanted him more. I trusted him more. I loved him more.

With my body already in overdrive from the moments leading up to this, he sent me over the edge faster than seemed possible. I cried out as my walls crashed around him, and when he made those small grunting sounds he always made before an orgasm of his own, I exploded again.

The hyper-sensitivity of my body seemed to carry my orgasm on a never-ending wave of pleasure that left me gasping, unsure now if I could handle anymore.

"Come," I told him. "I need you to come, Abram."

"Fuck," he grunted, my words sending him over the edge.

He bowed his sweat-beaded forehead against mine for a long moment, then gave me another kiss, sending small jolts thought my over-sensitive body. With another small kiss, he rolled off of me, and his head sank into the pillow beside my own as he stared up at the high ceilings.

For a long time, neither of us moved. After we finally we found the energy, we cleaned up and then huddled back under the blankets, him lying on his back, pillows propping him up, and me curled against him, resting my head on his chest.

His hand drew lazy patterns against my back, and he sighed. "I'm sorry I had to do that."

I raised an eyebrow at him. "Don't be. I liked it."

"I meant the first part." He shifted his gaze toward me. "I hurt you. I should have stopped sooner."

He looked away again, but I pulled his face back to mine and gave him a kiss. "You didn't hurt me, Abram. I told you. I liked it. All of it. Minus King Creeper hanging around outside the door."

He bit down on his lip, shaking his head. "You always surprise me, Charisse. But I think we should save any future 'punishments' for outside these castle walls. Please, please, just be on your best behavior while we're here."

"I don't know," I said, titling my head to the side. "Misbehaving has proven to be so rewarding."

Abram spun me onto my back and hovered over me, holding my hands above my head. "Maybe next time I'll make you say sorry the way I did back in New Haven."

"That wasn't so bad in the end, either," I challenged.

"It could have been," he said with a low growl to his tone. "Now please, I'm asking nicely. *Behave.* We have bigger things to worry about."

I nodded, my heart sinking as I remembered why we were really here in the first place.

"Good girl," he said, then he started to trail kisses along my neck, between my breasts, down my stomach…

But right as he was about to disappear beneath the covers, someone else appeared at the foot of the bed.

# CHAPTER 10

"Oh, my God!" I yelled, startled.

"Really?" Abram smiled, still staring at me. "I haven't even gotten started yet."

"No," I said, taking his head in my hands and turning it toward what I hoped was an apparition.

Satina stood there like a ghost. Well, like a ghost in a sundress wearing a pretty fashionable hat, looking as if she had spent most of the day at the beach. The idea of her loitering in our bedroom at this particular moment had too much weird ménage à trois energy for my tastes.

"Oh, for God's sake." Abram made a sound somewhere between a sigh and a growl. Even though we'd just had more fun than any lucky person could fit into a lifetime, let alone a night, the term 'blue balls' came to mind. This man was insatiable. And, when I was with him, so was I. "You *would* pick now for an informal pop in, wouldn't you?"

I pulled the covers up over me, making sure I was covered. Abram had no such modesty. Sure, all the best pieces were out of sight, but his chest, arms, and a tantalizing chunk of his left hip were on full display. And the way he moved around thoughtlessly in the bed said he couldn't care less who saw him.

Of course, who could blame him with a body like that?

"Like it would have mattered." Satina rolled her eyes. "The two of you are at each other more than rabbits in planting season." She reacted to my quizzical look with, "He knows what I'm talking about. Besides, I needed to wait until you were alone. The enchantment around this place is so strong that I can't stay very long."

"It's voided my curse," Abram said, leaning forward.

He seemed a bit upset at the prospect, which surprised me a little. It was a curse, after all. Shouldn't one be happy to see it lifted, even if only for a short time?

Satina huffed. "That doesn't say much for my skill set, does it?"

That was right. If the enchantment on this place was keeping Satina out most of the time *and* blocking Abram from going beastly, then it meant the Conduit who placed it was more powerful than her.

Not good, considering she was our 'big guns.'

Satina leveled her gaze at me. "I suppose it doesn't say much for *your* abilities, either," she added.

"Hey, I'm just a half-breed," I said, raising my hands unapologetically.

"And a pretty ill-informed one at that," she said smugly.

It was true. I hadn't found a way to tap into the Conduit part of myself yet. To be honest, I probably wouldn't have been able to tap into the Supplicant, either, if it entailed anything beyond the ability to bleed. There was some frustration there, though. While I had no interest in diving into this spooky world of magic and monsters more than I had to, I was stuck in it knee-deep, and the prospect of having some control over things didn't sound too bad.

Besides, I had all these Bewitched scenarios cooking up in my head. It was probably unrealistic, but what wasn't anymore?

"A teacher would be quite useful to you," she said, looking around. "Maybe quite useful for all of us, actually."

"Is that an offer?" I asked, raising my eye brows.

"Absolutely not." Satina scoffed. "I was never much of a teacher, and even if I was, I wouldn't be of any use to you. You're too tempting, Charisse. Being around you for too long wouldn't be in either of our best interests."

She looked at me again, some sort of hunger brimming in her eyes. "No Conduit could be trusted around someone like you."

And with that went my dreams of being some crazy witch's star pupil.

Abram put his arm around me, and I got the feeling he was going on the defense now. "Why are you here, Satina?"

"Well, it's not because I liked the show," she said, motioning toward his general nakedness. "Would you cover yourself? The last time you were this naked in my presence, the both of us ended up sorely disappointed. I'm not interested in a repeat performance."

Exhaling loudly, Abram pulled the comforter over his lap more thoroughly. "You didn't answer my question. Why are you here?"

"The same reason I'm always here. To stop you two from getting lost in the throes of your hormones." She moved around the bed, settling in front of me. She wasn't really here. I knew that. I had seen her face in the curtain during dinner, and now I saw her full visage. But she was still an apparition, even if it did seem like I could reach out and touch her. "I have information that will help you on your little…quest."

I sat up in bed. This I could get behind.

"About the curse?" I asked.

"About the suicides," she said, clicking her tongue in that annoyed, chastising way of hers.

I had to hand it to Satina. She might have sometimes relied too heavily on snark and pompous sarcasm, but she always came through with the good stuff.

"There have been fifteen in the last few months," she continued. "They've all happened on that far cliff, which was also the site of the original Grimoult castle."

"We're aware," Abram said gruffly. "Get on with it."

Satina quirked her eyebrow. "So you know about the beauty?"

"Sleeping Beauty?" I asked. "King Doucebag's daughter."

"King Archibald's daughter?" Satina shook her head. "That woman is long dead. She lived a good life, though. Met some prince in a forest and married him the next day, which is sort of ridiculous if you ask me."

Abram didn't correct her fairytale ending. Instead, he replied, "What 'beauty' are you referring to, then?"

"A quick bit of research on the victims would tell you that they had absolutely nothing in common. They were all of varying ages, sexes, races, belief systems. Some of them have lived here for years, while others—like yourselves—were on vacation. Some were married. Some were single. A few were children."

I shuddered.

"They have nothing in common...except one thing."

"What?" I asked, knitting my fingers around the blanket nervously.

"Most of them spoke of a woman before their deaths. She would come to them in a series of vivid dreams. I've spoken to a few of their spirits on my side, and it's my belief that, within those dreams, she guided them to their demise."

"The Conduit," I said in a whisper. "Did they tell you who she was?"

"Like they could figure it out." Satina rolled her eyes again. "But I've done a sweep of this island. Other than within this castle, I can't find any trace of magic. Unfortunately, that's not to say there isn't any. Dreams are not easy to manipulate. The sleeping curse that the original Conduit used on Sleeping Beauty all those centuries ago is some of the strongest magic known to man. It is so strong, in fact, that it was outlawed and lost eons ago." Her gaze met the floor. "If someone has managed to twist that magic outward, then it would be beyond anything I could combat, maybe anything that I would even be able to sense."

"Well, that's encouraging," I said, infusing a little sarcasm of my own.

Satina nodded. "But not impossible to deal with."

"I don't like where this is going," Abram answered.

He stood, taking a sheet from the bed and wrapping it at his waist, leaving me with just the comforter. He was like some fabled god standing before me, and knowing that I would get to spend the entire night with him sent a happy ache through my core. I promised myself not to fall asleep this time. He wouldn't be running off before he became the beast, and I wasn't going to miss it a second time.

"You haven't even heard my proposal," Satina said coyly, eyeing him up and down.

"I don't need to. I know you, and I know situations like these. I would throw myself in front of any dagger, lie down on any sword, but that's not going to be enough, is it?"

Satina's gaze didn't leave him. "I'm sure you've noticed the king is keeping a secret. I think it's somewhere in this castle."

"I think that's rather obvious," Abram shot back. "But what does it have to do with the suicides?"

Satina frowned. "If I knew, I would tell you. You're lucky I've figured out this much. Now you'll have to do the rest from the inside. The magic surrounding this castle is strong, so I've been forced to focus on what's happening outside the castle. I think whatever the king is hiding has to do with the beacon I'm sensing on the island. I can feel it whispering to me, but being in the after-life dulls my senses. I can't find it."

"A beacon?" I asked, my body tensing at the thought things were about to get a whole lot more complicated.

"Yes," Satina said. "Think of it as a mystical anchor, a stationary object that emits the magic like a...sort of like a pulse."

"Like a router," I finished.

Satina's eyes glazed over. "A what?"

"Like a router. You know, for the internet."

Abram swiped his hand down the side of his face, his fingers scraping against his permanent five-o'clock shadow. "She does this all the time."

Satina waved at him dismissively. "You have to find the talisman. Find that, and you'll find the Conduit."

"Fine. I'll find it," Abram said, one hand resting at the thin cloth around his waist.

"You know it doesn't work like that," Satina scolded. "You'll need more info from the king first, and to find it, you'll need someone to keep the mongrels inside this place busy, King Douchebag included." She grinned at me. "You know as well as I that there's only one thing she could give that would hold the king's interest. And we both know that you're not willing to put her through that."

Abram's expression twisted into anger. "Back off, Satina."

She raised her hands innocently. "I wasn't suggesting it," she said coyly. "You'll have to talk business or sports, or perhaps recount to him vividly some of your, uh...*training sessions*...with your princess. I suggest you spare no details."

A blush fired up in my cheeks. It was only moments ago that I was bent over this bed—half in agony, half in exhilaration—experiencing the sweetest pain I had ever felt.

Abram growled. "Those are private."

Satina picked an invisible piece of lint from her sundress, hamming up her boredom with Abram. "Whatever gets the job done, Beast."

"A-and what do I do?" I asked.

"There's a room at the end of the hall, by the entrance of the wine cellar. I've seen the king going in and out a few times while I was able to stay. He seems very protective of it. All you have to do—"

"Is break in," I finished.

"No" Abram said flatly. "What if they catch her in there? Somehow I doubt they will await my arrival to deal with her for an offense that large."

"They won't find me," I answered.

"You don't know that."

"This isn't my first rodeo, Abram. I'll be fine." From the bed, I reached up and took his hand into mine. "People are going to die if we do nothing. I can do this. You know I trust you. I've proven that. I need you to trust me, too."

"It's not you that I don't trust," he muttered.

I turned my attention back to Satina. "What am I looking for?"

"No idea." She chewed her lip. "It could be anything. The enchantment is stopping me from seeing in that room. It's as though that room has a secondary protection above and beyond the one put on the castle. I can't get in at all, for any amount of time."

"So how am *I* supposed to find these answers?"

"Do what makes you special." She flickered into and out of existence, like the flame of a candle that was about to go extinguish.

"What does that—"

"I have to go!" she said. "It's throwing me out."

And she was gone.

# CHAPTER 11

*W*hen I woke, Abram was standing at the window. He was already dressed, wearing a ridiculously loud purple suit that King Archibald had sent to him the day before. He was perfectly put together, clean shaven with his hair slicked back. Obviously, he looked younger than his century-and-a-half as the early morning sunrise filtered across his face. But more than that, he looked completely and fully awake.

"You didn't sleep again, did you?" I asked, stretching in bed.

His only response was a slight grin that perked up his ears.

"You have to sleep eventually," I said, noticing the way his eyes gleamed against the light.

"Do you have any idea how long it's been since I've seen a sunrise with my own eyes?" He exhaled slowly. "Or even been able to sit still in the quiet of the night? Or when next I'll be able to stand there and watch you sleep, watch you dream?" He shook his head. "I'll sleep later."

I dressed silently as Abram continued to watch the sunrise. It must have been strange and a bit beautiful to be him right now. To have so much of himself taken away for so long, and then to have that back; I couldn't even imagine. The sweetest joys often came tinged with pain. I had learned that recently.

"I was thinking," Abram said, turning toward me. There was a bulbous and gaudy golden lilac broach pinned to his jacket. "The magic in the castle, the way it deflects all other energy, I think I know what it's for." He followed by gaze to the ugly pin, then glared at me. "It came with the jacket," he added, noticing the distasteful way I stared at the broach.

"King Douchebag strikes again," I murmured. "So, the magic?"

"Yes," he answered thoughtfully. "At first, I thought it was defensive; something the king enforced to keep himself safe."

"That would make sense, given all he went through," I said, cinching a belt at the waist of a yellow dress that (if I did say so myself) fit like a dream.

"Right, but I don't believe that's the case. You were touched by magic, too. It made your life a living hell, and you have no interest in wrapping yourself in it."

I walked toward Abram barefoot. "Oh, God, no. I hate the damn stuff."

"As do I," he said. "And King Archibald has been dealing with it far longer than either of us. I can't imagine he would put much stock in it to protect him. And, if he did, I doubt he would spend so much money on a security detail."

"Maybe it's just for show," I suggested, settling in front of Abram and wrapping my hands around his neck. He was warm, hard, and inviting. And as I breathed him in, I caught a whiff of sandalwood and musk.

"Not likely. I used the window shopper on your mobile device while you slept last night."

"The browser," I corrected him, trying hard not to smile. He hated when I laughed at his mistakes.

"Yes. That," he said. "Do you have any idea how long it's been since the good people of Grimoult have seen its royal family?"

"No idea."

"Neither do they," he said, his hands sliding down to my waist. God, didn't he know how much that drove me crazy? "It's been decades since any member of the family has made a public appearance. In fact, other than press releases and the exceedingly rare dinner party, I couldn't find evidence of any royal sighting in at least the last fifty years."

"That's odd. I probably saw Kate Middleton on the cover of US Weekly ten times last year," I said, my eyebrows knitting together.

"Yes. Well, I doubt the Windsors have an ancient curse to worry about." Abram's head tilted up. "Though I suppose you never know."

"What does this have to do with the magic here?" I stepped away from him and settled between him and the window before our close proximity spurred a repeat of last night.

As I leaned against the sill, the sun beat against my back and, for the smallest of moments, I wanted to be on the beach again, free of the knowledge of all of this. Of course, at this point, that was about as likely as evening ponchos making a comeback.

"I don't believe the magic in this place is for defense at all. I believe it's to ensure punishment." Abram's perfectly coiffed hair moved just a fraction as he shook his head. "I know something about curses, and I know they're no good if they don't make the person suffering through them...well, suffer. I don't believe King Archibald *can* leave this castle. And I think the fact that no magic seems to be able to maintain itself inside these walls is intentional. Meant to keep the curse in effect, stop anything from breaking it."

"I gotta be honest with you, Abram. I really don't feel bad for the guy if that's the case. He's a rapey asshole."

"That's not fair, either, Char, and you know it."

I shrugged. "There's plenty of people who wouldn't disagree with me."

Abram's whole mood shifted so quickly that it was as though the room had taken on a sudden arctic chill. "I've been a part of this world for many years, much like King Archibald, and because

I've been given the opportunity, I've changed with the times. If King Archibald is trapped here, he's had no such luxuries. He's watched the world spin from the prison of this castle. He's never been part of the outside world, so how could he fit in with it?"

"You can't seriously be defending him."

"I'm—"

"Look, Abram. I don't buy it. The reason he's like that has nothing to do with being stuck in this castle—*if* that's even the case. The only luxury that pig has had is the luxury of being able to keep his island stuck in the dark ages. And generations and generations of women have suffered because of it."

Abram's hand found mine. "Are you suffering, Charisse?"

I pulled my hand away. "Don't. You aren't like him. I wasn't comparing. Just forget it and get on with your theory."

For a moment, I thought he would challenge my request, that he wouldn't let it drop. But when he spoke again, the defensive tone was gone.

"If he *is* trapped here by magic, that means he can't leave to find help, and if calls for help and they come to him, then whoever arrives finds themselves useless."

I pressed my lips together. "Like Satina. Her abilities here are about as potent as watered-down 7-Up."

A short knock came on the door. Before we had a chance a respond, it flew open. Good old King Douchebag himself was standing there, matching ugly flower broach and all.

"Ah, I see you're starting the morning off right," he grinned sleazily at me. "And by the window, no less. If you want to give the locals a real show, you should lose the dress."

He winked, and my stomach churned.

"Just reminding her to stay in her place," Abram said, giving me a swift swat on the ass.

Heat rushed through me, but I bit my lip, as if that would do anything to keep the redness out of my face.

"Good man," King Archibald said. "Now, if you're quite finished, I believe you wished to see the royal portrait room."

"Right. The royal portrait room, on the other side of the castle." Abram shot me a look. "I can't wait."

"Good." King Archibald motioned for Abram to follow him through the doorway. "Should I lock her in?" he asked, looking from me to the door. "We wouldn't want your little firecracker getting herself into trouble. She's already garnered a reputation as being something of a free spirit. Can't be too careful."

"No." Abram looked back at me. "She'll stay because *I* tell her to. Won't you, Charisse?"

"Yes," I answered, almost breathlessly. It was easier for me to say it this time, easier for me to play the game. Part of me wondered how much of that was because the game had become fun.

Abram turned to the king. "After last night, I don't think she'll give us any more trouble. But if she tries, she'll pay for it later."

King Archibald laughed as he led Abram out of the room. "Why do I get the feeling you hope she'll slip up?"

Abram turned to close the door and winked right at me.

\* \* \*

I waited a few minutes after they left before sneaking out—just long enough to be sure they were gone. Part of me wondered if, when exiting the room, I would find someone standing guard. But Abram would have warned me of that, and besides, they probably didn't think a woman was capable of outsmarting them.

I strode down the hall pretty easily. The entire area was an expanse of nothingness. No people. No movement at all, it seemed. Every few feet sat a dresser with some sort of plant that was turning brown (likely because of the drought), but that was all.

The drapes were closed. The only light in this half of the castle, much like the foyer, came from strategically placed lantern lights.

It seemed as though this would be a cakewalk. And why shouldn't it be?

If Abram was right, it was likely that no one other than trusted advisers had come into this castle in decades. And no magic, either, aside from Satina's neutered ghostly visits. King Archibald was, for all intents and purposes, an immortal. And anyone who could harm him had always been stopped at the gate. So it made sense security would be a little lax once inside.

I found the room Satina mentioned—it was located right at the end of the hall as she'd said. The thought that this might actually go smoothly crossed my mind right up until I jiggled the handle to find it locked.

Well, at least it didn't burn my hand the way Abram's bevy of locked doors had. Maybe things *were* looking up.

After peering around to make sure the coast was clear, I got on my knees (not easy to do in a dress that fits like wet paint) and pulled a pin from my hair.

*Okay, Char, time for that summer on the bad side of the Bronx to pay off.*

I broke my bobby pin in half and stuck the pieces in the keyhole, trying to get the pins in the tumbler down. I tried to think back to how Charlie Prince (the cutest guy I had ever seen before Abram) used to it do back when we went out. Okay, so maybe I'd done more than watch him do it. I'd been so fascinated, I'd had him teach me to do it, too, but only because I wanted to help myself if I ever got locked out of my own apartment.

It took longer than the last few times I'd done it—probably because it'd been years now—but finally the door popped open, and I let out a huge breath I hadn't realized I'd been holding.

Standing and walking in, I found that this room was unlike all the others. Where the rest of the castle was put away, sparse, and even unlived in, this room was chock-full of just about everything. Boxes lined the walls, stacked one on top of the other. Papers were strewn across the floor. An open notebook lay on a desk covered with what looked to be files.

If the rest of the castle was pristine, then this was a pig sty.

"I hope the talisman isn't a broom," I muttered, trudging through the mess. "Because it doesn't look like this room has seen one in years."

I had never been the type who did a lot of research. Hell, Lulu did most of my homework through high school. So the idea of digging into this pile looking for a vague 'something' wasn't my idea of fun. Still, a girl with magic blood had to do what she had to do.

I was twenty minutes and three boxes in when I felt like giving up. This was useless. I didn't even know what I was looking for and, even if I did, I wouldn't be able to find it in a place like this.

Sliding the last folder back into a box marked 'Autumn '63' (I was afraid to even ponder which '63 it referred to) one of the papers nicked my finger, giving me one hell of a paper cut.

"Damn," I muttered, staring at the trickle of blood that seeped out from my cuticle. I reached for one of the stray papers to blot it.

Light, golden and bright, swirled around the red blotch. It was like when Abram touched my blood and his entire body lit up.

And that was when it hit me. This entire place was cursed. My blood would react to this whole place the way it reacted when it touched anything supernatural.

And then, the gold light began to move. Like a lightning bug, it darted around the room, moving toward the back of the desk.

There was no way. Was this magic light, born from my blood, showing me where the talisman was?

And then I remembered Satina's words to me the night before: *Do what makes you special.*

"Well, I'll be damned," I mumbled. Apparently bleeding was what made me special.

But if Satina's visit and Abram's not-changing were any indication, I didn't have a lot of time before my magic would be cut off. I darted after the light. It settled behind the desk, floating to the floor and disappearing as it touched the hardwood. At this point, I knew better than to ignore mystical signal flares, especially when they were this big. So I knocked against the floor, and sure enough, I found a loose board.

Pulling it up revealed a small red box hidden beneath.

I sighed, grabbed the dusty-as-hell box, pulled it toward me, and opened it. A single letter lay unfolded inside. The script was a dark flowery thing and written with what looked like a quill and ink.

Picking it up carefully, I read its contents.

Dear Valued Customer,

While your request is still under advisement, it falls upon us to inform you of the innate difficulty of what you are asking of us.

The curse in which you have been placed is, as you know, no small matter. And the Conduit who placed it on you—again, as you know—is a near legend.

While it is true that the price you have paid has far outweighed the goods you were given, it does not discount the fact that you DID enter into this pact of your own free will, and as such, we can offer nothing by way of refund in this matter. As we've already lifted this curse once and yet you find yourself again in the same predicament, we find the situation requires further investigation before attempting to grant you immunity.

However, we ask you do not despair. Your matter WILL be resolved one way or another. Take this letter, and the gifts it gives you, as a beacon of hope in what must seem like a dark eternity. In the meantime, we have granted you a magical safe-haven within your home, so that you may protect all of your efforts and findings until we are able to assist you further.

And, as always, retain this correspondence. Any and all future decisions regarding this matter will appear upon it.

Best Regards,

The signatory was a blur. I tried to focus on it, but the name looked to be nothing more than a mishmash of symbols and letters.

As I held it closer to my face, something shuffled by the door. The turning of a doorknob soon followed.

I froze. Someone was here, and if I was found, that would be the end of this entire endeavor. Possibly even the end of my life.

Luckily, I was already behind the desk. Quietly, I slid into the crawlspace. All I would have to do is stay here and, with any luck, I could wait this out.

But then a spot of my blood touched the letter, and the entire thing started to glow, lighting up like Times Square on New Year's Eve.

*Damn mystical signal flares.*

# CHAPTER 12

The letter glowed brighter and brighter by the second, as if it wanted me to get caught. Which, as far as I knew, was exactly what the stupid thing wanted.

As the door to the room creaked open, I folded the damn thing up and sandwiched it between my palms. A few months ago, the thought of hiding from backwoods-thinking guards in a magical castle with a glowing letter in my hands would have been the craziest thing I could imagine. Now, as it turned out, it was a Tuesday.

Footsteps clunked into the room. Just inside the doorway at first, then after a pause, clomping even closer. The letter burned even brighter somehow, burning against my palms, but I knew better than to yelp or let go. Doing that would get me caught. And in a place like this, where women were about as valued as dish rags, that was not something I was keen on experiencing.

The letter brightened again. It started pulsating like one of those strobe lights Abram tried to convince me would have been a good fit back in his club. It was 'too '70s' then, and it was too inconvenient now. If there was one thing that was more notice-able than a bright shining light, it was a bright blinking one.

I really wanted to take this letter back to show Abram as evidence. But if I got caught here, that would be the least of my worries. I was going to have to rip this thing in half, and I needed to do it now.

Curling my fingers around the edges, careful not to let anymore of the light show than necessary, I ripped the letter in two as quickly as possible. I breathed quietly, hoping the light would go out.

And it did...for a second.

But as quickly as I had torn the note apart, some unseen force stitched it back together. It flew back into one piece right in my hands, burning as brightly as ever.

*Damn it!*

I had to press my lips together to stop the words from coming out. I was so furious at this damn thing, and I'd only found it a moment ago.

The footsteps fell quiet, and heavy breathing grunted from right over me, above the desk. Only a thin piece of mahogany separated me from sure disaster.

The breathing continued as did the pulsating light, my hands dulling the glow quite a bit but not snuffing it completely. It was only a matter of time before the breather found me, and with Abram on the other side of the castle looking at Douchebag's room of majestic paintings, I was going to have to fend for myself. Which meant one thing.

I was going to have to eat the damn thing.

Cursing my fate, I smooshed the white hot letter into the smallest ball I could.

Then I stuffed it into my mouth.

It tasted awful, and got even hotter against my tongue and the inside of my cheeks. It was like downing a burnt s'more while it was still too hot to touch, let alone eat. But there was nothing I could do. So I dealt with the pain (and the burnt taste) until the footsteps started to back up again.

This time, they were swift and deliberate. And thankfully, they were headed away from me. When the door squeaked open and closed again, I let out a sigh.

That was close. Too close.

As quickly as possible, I spit the burning ball of enchanted paper back to the floor, coughing and gagging, trying to catch my breath.

The letter straightened itself back out, pulled again by some unseen force, and slid unaided across the floor. I watched, mouth agape, as it literally hopped back into the dusty box and closed the lid behind it. The box slid back into the hole from where I'd pulled it.

Well, there went my plan to bring the stupid thing back as evidence. I stood, glancing around the room, then headed for the door.

The box clanged loudly against the hole.

Oh, shit. I'd almost forgotten to put the loose board back in place. If I was going to make careless mistakes like that, I might as well sound the alarms myself.

Quickly, I tiptoed over to the box, covered the hole in the floor, then ran back toward the door. The box was still clanging, though, and I had no idea how to make it stop. I just had to get out of here and hope it would give up once I left.

Sucking in a deep breath, I ducked out of the room and shut the door behind me, the whole time certain I was only moments away from being caught.

\* \* \*

The hallway was once again barren as I made my way back toward the room. It was at least a full minute before I even let myself breathe. By then, I figured I was so far away from the room in question that I could make a case for saying I got lost on my way to the bathroom and probably get away with it. Of course, I would have to deal with the fact that Abram told me to stay, and I had obviously disobeyed. But hey, maybe Dark Age thinking took pee breaks, too.

I slid back into my room unnoticed, sighing and leaning against the door and locking it behind me.

"Where have you been? I thought you were caught. Or worse."

Abram stood by the window. Stripped of that ridiculously royal outfit from this morning, he now wore a tight white tee and a pair of matching pants. They were glorified painter's clothes, but they looked sexy as hell on him.

"I almost *did* get caught," I said, making my way over to him. "But Satina was right. There *was* something in that room. A letter. I'm not sure what kind it is, besides freaky, but it definitely has something to do with the king's curse."

"Go on," Abram said, bridging the gap to meet me. He took my hand, and a world's worth of weight fell off my shoulders.

"First of all, you were right. And wrong. There is a spell on this castle trapping him, but there's also a spell inside the castle protecting him. Second, his curse has already been lifted once before. Kind of. I guess it didn't work? Sounds like he's trying to get them to try again."

"Them?" Abram asked, his eyebrows pulling together. "Them who?"

"Some magical business or something. But it sounds like they don't think they can help him this time."

"I'm not worried about whether they lift his curse," Abram said, his eyes narrowing.

"Then what are you worried about?"

"The cost. The people who dabble in the sort of mysticism it would take to break a Conduit's curse don't come cheap, and they wouldn't even attempt it without being compensated first."

"So?" I asked, looking around. "Check this place out. This moron obviously has more dough than he knows what to do with."

Abram's face darkened. "They don't take money, Charisse."

My mind went spinning before the pitch black truth of what Abram was suggesting settled on me. "Oh, God..." Tears pooled behind my eyes. "He's killing them, isn't he? He's having them murdered as payment to get his curse lifted."

"We don't know that," Abram said firmly.

"The hell we don't!" I snapped, pulling my hand out of Abram's "He's a monster, and he's killing people!" I started toward the door. "I'm gonna kill him myself."

"Stop!" Abram jumped in front of me. "Keep your head on straight, Charisse. Even if he wasn't surrounded by guards, you couldn't kill him. He's immortal, remember?" Abram ran a hand through his hair. "Besides, if he's responsible, he's not the only one. He would need help. He can't leave this castle, and no magic can enter. All the magic here is either from the Conduit or the company in the letter. That means if King Archibald is responsible for people throwing themselves off that cliff, then he's got help from someone on the outside."

"Sleeping Beauty," I muttered. "The woman in the dreams. She's the one who's helping him. That's why she appears three days before they die. That's why she guides them to their deaths."

A slight and maybe even prideful smile tugged at Abram's lips. "That's what I was thinking. Look at this." He turned toward the bed and picked up my cell phone. "While you were gone, I did some research on the internet."

"The internet?" I asked.

"That's what I said, Charisse."

"So...not the window shopper this time?" I giggled.

"This isn't the Stone Age."

"Could've fooled me," I muttered.

"Need I remind you, *Ms. Bellamy*, that I'm over a hundred and fifty years old? You don't get to be my age without more than a fair share of adaptability."

"Okay, then. Get on with it. What did you find?"

He hit (way too many) buttons, fumbling with the phone like

somebody's grandfather. Finally, though, he handed the phone over, beaming with pride.

"Her," he said.

A woman's picture graced the screen. She had red hair, cat-like green eyes, and a bitchy face that I remembered the instant I saw it.

"I know her," I said.

"What?" Abram asked, his eyebrows pulling together. "You can't know her."

"That's Briar Templeton. We had the same agent. I hated that bitch!"

"She's in a coma," Abram said.

"Well, she wasn't *that* bad..." I said. I wouldn't have wished a coma on her. Maybe a kick to the head, but nothing that would cause permanent damage. "What happened to her?"

"She was found several months ago, lying face down in a rose-bush, of which she apparently has a severe allergy," Abram said. "She's been unresponsive ever since. Word is her husband is one of the few people who knew of her allergy, too. They have him in custody now."

"They think her husband did this?" I asked.

"Apparently she had quite the life insurance policy," Abram said, spreading his hands.

I pointed to her picture on my phone. "And you think she's connected to this?"

"The magic, the drought that coincidentally started the day Briar fell asleep, and now the letter you found... Isn't it obvious? Someone—my guess is King Archibald—is setting all of this in motion again. Not only do I think your old rival is a Supplicant, but I think she's the new Sleeping Beauty."

I stared at Abram, a million questions running through my mind. Unfortunately, one bubbled to the top above all the others. "You think she's beautiful?"

"Charisse—"

"I mean, cute maybe," I said, looking at the picture on the phone again. "Unique if you wanna stretch it. But beautiful?"

"You have nothing to worry about," he said, taking my hand again. "I prefer my women alert and well."

"Uh huh."

"Please, Charisse. There's been fifteen deaths this month, and I don't think there was even that many Supplicants on the island to begin with."

"Wait--you think the victims are Supplicants, too?"

Abram's eyebrows pulled together. "What did you think?" he asked. "OF course they are. What other purpose to kill them, if not for their magical blood?"

"But doesn't that mean..." I shook my head. "I'm a Supplicant. Am I next?"

"You haven't had any dreams," Abram reminded. "We need to focus. At this rate, there will be no Supplicants by the end of the month, and with so many deaths, it might not be long before it makes international news."

"Well, then," I said, heading toward door, "sounds to me like we better pay the new Sleeping Beauty a visit."

*Before I'm next.*

# CHAPTER 13

*P*art of me figured getting out of the castle the next day would be a problem. Although we'd been taken off of lockdown after that first night, and the king had stopped treating us like prisoners, I still worried he would deny Abram's request to survey the grounds.

And yet, King Archibald was more than willing to send us on our way. He even insisted we take a pair of overdressed (and conveniently dimwitted) bodyguards with us for the trip.

I was unnerved by how easy it had been. It was as though he wanted us gone for the day, and I didn't want to think what he was up to if that were really the case. But we *needed* to go.

And now we also needed to ditch two bodyguards.

Thankfully, one-hundred-and-fifty years of hiding in the shadows had taught Abram a thing or two about being stealthy.

Five minutes and two turns after we'd left the Castle, King Archibald's henchmen were a distant memory.

"What are you going to say when that royal pig asks you why we ditched his guards?" I asked as Abram held the door open for me to enter the hospital.

It was a small place—certainly much smaller than any of the vast

CONNER KRESSLEY & REBECCA HAMILTON

medical complexes in New York City—but it was even tinier than the hospital that sat on the other side of New Haven. It made me shiver to walk through the halls. I had never been the sort of person who liked hospitals, and after Mom had died, I could barely walk through them. Of course, the whole 'Dalton' ordeal, with me being forcefully medicated and put in a paper gown, hadn't done any good.

Still, there was something even worse about this place, something very rudimentary and third world. If Briar was in here, then part me of might actually feel sorry for her.

"I'll tell him I was testing them, and that they failed," Abram answered, keeping pace with me. "King Archibald could never listen to someone question the competency of his pack and think of anything else."

"Pack?" I asked, looking over at him. "Is he a king or the leader of a lion pride?"

"You know what I mean, Charisse."

"Were you speaking from personal experience?"

Abram clicked his tongue. "I'm more of an oddity, and oddities don't get company."

I found my hand drifting toward his. I loved this man with all of myself, more than I had ever loved anyone, more than I even thought possible. But the truth was, I knew next to nothing about his life between the time he was turned into the beast and the day we met, let alone the years before that.

I squeezed his hand. "You have company now."

Once we reached the receptionist's desk, Abram asked where we had to go to sign in for volunteer work. A large woman with chin hair and a bad disposition grunted and pointed to the left. We marched down the corresponding hallway, eerily alone.

Where were all the nurses? Where were all the doctors? Where were the crying family members sitting vigil, like on all the medical soaps I watched in the fall?

"I don't like this place," I said, biting my lip.

"I know." Abram's hand slipped from mine and slid down my spine toward the small of my back. He guided me through the halls. "Your heart's practically doing somersaults in your chest."

He could hear my heartbeat again. But that meant... "Your abilities are back?"

"They're returning," he said. "Though not nearly as evenly as what's normal for me. I think whatever magic is concentrated in the castle also exists, in some quantity, throughout the island."

"Well, isn't that convenient," I murmured, looking through each room as we passed and checking for Briar. "Why?" I asked, turning to Abram. "If King Archibald can't leave the castle, then why did the Conduit put it throughout the island?"

"Maybe it wasn't the Conduit," Abram said. "Maybe the king had a hand in it. Altering magic on an entire island would keep those who hoped to exploit his condition at bay." Abram shook his head. "It's smart. It's something I would do, if I were ever in his shoes."

I bristled. "You're not like him at all." Something—maybe anger, maybe disgust—rose up in my throat. "He's a son of a bitch. He doesn't deserve a box under a freeway bridge, let alone a whole damn castle." My teeth ground together. "Anyone who'd treat women like that, like they don't matter, I don't even know what to say about that."

"Really?" Abram narrowed his eyes at me. "Is that what you think? That he's treating them like they don't matter?"

"Of course," I answered, nearly stopping dead in my tracks. "Isn't that what you think?"

He frowned. "Not necessarily."

"Abram!"

He raised his free hand as though he were about to tell a child to settle down, and if we weren't in public, that would have been the thing to send me over the edge. I almost fell over when he actually proceeded to speak after that.

"He's forceful, and his beliefs are unarguably archaic," Abram said, "but I'm not sure it's fair to say he doesn't value women."

"He treats them like objects!" I couldn't keep my voice down, hospital setting be damned. At least we weren't in a library.

"Like *precious* objects," Abram said, hurrying me along the hall as he stole a glance over his shoulder. "I know this is hard for you to understand, and it's hard for me to explain, but for men like Archibald—men who grew up in a time much different than the one we live in now—women wanted this. They wanted a man to take care of them, a man to serve, a man to encourage the best from them. And a man had to earn that kind of devotion and trust. If you think about it, the man has to be good enough for the woman. Not the other way around."

"Don't be ridiculous." I scoffed. Leaning in, I whispered, "He had you spank me like some spoiled child, for God's sake. Is there something you'd like to explain to me about that, too?"

"I don't mean to offend you, Charisse. You know me well enough to know that I wouldn't hurt you for anything, least of all to defend the honor of a man who most certainly doesn't deserve it."

"Then why are we even having this conversation?"

"Because I want you to understand the man we're pitting ourselves against." His gaze trailed the floor. "And I want you to understand me, too, Charisse. All of me." When he looked back at me, his jaw was set. "When I was young, things were different, times were different. Men ran the world and were unopposed. We treated our women the same way we treated our children because they needed us to. The world needed us to."

"Oh, for Christ's sake, Abram. Don't be so self-important."

"I'm not," he said, and now he sounded a little angry. "You just refuse to see it any other way than how you were raised to see it."

"I could say the same to you," I mumbled.

Abram stopped short, grabbed my wrist, and spun me toward him. "You liked it," he said, his gaze confronting my soul. "You don't think other women could like it, too? You don't think they could want that?"

He always had to have some damn point that could infuriate me and make me want him all at the same time. But I wasn't going to let him oversimplify this. "You don't treat someone you love that way, Abram."

One of his eyebrows arched challengingly. "Just because you discipline your children does not mean you don't love them. In fact, you discipline them *because* you love them."

"What about this aren't you getting, Abram?" I said, surprised at how angry I had gotten in such a small expanse of time. "I'm not a child!"

Somehow he was able to keep the calm I could not. "Well, you're sure acting like one," he said coolly.

As he turned and continued down the hall, a big part of me wanted to just drop it, but it was as if something had come over me. I wasn't letting this go. I grabbed his arm and pulled him back to face me again. Of course, it was entirely by his choice that I got any result.

"There's a difference between love and lust," I said firmly.

He shook off my grasp. "I thought we had both," he said, and now I couldn't tell if he was hurt or angry. "We'll talk about this later. This isn't the time or place."

He stopped in front of a door in the middle of the hall. It was open, and by the way he stared inside, I knew it was her. I closed the distance between us, coming up beside him to peer in.

Briar lay flat on her back. Her red hair sprawled in lifeless strands across her pillow, and her skin—always pale—looked sallow now. She was nothing like the girl I'd known back in New York, the one who seemed to make it her mission to make my life a living hell.

Back then, she snagged every job she could right out from under me. She spread lies about me to all of my friends and even tried to convince our shared manager to drop me. She was a grade

A bitch, and there were more than a few times when I wished she would just drop dead. But now, seeing her like this, so close to that death I wished for, made my stomach churn. All of my issues with Abram seemed so insignificant in that one moment.

I made my way over to her. The monitors connected to her chest beeped in a steady rhythm that seemed to match my own.

"I had a boyfriend back in New York," I said softly, staring down at her. "His name was Charlie. He was in a band, and I thought he was just about the sexiest thing ever." A sorrowful smile split my lips. I had been so young back then. In truth, I had no idea what sexy was. I had no idea what love was, not until Abram. "But Briar seduced him. She slept with him and convinced him to leave me." Tears burned my eyes. "I never knew I could hate someone as much as I hated her back then. I mean, I thought my father abandoned me, and I still didn't hate him as much as her. But this"—I motioned to her near lifeless body—"I didn't…I would never wish…"

"I know," Abram said solemnly. "And I'm sure if she was awake, she would know that, too."

"I wish I could be sure."

"Then we'll tell her," Abram said, sliding his arm around me. "When we wake her up and open these damned dry skies, you'll go out for a drink and talk how stupid you both were." He gave me a wink. "And you'll tell her how you got a better one than whoever Charlie is."

Abram left my side and pulled open drawers until he found a needle and vial. That must have been some backwoods hospital thing, because New York would never leave needles sitting around in the actual patient rooms.

"We need to move quickly," he said. "If we're found here, we have absolutely no excuse. I doubt they'll believe we volunteered to help the sleeping. Besides, the Conduit could be anyone, anywhere. We can't let him or her know we're on their trail."

I winced as he stuck a needle into Briar's arm and drew an

entire vial of blood. Something pricked at my mind. To my aston-ishment, I found that it was a bit of jealousy. Could this woman—this woman who had been so horrific to me—actually be a Suppli-cant. Could she be the thing that made *me* so special? And if she was, did that mean I wasn't so special after all?

"Do you really think she's like me?" I asked in a small voice.

As if he had (finally) taken a class on knowing the exact right thing to say, Abram answered, "She might be a Supplicant, but she's nothing like you. Nobody is."

And that was all it took. All my insecurities melted away. I wasn't that young thing anymore. I wasn't throwing myself at loser lead singers who didn't deserve me. I was Charisse Bellamy, and the most exquisite man on Earth called himself mine. I had nothing to be jealous of.

Of course, as the jealousy waned, the empathy kicked back in. When I saw Abram ready to extract the vial of blood onto his arm to test the potency of her blood, I raised my hands.

"Not here," I said, looking at her. "Not in front of her...like she's a thing. Like she doesn't have any control over any of it."

"Okay," Abram said, carefully wrapping the needle in gauze and placing it in his closed fist. "Let's go."

Following Abram out the door, I chanced one more look at Briar.

"I'll get to the bottom of this," I muttered. "And then you and me, we're gonna have a talk."

# CHAPTER 14

*G*etting out of the hospital proved even easier than getting in. Abram and I moved out the back way, weaving from one long, empty hallway to the next until we found a small silver door with a flashing exit sign overhead.

As we burst through the door and into a back alley like a pair of wannabe socialites at a Barney's sale, we ran into a familiar face.

Satina twirled blonde curls around her finger. "Did you get it?" she asked, smacking a gob of gum between her teeth. "The girl's blood?"

"You knew about that?" I balked breathlessly, wondering why Satina hadn't just swiped a bit of the stuff on her own—since, you know, she was already out here.

"Do you really think anything happens anywhere that I don't know about?" She quirked one of her perfectly plucked eyebrows.

"I hope so," I muttered, thinking back to some of Abram's and my less demure moments.

"The blood," she repeated, this time looking to Abram.

He held up the vial. "I got it."

The way Satina eyed it, as though it was ice cream on a hot

day, made me more than a little uneasy. That may as well have been my blood. God knows mine was just as potent. At the end of the day, no matter how much Satina helped me, I would always be that to her—a giant freaking ice cream cone. And that worried me.

"I'll take that," she said hungrily, holding out her hand.

Abram grimaced. "I don't think so. I'll test it out myself."

"And why would you do that?" She narrowed her eyes. "You know how that stuff burns."

I thought of my own blood, how it scalded Abram wherever it touched him. A twinge of pain ran through me. I could hurt him. The very thing keeping me alive (and putting me at the top of the mystical world's most wanted list) was poison to the man I loved, and there was nothing I could do about it.

"And whose fault is that?" Abram asked, his arms folding across his broad chest.

"I'm just trying to save you pain, Beast," Satina answered.

"You're trying to give yourself a power up." His tone had dropped to a growl now. "You must be out of juice."

"And so what if I am?" she asked, smiling. "I'll admit that keeping my magical presence in this place has been a bit of a challenge, what with the mystical barriers and restrictions on this damned place. But I assume you would want me to be at full-strength. Unless you would rather deal with them on your own."

I was about to ask who 'them' was, but Satina pointed to her right, where the two bumbling bodyguards we evaded earlier were, at present, running down the alley toward us. The one on the right shouted something into a walkie talkie that was either foreign or so thickly accented I couldn't understand it. The second one shouted "Stop!"…which I understood just fine.

"Damn it." Abram shot Satina a condescending look and tossed the vial over to her.

She caught it with aplomb, popped the top, and doused herself in the red liquid. Closing her eyes, she took a deep breath, as though she was savoring something. Then, just as quickly, her eyes popped open. "Oh."

"Oh?" I repeated. "What does 'Oh,' mean?"

"Not really the time to worry about that now," she said, tipping her chin toward the approaching guards. "You'd better run, little Supplicant, unless you would like to explain exactly what you're doing back here."

"No," Abram said. "I'll tell them I was seeing the town. I'll blame them for not being able to keep up with me, strike at their pride. They won't be able to—" Abram grunted and keeled over, clutching his gut.

"Abram!" I rushed to his side. "What's wrong?"

"What time is it?" he muttered, sweat beading on his brow.

I looked up. The sun was setting in the sky. How could I not have remembered this? How could we have let it get this far? "Almost sunset."

But this didn't make any sense. Abram's curse was tied to the moon, sure. But he was supposed to be able to keep it in control until midnight. This—him writhing in pain and sprouting fangs— wasn't supposed to happen this quickly. We should have had more time.

"Why is this happening?" I asked Satina hurriedly, looking behind me at the quickly advancing guards.

There would be no way to talk ourselves out of this. If they saw Abram like this, our secret would be out. Whatever chance we had of saving the next suicide victims would be as gone as the rain.

Satina scowled. "Oh, she's good."

"Who?" I asked as Abram let out an actual howl.

"The other Conduit. The one who tampered with this place." Satina shook her head. "But it's personal now. She's messed with *my* creation, with *my* art." She turned to me. "Quickly. Open a vein."

"What? No!"

"I need magic to stop these morons." She pointed to the nearing guards.

"Then use Briar's blood," I said, shying away.

"It's worthless. She's not a Supplicant. She's not anything."

"What?" That couldn't be. Briar was the new Sleeping Beauty. She had to be a Supplicant. That was the only way any of this made sense.

Abram fell to his knees. He peered up at me, eyes red as they had been the first night I saw him back in New Haven. The beast was coming, and there was no stopping it.

"I don't have time to placate you, girl!" Satina yelled. "Your entire mission, all your missions, ride on the coming moments. Now give me your blood, or so help me, I'll take it!"

It wasn't her threat. Honestly, Satina couldn't threaten me at this point. I was beyond that. But Abram was about to get ruthless. He was about to go primal and, if history was any indicator, he would take out anything that looked like it meant me harm, guards included. I didn't want him to have to live with that.

"Fine," I said, and I ran my hand down the concrete hospital wall, scraping my palm. A tear of blood pearled from the skin. "It's not much."

"It'll do," Satina said, swiping it up with her finger. She stepped past me, her body glowing golden. "Suspend!" she shouted.

The guards stopped dead in their tracks.

"What did you do to them?" I asked, wiping the excess blood on my jeans. No need to arm Satina more than necessary.

"I stopped time around us. It won't last for long, especially in this place. But it'll give us enough time to get Abram out of here."

"No." His words muffled against oblong teeth. "You have to go!"

I shook my head. "I won't leave you like this. What if the townspeople find you?"

"I survived for well over a hundred years before I met you,

Charisse. I can make it another night." He wretched in pain again. "Besides, I don't know what this place will make me capable of. I don't want anyone around me when midnight comes, especially you."

"We can get you to the castle, sneak you in somehow," I pleaded. "The castle will stop the turning."

"I won't make it that long," he said, now panting. "I won't make it another thirty seconds." He touched my shoulder. His hands trembled, but they also felt stronger than I had ever known them to be. "I need you to listen to me, Charisse. Get to the castle. Tell them I found another woman, that I'm spending the night with her, and that I told you not to leave the castle again without my permission. It's such a dastardly thing to do, that I doubt they'll question it. I'll find you in the morning. I'll—" He grunted in pain again. "I have to go."

In a flash, he bounded around the side of the hospital and sprinted into the darkness in the trees beyond. He was out of sight. Gone. And I was left with tearful eyes and a trembling lip.

I had to go to the castle—that wretched, disgusting place— alone. I just couldn't.

"He ruined my life," Satina said, looking to where Abram had darted off. "But I have to admit, he's sort of sexy when he does that."

"What do I do now?" I asked, ignoring the inappropriate (if true) sexy talk.

"What he told you to," she said. "Return to the castle. We'll figure out the rest in the morning."

\* \* \*

When I got back to the castle, I found that all of Abram's suggestions worked as promised. They totally bought the 'sleeping with another woman' thing, and the king was so ashamed of his own henchmen that he paid no mind to them when they talked about Abram moving 'at the speed of lighting.'

Of course, he was curt and dismissive with me, but who was I to split hairs? I just wanted to get away from them and to my sleeping quarters as quickly as possible.

The night stretched out long and slow for me. I worried whether Abram was okay, whether the people around him were okay. I worried about what I would do if the king or any of his men tried anything while Abram was gone. I worried about the next 'suicide' victim, and I worried that we would never get to the bottom of this.

As I always did back in the city, I took to a hot bath to clear my head.

The drought made the luxury of it impossible, as I was rationed to a mere four inches of water. Still, as the steam from the water drifted up into my tired body, it felt good all the same.

My mind started to clear. My muscles relaxed, and my eyes began to droop and feel heavy. I should have gotten out. Falling asleep in the bath was dangerous. But I was a super magical creature, so I figured it would take more than four inches of H2O to do me in, even if they did say all it took was a few inches of water to drown.

Before I could stop myself, I had drifted off into the sweetest sleep.

The next thing I knew, I was staring across the island at a cliff. The castle I was supposed to be inside sat atop, stretching up toward the heavens. Slowly my gaze shifted toward the beach-side of the Island. And that's when I realized where I was.

On the cliff. Not the cliff where Archibald's caste resided. The *other* one.

The one where people jumped to the jagged shore below. Where people jumped to their death.

I was standing on the suicide cliff.

A nervous energy spun a web through my veins. This wasn't right, though. I could see the shore, but I couldn't feel the ocean breeze. This was a dream.

I reminded myself that I was asleep, that I could wake myself up if I wanted. But when I tried, nothing happened.

Briar stood ten feet away. She was wide awake and looking every bit the nosy back-stabbing bitch I had come to know and loathe.

"You couldn't leave well enough alone, could you?" She sneered, hands on her hips. "Saw me in a bit of trouble and thought you'd come and be the big bad rescuer." She rolled her eyes. "Even now, you can't stop yourself, can you? You *have* to prove you're better than me."

"This doesn't have anything to do with you."

"That's where you're wrong," she whispered.

"I'm here to save those people, those people who hurl themselves off that cliff three days after they—" My mouth went dry.

"Three days after they see me in a dream?" Briar finished, arching her eyebrows.

This was it. I was marked. If we didn't find a way to stop this thing, I would be dead in three days.

"Catwalk got your tongue?" She grinned. "Come on, Char, you're the one who said you wanted to talk."

# CHAPTER 15

*T*he next morning, I woke shivering. It took me a second to remember why. But when the visage of Briar's face came hurtling back into my memory, my stomach flipped.

Three days; that was all I had. Three days, and then I would be just like those poor bastards at the bottom of the cliff, scarred and splattered across the sand.

"Are you all right?" Abram asked, startling me with his closeness.

He had run away last night, hiding in whatever shadows this God-forsaken island had to offer and waiting out his magically enhanced transformation. He must have moved me to the bed when he returned, because I was no longer sleeping in four inches of water.

On one hand, it did me good to see him there, standing above me, recently showered and dressed in fresh clothes. It meant that whatever happened last night wasn't enough to take him out. And the fact that he had such an easy-going smile on his face meant that he had very likely made it through the night without maiming or murdering some innocent bystander.

Of course, there was the other hand to think about—the hand

that knew how crushing the news of the dream would be to him. In the time I had known Abram, the only situations where I had even seen him lose control were the ones that involved my safety.

Telling him this—telling him about my death sentence—wouldn't help anyone. It would render him useless. He would see red. He would get tunnel vision. Nothing would matter but saving my life. In a heartbeat, he would pull me off this island, shackle me to something stationary, and wait the three days out. He would guard me like some suicidal treasure, ensuring my survival.

And while that might be good for me, it would spell doom for all the others afflicted by Briar's fatal visits.

No, I couldn't tell him about this. Not if it meant the deaths of the people we were brought here to save. We just needed to hurry up and get this situation sorted sooner than later.

"Char," Abram said, sharper this time. "Did something happen?"

"I'm fine," I murmured, shuffling under the covers. "Just tired."

"No one laid a hand on you, did they? Because I swear to God—"

"I know," I said, my voice a ghost of a whisper. Boy, did I know. And that's why I couldn't tell him about the dream. "I'm okay, really."

"You were shaking," he said, narrowing his dark eyes at me.

"I was afraid," I answered. "That you wouldn't make it back."

He ran a strong hand up my arm, tickling my skin and resting his touch on my shoulder. He smoothed the strap of my night-gown away, leaving the soft skin of my shoulder exposed.

"I'll always come back," he said firmly. "Always."

Instinctively, I cleared my throat and brushed away from him. He might always come back, but in three days, who knew if I was going to be able to say the same?

"What happened last night?" I asked, fixing my strap back in place.

Hurt flashed through his eyes, but he steeled himself just as quickly. "I'd rather not discuss last night. No one was hurt, but I..." He stared at the floor. "I'd rather not think about it. Let's just say the beast got the better of me and leave it at that." He pressed his lips together and turned his attention toward the window. "I need you to get dressed. I've cleared it with King Archibald, and we'll be going out again today. And, because of the guards embarrassing ineptitude yesterday, we have the added boon of going unaccompanied."

"You mean Archibald didn't decide to assign more apt guards instead?"

"I think he's worried how it will look if the second round of guards prove as useless as the first. I told him we wanted some privacy, and he seemed relieved."

"Yeah, right," I said. "He sent those first guards to keep us out of trouble, not to protect us."

"I know that, Char. I'm not defending him. But he wants us to believe the guards were for our sake, not his, and he's not going to show his hand that easily. Especially since we did return on our own accord. This is all about appearances. We have to pretend to buy into his charade, just as he's pretending to buy into ours."

"You know, I don't even care anymore. I'm just glad we can get out of here without any stalkers." I flung off the covers and stood. "Where are we going anyway?"

"To get to the bottom of this," Abram said, standing to meet me. "We have a lot of information and nothing to piece it together."

"So...?" I asked, leading him to what I assumed would be the next logical thought.

"So we're going to have drinks," he answered.

"Oh, great!" I chirped, brightening up. "But how is that going to help things?"

"Because of who we're having the drinks with," he said evenly. "Satina."

"Oh," I said, less enthusiastically. "Great."

* * *

It was nice to get outside again, especially this early in the day. Sundown was far enough away that I didn't have to worry about Abram losing control, and the island was bustling with people.

Still, everything looked different now. What was once a Mediterranean paradise was now a dry, desolate place strangling against the chokehold of repeated magical attacks. The tanned people looked tired and burned. The stretches of beach looked empty and fruitless. This wasn't the vacation I had been hoping for. In fact, it turned out this wasn't much of a vacation at all.

That didn't seem to bother Satina, though. When we found her, she was stretched across a beach towel, sipping gingerly from a drink with an umbrella in it and wearing a barely there bikini that I was sure the original owner of that body wouldn't have been too happy about. You know, if she wasn't dead.

Abram scoffed, settling in front of her. "Good to see you're not taking yesterday's failures too hard."

"Who said they were failures?" She looked at him from over the top of a pair of heart shaped sunglasses. "Knowing where not to go is just as important as knowing the right place. Now will you move? You're blocking my sun."

"This is serious, Satina," Abram said, not budging an inch.

"Oh, I know that," she said, resting her drink glass against the sand with two fingers. "I'm not sure you're going to share that sentiment once you hear what I've got to say, though."

"What does that mean?" I asked, catching a glimpse of Satina's stylish sandals and actually envying her taste. Damn her.

"Desperate measures, Supplicant." She smiled, standing and brushing a bit of sand from her sun-kissed skin. "Let me ask you, how much do you know about your Conduit abilities?"

"No!" Abram growled, moving closer to Satina menacingly.

"Let the girl answer the question, Abram." Satina clicked her tongue. "Or has the dom/sub aspect of your relationship extended outside the bedroom now?"

"Nothing," I said quickly, hoping the hot flush in my cheeks wasn't noticeable. "I don't know a damn thing about it."

"And it's going to stay that way," Abram cut in.

There was a hint of the commandeering nature he displayed the other night at the dinner table: strength, stubbornness, undeniable masculinity. And though I would never admit it in front of Satina, I sort of liked it.

"Well, that's stupid," Satina said, smoothing her hair with her fingertips. "Seeing as how her latent abilities are the best chance you have at defending yourselves."

"Bull," Abram said through gritted teeth. "The castle is enchanted. No magic will pierce it. As long as we're in there, we're safe."

"Unless the people in there decide to slit you from neck to navel, which just might happen if they learn you've been lying to them. And without that oh-so-special magic of mine that makes you all fearsome and sexy, you'd be about as useful as a mountaintop outhouse. Besides, who placed the enchantment there if not a Conduit? Which means we'll need Charisse's Conduit abilities to undo it."

"Then you should be able to undo it, seeing as you are one yourself," Abram said, standing his ground.

"I'd have to bleed your girlfriend dry to power something like that. But her..." She tipped her finger toward me. "...she's her own never-ending energy source. If she'd just learn to tap into it—"

"I said no!" Abram's shouting garnered the stares of passersby on the beach, but none stopped to intervene. Maybe this place wasn't as unlike New York as I thought. "You would have me train her? To what end?"

"*You* couldn't train anyone, Beast!" Satina was shouting herself now, and the conversation was surely seeming stranger and stranger to anyone who heard it. They would need to reign it in soon. "But if she did get a sense of what she was capable of, you might be able to—"

"To put her in the path of a much stronger Conduit?" Abram's voice was heavy with disgust, but quieter. "Whoever set this up has immense power. You said so yourself. We would be signing her death warrant."

"And whose are you signing now?" Satina asked with arched eyebrows. "There's always the next. Sleeping Beauty will visit someone again, and my guess is that will be sooner rather than later, if she hasn't already. And when she does, the poor soul will have—"

"Three days," I murmured, careful not to give any outward sign that the person in question was me.

I didn't know what I was going to do about all of this yet, but with Satina and Abram at each other's throats, I knew they couldn't handle this new twist of fate.

"Exactly," Satina answered triumphantly, "and you've no way to help them."

Abram shook his head. "It's not necessary. I have a plan."

"Hallelujah." Satina scoffed, crossing her arms over her chest.

I put a steadying hand on Abram's forearm. "What is it?"

"Briar's husband, Ramsey Duldridge."

"The one who very likely tried to kill her in the first place?" Satina asked.

"We don't know that. We don't know anything. But he might," Abram said, turning to me. "I used the phone to look up some of his information, including his address."

"Do you think we can trust him?" I asked, ready to accept whatever answer he gave me as fact.

"Probably not, but we don't have to. He's still in police custody, awaiting trial. All we have to do is get into their home. There has to be a clue to what's going on with Briar somewhere."

"That's your plan?" Satina threw up her hands. "You want to go mucking around his house like...like..."

"The Hardy Boys?" I suggested.

"Who?" she asked.

"Nancy Drew?"

"What?"

"Veronica Mars?"

"Is that a car? You know what?" Satina motioned with her arms like a referee calling safe. "Do whatever you want. If it's your intention to go searching for needles in haystacks, then I suppose I can't stop you. But you, Charisse…sooner or later, you're going to have to be who you are. Whether you want to or not."

\* \* \*

Turned out Briar and her husband Ramsey lived in a really posh house right on the beach. Seemed like the bitch had done well for herself, if you discounted the fact she was in a magical coma.

I thought when I left my modeling career, she would finally be out of my life. Instead, she somehow ended up living on the mystical island I had chosen for my vacation. The same island that now had some kind of supernatural suicide curse. This had to be connected somehow, and damned if I wasn't going to get to the bottom of it.

Abram and I moved like shadows toward the back door.

"Even her backyard is immaculate," I said distastefully. "She's in a coma, and he's in jail. How good would this place look if everything was going well?"

"Hopefully we'll get to find out," Abram said, crouching beside the door. Reaching into my hair, he quickly pulled a pin from it, sending my dark locks spilling around my shoulders. "May I?"

"It's a little late for me to say no," I quipped. "But why not just pull the damn thing off the hinges. You have your strength out here."

Plunging the reshaped pin into the door handle, he said, "Because this is someone else's property and, regardless of what's happening around us, that's something that should be respected."

Before I could point out that breaking and entering wasn't exactly respecting someone else's property, the door sprung open.

"Impressive," I said coyly. Damn, that was faster than Charlie Prince ever made that happen. Abram really had him beat in every way.

"Skills of a misspent youth, paired with years of evolving practice, I suppose."

As beautiful as the outside was, it couldn't hold a candle to the interior. As we crossed into the house, covered in classic art and décor that made me wince with jealousy, it was clear that what Briar lacked in personal warmth, she made up for in taste.

"What are we looking for?" I asked, sticking close to Abram.

"Whatever doesn't belong." He pointed to a bookcase in the far corner of the foyer. "Like that."

"Good eye," I said. "Briar could barely read the nutrition facts on a Special K bar. She's way too stupid for actual books."

"Not that," he said, moving over to the oak structure. "This."

He pulled a weathered book from the shelf. In the smallest print I had ever seen, it said *Hidden Truths: Cornerstones of the Majestic.*

"You think they're in a cult?" I asked, crinkling my nose.

"This is a rather famous manual," Abram said, flipping through the pages. "It details Conduits, Supplicants, and the entire magical realm."

"But Satina said Briar wasn't a Supplicant. She said she was just a human. Why would a human have a book like this?"

"Briar's a human," Abram said, still inspecting the bookcase. "The question is, what is her husband?"

"I could ask the same thing of the people who just broke into my home," said a gravelly voice, followed by a loud clicking sound.

I startled at the sudden presence before turning to find a man standing right next to me. He was tall and thin, but his features were striking. He looked a lot like Charlie Prince, actually. Which was to say, he was just Briar's type.

His hand was outstretched, but not to shake hands and make

introductions. Instead, in his grip was a pistol, cocked, ready, and pressed to my temple.

My entire body turned to stone. My heart fell through my feet, and a shock of fear threatened to tear me apart.

"Ramsey Duldridge, I presume?"

# CHAPTER 16

*T*he cold metal of the gun barrel pressed against my temple. It seemed strange after all the times I had cheated some mystical and fantastic death that this was how I would go...in such a normal and mundane way.

I squeezed my eyes shut. Only I would think of being shot to death after breaking into a house as mundane.

"I would drop the gun if I were you," Abram said, a low growl to his voice. Even now, in broad daylight, he was doing his best to keep the beast at bay. What sort of island was this?

"But you're not me. And if you were, you would know that I'm the one with the upper hand, and you are in no place to make idle threats." Ramsey Duldridge pushed the gun's barrel harder against my head. "So unless you'd like to see your accomplice's brains splattered across my brand new rug, I'd stop giving orders and answer the question. What are you?"

"Thieves," Abram said. "And if you let her go, we'll be on our way."

I opened my eyes to see him nudging ever closer. A few more feet, and he would snatch the gun from Ramsey. Hell, given the look on his face, he would probably take the hand with it.

"Bullshit," Ramsey said. "You passed by three antique vases *and* a dresser full of Waterford crystal so you could peruse my bookshelf? What sort of piss poor thieves would do that?"

"Briar has Waterford?" I bemoaned instinctively.

"You know my wife," he said accusingly. From the corner of my eye, I saw Ramsey's finger graze the trigger.

"Or she's seen the news," Abram said. "You and your wife aren't exactly low key these days. We saw what happened to you, knew you would be in jail, and figured this would be an easy hoist." Abram edged even closer. "The fact that I like books is just an added fold."

"Books that detail the secret history of magic?" Ramsey asked with raised eyebrows. "I'm not buying it. Also, I suggest you stop closing in on me. Judging by your height, weight, and the general nonchalance with which you carry yourself, I'm guessing that whatever you are, you have both enhanced speed and a resistance to bodily harm. But judging by the way your girl here is shaking like a leaf in a thunderstorm, my guess is that the same cannot be said of her. Like me, she knows that however fast you are, it won't be quick enough to stop a bullet."

Well damn if this son-of-a-bitch didn't have things down.

"I'll kill you where you stand," Abram said loudly.

"Probably," Ramsey answered. "But it won't matter by then, will it? Now what are you?"

I bit my lip, trying to work up the courage to speak. Finally I forced out the words, "It doesn't matter what he is."

I sensed Ramsey falter, likely surprised I had the gall to speak, and took advantage of his pause. I spun toward Ramsey, grabbed his pistol-holding hand, and wrenched him hard enough to twist him to the ground. The gun fell from his grip.

"Because every smart city girl has taken self-defense classes, and if you think this is the first time I've had a gun to my head, you're stupider than I thought. Which says a lot given you married Briar."

As I gave his arm a twist, he grunted. "Get off me!"

"Soon. First tell us what *you* are." I wrenched his arm a little harder. "I suggest you answer me before something snaps."

"He's a mage," Abram said. He had picked the book back up and was flipping through it. A rush of pride shot through me. Not only had I disarmed this loser all by myself, but Abram felt secure enough in my abilities that he had taken his eyes off us. "You can let him go."

"I'm not sure that's a good idea. He *did* just try to kill me."

"He was bluffing," Abram said, slamming the book shut. "I didn't know it before, but now that I know what he is, I know there's no way he would have harmed you. Mages have strict codes against that. Isn't that right, Mr. Duldridge?"

"What would you know?" he asked, still on the floor, still at my mercy.

"I've been alive for quite a long time," Abram answered, his voice calmer now. "You're not the first mage I've run across. The crest I saw at the back of your book—it's from the Appalachian Sect, is it not?"

Abram shot me another look and nodded. Hesitantly, I released Ramsey's arm. He pulled it to himself and slowly got back to his feet.

"It seems I'm at something of a disadvantage." Ramsey coughed. "You know who I am, but I don't know who—"

"This is Charisse Bellamy. She knew your wife several years ago in New York City. My name is Abram Canavar. I was, for lack of a better word, sired by the Conduit Satina over one hundred and fifty years ago."

"You're *them*," Ramsey said, a curious smile spreading across his face. "The Beauty and her Beast. The Supplicant and the Wolf."

Abram scowled. "I'm not a wolf."

"So you say."

"You've heard of us?" I asked, trying to keep the surprise out of my voice.

"Who hasn't?" Ramsey shook his head. "You made quite a splash back in America. You're on a lot of peoples' radars now."

Abram's mouth tightened, and I could tell what Ramsey said wasn't something he considered good news.

Ramsey tilted up his chin. "Well, now that we have that out of the way, do you care to tell me what you're doing here?"

"I could ask you the same question." Abram's eyes narrowed. "You're supposed to be in jail."

"A Conduit owed me a favor," he said, looking over at me. "He used some of his magic to coerce the judge into reconsidering my bail. Now would you please tell me why you broke into my home? The *real* reason, if you would be so kind."

"To save your wife," Abram said evenly.

Ramsey rocked back on his feet. "Sure. Yeah. You want to help me. Your girlfriend here hates her. But you want to save her. Of course."

I folded my arms over my chest. "I may not be your wife's biggest fan, but I don't want her to die, and we need to stop whoever is using her to kill everyone else around her."

"Ah, so the enemy of your enemy is your friend?"

"Not exactly," I said evenly, thinking that applied to more than just Briar. King Archibald fit that bill, too, and frankly I didn't give a crap about saving him. "Before you get all shitty with us, maybe you should consider the Conduit you made a deal with is the one responsible for all the craziness going on around here."

Ramsey raised his hands as though trying to get me to calm down. "That kid barely has enough power to light a candle. Even the spell to get me out of jail took everything he had. I should know. I taught him myself. Besides, I sent him back to the mainland. As you said, things have been strange around here. I figured it was no place for a kid."

"Then why are you here?" Abram asked.

"That's a stupid question." Ramsey clenched his jaw. "My wife is here."

"The wife you nearly killed?" I spit out.

"No," Abram said. "He couldn't have. The codes would have prevented it."

"Please." I scoffed. "I know you're old school, and that back in the day somebody's word was worth something. But nowadays, anybody'll just break a code."

Ramsey shot a look to Abram and then back at me. "You are green, aren't you?"

He reared back and, before I could react, he leveled his fist at me.

I flinched, but instead of being hit, I heard a yell. My eyes flew open. Ramsey had stopped mid-punch, pain etched into his expression. His hand lowered, and he keeled over, resting his hands on his knees and sucking in deep gulps of air. The hand he'd used to try to punch me was shaking.

"He *can't* break the code, Charisse," Abram said. "He physically can't. Which means someone else is responsible for what happened to Briar."

"Not that I would've done anything to her even if I could have," Ramsey said. "I adore that woman. Always have. God knows I've proved it more than a few times."

"What does that mean?" Abram and I said at once.

Ramsey sighed, brushing his copper-brown hair out of his eyes. "Things weren't always good between Briar and I. Even before we came here, the modeling jobs started to dry up."

"No way," I murmured.

Briar had always been the top model at our company. It was part of the reason I hated her so much. She could (and often did) book any and everything, even to the extent of stealing gigs right out from under me—even after contracts had been signed.

"It's true," Ramsey answered. "She was getting older, I suppose. But I could feel her growing dissatisfied with her life and, as a result, she started to pull away from me. She started talking about taking some time apart, said she needed to find herself. So I did the finding for her."

"What did you do?" Abram asked, his voice dropping an entire octave.

"Another Conduit, another favor. I had them place a light enchantment on her. Persuasion. It made her endearing. People couldn't stop looking at her. It was harmless—just made it so everyone saw her the way I did."

"Everyone but me," I answered.

"Well, there are reasons for that, aren't there?" he asked, looking at me intently.

Abram stepped in front of me, blocking me from Ramsey's view. "What does that have to do with what's happened to her now?"

"I don't know," Ramsey said, his voice quiet.

"Is it the Conduit you bargained with? Is that who's doing this?"

Ramsey shook his head.

"How can you be sure?" Abram asked.

"Because your girlfriend took his head off," he answered.

"You knew Dalton?" I asked breathlessly, my heart dropping.

"He was desperate. He wasn't true born. He had come by his powers illegitimately, and he didn't know anything. He promised that, if I taught him, he would give me whatever I wanted." Ramsey licked his lips quickly. "I swear, on my name as a mage, I had no idea what he was up to."

"And you didn't bother to ask!" Abram yelled. "You didn't care! So long as you got what you wanted! And where did it get you?"

"Nowhere!" Ramsey screamed, tears welling up in his pale blue eyes. "She still pulled away. After everything, after all I had done for her, she still started spending the night with that woman. But I still loved her. God help me, I still do."

"Come on, Charisse," Abram said, taking my arm and leading me toward the door. "We're leaving."

"No, wait." I pulled my arm free and crossed the room back toward Ramsey. "What woman?"

"Charisse, I said *let's go*."

I put my hand up, not even bothering to turn back toward Abram. To Ramsey, I said, "Well?"

"Briar was having an affair. Look, I knew she was bisexual. We've had an open relationship for years—for her, not me. I was happy with only her, but she wanted...more..."

"And you think this has something to do with what happened to her?"

Ramsey frowned. "She was hiding it from me. This other woman. Why would she hide it from me?"

I pressed my lips together and shook my head sadly. "I don't know. But that doesn't mean that woman is responsible. Not for that."

"Maybe not. But she was with her when it happened. For hours I couldn't reach her, then next thing I knew, I got a call from the hospital that they found Briar in a rose bush near the hotel. She's deathly allergic."

My eyes widened. "And they think you did it. Because who else would know that."

"That's how she ended up in a coma...but to still be in one?" Ramsey asked, spreading his hands. "Someone very close to her at the time it happened must have done something to make sure she stayed that way. And now the police want to pin it on me."

I felt Abram's presence at my side. He was nearly growling. "You got framed, probably to get you out of the way of whatever that Conduit has planned. But you know what? They got one thing right. You deserve to rot in jail."

"Abram," I hissed sharply.

His gaze bore down into mine. "It's time to go, Charisse. For all we know, he created this problem. Given his history with

CONNER KRESSLEY & REBECCA HAMILTON

Dalton, my guess is he's not the person to help fix it. If this is Briar's fate because of his actions, he's gotten what he deserves for helping a Conduit."

I pivoted toward him. "It's not Briar's fault or anyone else's who is dying."

Abram's jaw clenched. "And we will help those people. We're just not going to help *him*."

With that, Abram led me back toward the door, and this time, I let him. Not because I agreed with him, but because I thought Ramsey had heard enough. I would have to talk with Abram about this later.

As we left, Ramsey yelled after us. "You'd really run away from this just because I had a few conversations with a dead man? Do you have any idea what's going on out there? Have you even seen the news?"

My feet stopped moving, and I turned around. I needed to know. I needed to know because I was next.

Ramsey scrambled for a remote control that sat tackily close to the Waterford. When he flipped on the television, my breath caught as I saw what was on the news. A man lay disfigured and bloody on the ground. Familiar words were carved into his forehead.

"It's happening more frequently now. I've done the math," Ramsey said. "Even now someone else is in waiting. Today and two more, that's how long we have until whoever that poor bastard is throws himself off the cliff, too."

*Herself*, I mentally corrected him.

Abram didn't let him say another word. He pulled me outside and slammed the door shut. I followed after him blindly, the vision from the television still playing in my mind.

My chest tightened. I was looking at my own future. In two days, I would be where that man on the news was.

Poor bastard, party of one.

# CHAPTER 17

*I* should have anticipated having another dream that night. After all, that *was* what happened to people after they saw Briar around here. Perhaps some part of me had hoped that first dream was a fluke. Maybe another part of me would hold onto that idea until I was plummeting to my death. Still, that night—when my dreams landed me even closer to that horrible cliff with Briar folding her arms in front of me—I was just as shaken as I had been the night before.

"Do try to hold it together." Briar rolled her eyes. "For some reason, I expected more from you."

"It's because I'm not exactly normal," I answered, looking past Briar and noticing the way the trees swayed in the breeze even though I felt no wind.

"I guess we can agree on that." She scoffed, digging a jeweled heel into the ground.

She was so angry, so dismissive. And the thing was, I couldn't really blame her. What she was going through—be forced to murder by proxy—was insane and, even if we did hate each other, fate and magic had tied us too tightly together for me to overlook that now. Though it churned my stomach, I found myself actually relating to Briar...*and* feeling for her.

"Do you know what's happening to you?" I asked, moving closer to her and, as such, closer to the cliff.

"I know what's happening to *you*," she said. "In two days, you're going to take a header off this cliff. I'll never see you again, and you'll be reduced to a tacky overcompensating splat on the ground. Does that answer your question?"

Her words stung, but I couldn't let them derail me.

"You're being used, Briar," I said, running a hand through my hair. "I don't know by who, or why, or even to what end. But it's the truth. And I'm going to need your help if I'm gonna have even a little bit of a chance of getting either one of us out of this. So could you pretend your attitude is one of your ratty old coats and check it at the door?"

"What do you mean by get *us* out of this?" she asked, blinking hard.

"Well, I'm a couple days away from becoming the next in a string of history's weirdest suicide victims, and you're lying unconscious in a hospital bed. So I think my words speak for themselves."

"I-I'm alive?" she asked almost breathlessly. "This has been going on for so long. It's been an endless parade of death after death. The last thing I remember is falling. I figured it was some eternal punishment for—"

"Being a bitch?" I finished.

"Like you're one to talk," she shot back.

"Look," I said, "I'm not here to fight with you. I know we've had our differences in the past, but that's over now. I met your husband, Briar. He told me everything you guys have been going through, and everything he did for you...magic-wise, I mean."

She scrunched her nose. "What nonsense are you rambling on about now?"

"You know, how he had a Conduit spell you to be extra persuasive, to help you with your modeling career and all."

When her eyebrows pulled together, I instantly realized I had misspoke. Not only did Briar have no idea what I was talking about, but she also was pretty disgusted that I thought it.

"Seriously?" she yelled. "I should have figured. I should have known that you'd have to resort to cheap lies and misdirection to make yourself feel better. Even now, you can't take the fact that I was just better than you!"

"That's not what I meant." I sighed. "None of that's important."

"Which is why you brought it up, right?" She sneered. "You know, it's my own fault. For a second, I actually thought you were on my side. I thought that you might have been brought here for a reason. But you're just like the rest of them, with your 'I'm so special and different' garbage. You're all the same." She stomped the ground. "Have fun ending up like the rest of them, Charisse. Dead and gone."

As I floated back to consciousness, my entire body shook. Two days, that was what I had left now. Two days and, like Briar said, I would be dead and gone.

"What's wrong?" Abram asked from beside me. His hand brushed against my cheek. Looking over, I could only imagine what he saw in my expression. He stared at me, his dark eyes tracing my face. He was bare-chested, and his skin glistened in the morning sunlight.

Just once more. I would only see him like this one more time.

"Nothing," I answered quickly, though unconvincingly. "I didn't sleep well. That's all."

I couldn't tell him the truth. It would weigh on his mind until nothing else was able to reside there. No. All I could do was see this through. One way or another, it would be over very soon.

"Abram?" I asked, but I continued before he answered me. "Why do you think the cops aren't more involved? Why don't they physically stop people from jumping?"

"Oh." Abram's expression fell. "You didn't read the earlier articles?"

I shook my head. Truth be told, I couldn't stand to keep reading about it, knowing I was next.

"They tried, Charisse. They weren't strong enough to hold the jumpers back. Explained it as some kind of increased strength caused by adrenaline, or something. One of the cops went over the cliff with one of them."

So much for hoping someone could physically save me. We needed magic on our side for this one.

"Wh-what's on the agenda today?" I asked, switching the subject before Abram had a chance to delve into it anymore.

"I'm going to go over the list of victims again and hopefully find a common denominator that I overlooked before."

He got out of bed. His body might as well have been a painting or a sculpture—some perfect masterpiece that only came along once every dozen or so lifetimes. A pang of hurt ran through me. It wasn't long enough. I hadn't known him—known this feeling— for nearly long enough yet.

"There has to be connection," he said, standing there naked and letting the sunlight kiss every inch of his body. "There has to be something that links them."

A thought tickled the back of my mind. Briar told me something in the dream when she was chewing me out...something about everyone being like me, about everyone thinking they were special.

My heart sank as the realization came over me.

"A-Abram," I stammered, trying to collect my thoughts. "I think I know."

"You think you know what?" he asked, turning toward me with beautiful, narrowed eyes.

"I think I know who the Conduit is targeting."
　＊ ＊ ＊

128

"Tell me again," Satina said, twirling a curvy straw around an electric blue drink. "I just want to make sure I understand."

After I told Abram my theory (albeit without telling him exactly *how* I came up with it) he thought a return trip to Satina might help clear things up. Although, given the way she was looking at me now—as if I had suggested pink was a neutral color—something told me that maybe she wasn't going to be as helpful as we had hoped.

"I've told you three times already," I answered, sitting between her and Abram under the shade of a beach style umbrella.

The sand looked unbearably dry, and the tourists were all but extinct—not too surprising, given that we were sitting on an island that was experiencing both a legendary drought and an unprecedented spike in mysterious suicides.

"Humor me," she answered, taking a sip of the blue tonic.

"The victims." I sighed. Repeating myself made me uncomfortable. Like Satina knew I was hiding something and was hoping I would reveal it one of these times. "I think they were Supplicants."

"Because that's your answer for everything?" She arched her eyebrows. "First Sleeping Beauty was a Supplicant and now all of her victims are?"

"They're not her victims," I answered. "She doesn't have any ill will toward these people. She's as much a chess piece in this as anyone. Or, at least that's what I assume," I finished, covering my tracks.

"And do you have any proof of this?" Satina asked.

*Yes, just none I can speak of at the moment.*

"Look, what else could it be?" I asked. "The Conduit must have some, albeit warped, reason for doing all this. Based on what I know about Conduits, all they care about is power and vengeance. And since Ramsey didn't say anything about Briar pissing off an extremely magical being, then my guess is that the Conduit is using Briar's gift of magical persuasion to get the Supplicants to kill themselves as a means to collect their blood for magic."

"And it's just a coincidence that all of them showed up here?" Satina asked, shaking her head. "That's a bit of a stretch."

"Unless the Conduit is also drawing them here somehow," Abram chimed in. "It would explain what we're doing here."

"What?" I asked, turning to him. "I came here because you said it was beautiful."

He narrowed his gaze. "This place is a hole," he answered. "I hadn't been here in over seventy years, and it was a hole even then. You pointed this place out to me on a map and said it looked like fun. You told me you saw a television special about it."

"No, I didn't!" I said, leaning back in my chair. Why was he doing this? We didn't have time for games! "Coming here was your idea."

"They're drawing Suppliants here," Abram answered. Looking at me, he added, "They drew *you* here, Charisse. I swear to you, I never suggested this place."

My heart sunk to my stomach. I thought for sure it might drown in the acid sloshing around down there. I certainly felt like I was drowning. Unfortunately, history dictated that wasn't quite how I would go.

I wanted to tell him everything right then, but we were finally getting somewhere. I needed him to be clearheaded, not worried about me dying. If he thought I was in danger, he would have me off this island in the blink of an eye—which for all we knew would not be enough to save me and certainly wouldn't be enough to save anyone else.

"Well," Satina said, taking another sip. "Looks like your girl-friend's hypothesis just gained a little credence. Maybe it's that beacon I was telling you guys about."

I shook my head. "I already found it, remember?"

Satina rolled her eyes. "You found a magical letter in a castle. That hardly counts."

I gritted my teeth. "That's where you told me to look."

"For a clue, not for the beacon." She waved her hand dismissively. "Char, you do realize you aren't even close to solving this one, don't you? That's why I said we needed you to work on your abilities. And now that we have an idea what's going on, finding that talisman seems more important than ever, wouldn't you say?"

My mind started swimming...or more like drowning. I'd been wasting precious time—time I couldn't get back, and with only two days left to live, time that I didn't have to spare.

Abram, scowl firmly in place, stood and started to walk off.

"Where are you going?" I called after him.

"To the morgue," he answered. He stopped to turn back and face me. "I need to test the bodies of the victims. If they are Supplicants, then their blood will confirm."

I stood to meet him. "Then I'm coming with you."

"You're damn right," he replied. "From this moment on, I'm not letting you out of my sight.

Dropping her finished drink on the table, Satina added, "At some point, you have to let Char be who she is, Abram!"

Abram didn't so much as acknowledge her.

"Good luck, young lovers," she added. "I assume you'll keep me posted."

With that, Abram grabbed my hand, and we were gone.

\* \* \*

Getting in and out of the hospital was almost a joke at this point. We weaved through the halls once again unnoticed. We navigated to an eerie silver door that stood out in the sea of white. *The morgue.* A lump rose in my throat.

Other than Dalton's body and the expired one that Satina wore around like a prom dress, the last dead body I had seen was my mother's. She had died right in front of me, a shell of the vibrant loving woman who had been my everything. Even now, with all the time that had passed, I still couldn't really process that loss. It was bigger than me, bigger than anything I had ever gone through before or since...and that said a lot.

"Your heart is racing," Abram said. "Not in the good kind of way."

I nodded slowly, careful not to look at him out of fear I might crumble right then and there.

"Wait out here if you like," Abram said to me softly. "Just stay by the window where I can see you."

"No," I answered. "I need to see this. I need to see what we're fighting for."

Opening the door didn't do much to still my heart. It was cold and unbearably still in this place.

Abram pulled open two large drawers. Long figures covered in sheets lay on each of the boards, each one the evidence of my own impending fate.

Abram glanced at their toe tags. "These are them."

Moving over to the counter, he pulled out a needle, ripped off its seal, and took it to the first body.

I tried not to look, but I couldn't resist. I would be here in two days. Abram would likely be standing over me. Was it fair to do this to him, to rob him of the knowledge that these were very likely his last moments with me?

"What the hell..." he murmured, and then moved on to the next body.

As quickly as he had moved to that one, he went to the next.

"Unbelievable," he said.

"What is it?" I asked.

"I think you may have been right."

"They have Supplicant blood?" I asked, pulling nervously at my fingers.

"I assume they did at some point," he answered, holding up a decidedly empty needle. "Though I can't say for certain, as it appears all of their blood has mysteriously vanished."

# CHAPTER 18

*bram* and I were pretty silent as we made our way back to the castle. Any other time, it would have been nice. We had an unspoken connection, the sort where you didn't need to talk to be comfortable. And, given that we were actually going on a long walk on the beach, I couldn't have painted a more romantic, even if cliché, picture.

But this wasn't romantic. It was terrifying. Taking away the idea that if we didn't find an answer for every one of the thousand questions we had, I would be dead in two days, we now knew for sure that we were in the clutches of one of the most powerful Conduits either of us had ever encountered.

He or she brought us here on purpose. They weren't afraid of my untapped potential. They weren't afraid of Abram's very formidable skill set. They knew who we were, and they brought us into this fray regardless. And that scared the hell out of me.

"How are you?" I finally asked, looking at the late afternoon sun and trying to clear away the darkest of my thoughts. "I never know what to expect here—if you might just turn in the middle of the day or something."

"I'll be fine," he answered, eyes resting on the gently cresting waves. "I'll admit, the magic here is pulling at me, but I've been through worse. I was caught off guard last time, but I'm expecting it now, and I'm not about to lose control again. Not with everything that's at stake."

And there it was. This was about me now, and that changed everything for Abram. Knowing that the Conduit brought me here specifically to drain me of my blood and, as such, my life, had already seeped into Abram's thoughts. It was already making him anxious and fogging up his mind, which solidified what I already knew. If this was all it took, then telling him I had *already* seen Briar in my dreams was definitely off the table.

I intertwined my fingers with his. I wasn't gone yet and, if I could help it, I wouldn't be going anywhere anytime soon. My life would not be ending in a day and a half. I needed him to know that.

I needed to know that.

"What do we do next?" I asked.

He cleared his throat, his eyes moving from the water back to me. "We know a lot more than we did two days ago. We know why and how Briar is being used as the new Sleeping Beauty, and we know to what end. At least in part."

"What do you mean?" I asked, keeping pace with him.

He frowned. "Well, we know that the Conduit is somehow pulling Supplicants to the island, and we know they're somehow using Briar to murder them and harvest their blood. But what is the Conduit using that blood *for*?"

"I figured all Conduits were greedy when it came to blood. Sort of like that creepy Lord of the Rings guy and his precious."

"Gollum," Abram answered absentmindedly.

"Oh, I finally stumbled onto a reference you're aware of." I chuckled. "I'd never be presumptuous enough to think you knew the movie. I'm guessing you're familiar with the book."

"You could say that. I helped Mr. Tolkien with the editing," he said as if it was no big deal.

I smiled, peering over at him. "You enjoy being a mystery to me, don't you?"

"More than you know, Ms. Bellamy," he said, dropping his tenor to that seductive note.

Normally his tone would make me feel giddy and aroused, but given my impending death, it only made me uneasy.

"Now," he said, continuing on, "about our next move. As I mentioned, we don't know what the Conduit's ultimate goal is. This many Supplicants have never been in the same place at the same time before. So, whatever the Conduit is after, it must be quite the lofty endeavor."

"Sort of like the Mount Doom of evil plans."

"Don't push it." He smiled and squeezed my hand. "We also don't know who the Conduit is that King Archibald very likely has something to do with. Is it the same one plaguing this island, or a random one that works for the company that wrote him that letter?"

I groaned at the mention of the king's name. He was the *last* person I wanted to think about right now.

"I understand he isn't your favorite person in the world, but the letter you found is more than enough incentive to believe he has something to do with this, at least tangentially."

"The letter made it sound like the Conduit's working against him."

"But that doesn't mean it's the same one working against the Supplicants on this island. I'm certain it's connected, though," Abram said, "and the King knows it. I can sense it—he's been acting strange lately."

"How can you tell?" I scoffed, remembering the bound woman and the way in which King Douchebag thought of women in general. If that was normal for him, what could possibly be strange?

"He's gotten lax about keeping an eye on us. Too lax. In fact, this morning he suggested we go see more of the island."

"So?" I asked, quirking my lips.

"So, as far as he knows, we're his familial enemies. If my sworn adversary was under my roof, very likely plotting against me, I would want to keep him as close as humanly possible."

"Maybe King Archibald isn't as smart as you," I suggested, melting against Abram as the ocean breeze fluttered through my hair. Why couldn't life just be this? This feeling of complete belonging I had with Abram?

"He's been alive for five hundred years," Abram said. "He's as smart as anyone who walks the Earth. If he wanted us out, it was because he was doing something he didn't want us to see. So, before we left this morning, I snuck into his private chambers and checked his day planner. He has a meeting scheduled with someone referred to as Huntsman in the East dining room."

We came to a stop, and I realized we were standing in front of the castle. No, not in front of it. We were in the back, on the eastern side. How long had we been walking like this?

I stared up at the castle. "I don't like where this conversation is going, Abram."

"Then you'll absolutely abhor the next part," he said, straightening his posture so that his shoulders pressed squarely back. "We need to find out what that meeting is about. There will be guards surrounding that room, but we can listen from the outside."

"You want to scale the building and eavesdrop on them?" I asked, raising my eyebrows.

"Not just me," he answered. "*Us.*"

"What good would I do? In case you haven't noticed, I'm not exactly a gymnast," I said, motioning to my full figure.

"But you're smaller than me, and that means you can fit on the ledge under the windowsill. Something I decidedly cannot do."

Of course I was smaller than Abram. Everyone was smaller than him.

"Abram," I started.

"I'll get you up there, and I won't be more than five feet away at any time. There's a fuller fold in the wall where I can sit. But unfortunately, it's not close enough for me to hear anything going on inside, not with the enchantments on this place."

"So you want me to dangle midair while listening to a conversation that will most likely kill my appetite for the next century?" I asked.

"Yes," he said, matter of fact. "Are you ready? We don't have much time."

After a second and a half of thinking, I extended my hand, motioning for him to pick me up.

"The things I do for you," I muttered.

"Don't think they go unnoticed," he answered, scooping me up.

As every time I had ever been in Abram's arms, the rest of the world fell away. There was only me and his grip, strong and unyielding. I was safe here, with him. And I always would be. A sense of calm filled me, tinged with a carnal hunger that also accompanied any contact I had with him.

"Hold on tight," he breathed against my ear.

And he was off.

There were some abilities Abram might no longer have since the castle's enchantment thwarted his beastly nature, but apparently some of his skills remained, perhaps his body having learned them from years of practice. Surely there was a time, back when he was human, that he wasn't able to scale walls with all the ease and silence of a movie assassin?

If catching my breath while in his presence would have been possible, I wouldn't have time to do it. Mere instants passed, and I was perched on the ledge. Looking down, I saw that I was fifty feet in the air, with Abram resting a few feet under me on the fuller ledge.

"Don't look down," he whispered.

"Too late," I mouthed back.

Trying to settle my racing heart and jittery fingers, I edged closer to the window and peered over just far enough to see what was going on. Large drapes blocked most of the window, which I hoped put me at a slight advantage of peeking in without being easily spotted.

The East dining room was smaller than the one we had eaten in since we got here, but it was no less fancy. Decorated in ancient art, the room was filled with trinkets to redecorate the castle, should King Archibald find himself in the mood.

The king stood at one end of the table with a younger-looking man standing at the other. This man—Huntsman, I presumed—had shoulder-length brown hair that spilled across his broad shoulders. His face, sharp and striking, was without blemish or flaw. The words Calvin Klein sprang to mind while looking at him. And when he turned, and I saw the ax strapped across his back, the word 'terrifying' replaced them.

"I told you this wouldn't be easy," the man said, an English accent toying with his words.

"I never imagined it would be," King Archibald shot back testily. "If it was easy, I would get one of my people to do it. No one pays you for 'easy,' Huntsman. That's why you're so expensive."

"I'm expensive because I produce results," Huntsman answered, running a thumb over his bottom lip.

"So where are mine?" Archibald demanded, jabbing his finger into the table. "I'm in a particularly sensitive place right now. These suicides—I can't have it. It brings too much attention my way. If I'm going to get out of here, I need to convince the Company that I'm a valuable commodity, that it's in their best interests to facilitate my needs. And if I can't put a stop to a witch running amok in *my* backyard, I'm going to have a hard time proving that."

"You do realize," Huntsman said, "that you are essentially paying me to stop the witch so that the Company will see fit to stop her. That doesn't make much sense now, does it?"

The king bristled, then slammed his fist on the table. "I'm

going to ask you one more time, can you find her for me or not?"

"Patience," Huntsman said easily, amusement lighting up his eyes. "Rome wasn't built in a day. You should know, right? I'm sure you were there."

"I was a lot of places before this blasted curse, Huntsman! And now look at me." The king's posture deflated. "Imprisoned to this castle. *Again*. No sooner did I break the curse than it came back. I didn't so much as make it down the castle's walkway before I was violently thrown back inside by a similar curse—and this time, one the Company doesn't feel is their place to remove. Tell me, Huntsman, what could I have done to deserve this between my front door and the mail post?"

Huntsman shrugged, though his expression said he could think of a few ways to answer that.

"Nothing, that's what!" the king said. "I know this curse inside and out. I have lived it for decades, and I'm telling you, there's another Sleeping Beauty on this island."

"I don't doubt it," Huntsman said passively. "And I'll find her."

"When?" the king asked, his voice nearly a growl. "If I could leave this damn castle, I would have found her myself by now. What's taking so long? I'm starting to get the feeling you are giving me the runaround."

Huntsman's thumb rubbed across his lip again. I chided myself inwardly for thinking his lips were nice. They weren't as nice as Abram's.

"Let me ask you something," Huntsman said, dropping his hand away from his face. "If you doubt me, why is it you hired me?" He made a dismissing motion with his hand. "Don't answer that. Why, I think you already have, don't you?" he asked, tilting his head to one side. "You're stuck here, and I am not. I can do this job, and you cannot. You're the idiot who got cursed in the first place, and not me."

The king pounded his fist on the table. "Enough! I'll remind you who you're talking to."

"No need," Huntsman said coolly. "Let me be clear. You, king or not, are afraid. This whole incident is unusual, and your people's support is waning."

"Watch it," King Archibald warned. "You came highly recommended as one of the few people able to do what I need done. But make no mistake—I won't hesitate to act should I find your work lacking."

"You would be hard-pressed to replace me, and we both know that. We also know that when all is said and done, I don't need your money. I'm doing you a favor. *You* are the one with everything to lose. If the people found out your greedy desire to escape a curse you brought on yourself was in any way tied to the drought and suicides, your life would be over." Huntsman crossed his arms and stepped ever-so-slightly closer to the king. I trembled on Archibald's behalf, as he didn't seem to be adequately enough afraid of this rather intimidating man. I thought Huntsman was going to do something, but he just tilted up his chin. "So maybe it is *I* who need remind *you* who you're talking to, Jacob. I'm your lifeline."

Something about the king's expression faltered, but I couldn't place my finger on his emotion. "I haven't been Jacob in quite some time," he said, "and I'll thank you to remember that."

"So long as I get what's coming to me at the end of this, you can be whoever you want." Huntsman grinned. "Now what about the other two? The visiting prince and his concubine?"

"Concubine?" I mouthed. I wasn't sure what that word meant, but I was sure I wasn't one.

"For the time being, they distract people. We need that," he said, moving toward Huntsman. "But we can't have them running around telling the world what they've seen. Once the main objective is completed, dispose of them." King Archibald slid a finger down Huntsman's ax, which I was pretty sure glowed a little at the touch. "Unless they get in the way before, in which case, you're to waste no time silencing them. Permanently."

# CHAPTER 19

"What are you doing?" Abram asked.

He had a newspaper in his hand and a bemused look on his face. I couldn't blame him. I probably looked pretty foolish, sitting cross legged on the floor with my arms outstretched at either side.

We'd managed to get back into the castle while King Archibald was still tied up with Huntsman. As far as we knew, neither of them had realized anyone was listening in on them, and we thought it best to quit while we were ahead. But that didn't mean we were out of the woods. And it didn't mean I could afford to sit on my fashionable laurels while some unknown Conduit moved us around like chess pieces. Especially now.

"I'm meditating," I answered after another slow exhale.

"Yoga?" He pursed his lips. "I never thought of you as the New Age type."

"I'm not meditating for exercise or enlightenment," I answered, my arms still outstretched. "This is purely business."

He moved closer, setting the paper on the bed and kneeling in front of me. "I'm going to ask you to explain what you mean by that. I'm absolutely sure I won't like the answer, but God help me, I'm going to ask you anyway."

"I have power, Abram," I said, staring him straight in the face and finally lowering my arms. They didn't seem to be doing much good anyway. "I have power that I can't control, that I can't even tap into. And every time I see a movie or read a book about someone unlocking their hidden potential or whatever, it always starts with this sort of meditation crap."

Abram's jaw set. His eyes darkened. "I don't want you diving into that. It's too dangerous."

"You're not serious," I said, all my calm being ripped away on a current of irritation. So much for meditation being the path to tranquility.

"More than you know," he said, standing and looking down at me.

I scrambled to my feet. Even though he was as sturdy as an oak and stood nearly a foot taller than me, I wanted to even the playing field as best I could. "You want to know about dangerous? There's an assassin with an enchanted ax and abs of steel out to kill us."

"You saw his abdominal muscles?" Abram asked, raising his eyebrows.

I waved him off. "Context clues. Doesn't matter. The point is, he wants to kill us."

"Huntsman doesn't scare me."

"Maybe he should," I said, stepping closer. "In case you've forgotten, you don't have any powers here—none that you can control, anyway. You're just you."

"*Just* me," he repeated, frowning. "If you think I need powers to keep you safe, then you haven't been paying attention."

"And if you think we're not in over our heads, then *you* haven't been paying attention," I shot back.

His glare didn't change, same as I knew his mind wouldn't. Not like this. Abram was stubborn. He knew what he wanted, what he thought was right, and what he considered important. And banging against him like a wave against a rock wasn't going to change that. We had done this dance enough times for me to know that. If I was going to change his mind (and that was a big if), I was going to have to be honest.

"Abram…" I started, my voice trembling a bit at the thought of what I was about to confess. "We-we don't have as much time as you think."

"What are you talking about?" The fire drained from his voice. His face grew pale and expressionless.

I opened my mouth to speak, but nothing came out. Could I really do this to him, lay this on him and expect him to fix it? No. I knew him better than that. I was his soft spot—his Achilles' heel. This information wouldn't kill him. It wouldn't even knock him down. No, it would invigorate him to the point of overload. It would blind him from the truth of what was happening here and halt the necessary steps we had to take if we were ever going to get out of this.

"It's just…" I shook my head.

"What?" He placed a rough hand on my arm and squeezed. "Tell me what's going on."

No. He couldn't know this. Not now.

"We don't know how long until the next person dies."

"There's going to be casualties, Char. I know you care. Believe me, I do, too. But we can't save everyone.

I bit my lip. "That's not fair, Abram. That's—"

"Life," he said. "That's life. This life, anyway."

I swallowed hard. I needed to get through to him. "Fine. I get what you are saying, Abram, but think for a minute if it was me. What if *I* was next? What if there was someone like me, right here on this island, who could help me…and she chose to do nothing. What would you think then?"

Abram's lips pressed into a thin line. "You know the answer to that, same as you know why I'm not going to change my mind. If there was a person who could help you if, God forbid, you found yourself in that situation, I would personally move heaven and hell to make sure you got what you needed. But you're *not* in that situation, and it's because I don't want you in that situation that I want you to be careful in the first place!"

My whole body burned to tell him how wrong he was. But this wasn't only about me, and he would make it that way if he knew the truth. Somehow I needed him to treat this situation as though it was my life on the line, but without the single-minded rampage that would occur if he knew that was actually the case.

He was still ranting when I tuned back into his tirade. "—and throwing yourself headfirst into a very dangerous world that you couldn't even begin to understand will only serve to get you killed." His dark, deep eyes pinned on mine. "You're more important to me than those people, Charisse. I won't apologize for that. And I won't let you lose yourself trying to save people you don't even know."

"Abram—"

"No, Char. Listen to me. The Conduit lured you to this island because you're a Supplicant, and if it weren't for your Conduit nature blocking dreams, you might have seen the new Sleeping Beauty yourself by now! Just the thought of that—" He swallowed hard and shook his head. "We can't go down that road, okay?"

I chewed on my lip, biting back the words. Stopping myself from telling him that my Conduit nature hadn't protected me. That I had already seen Briar. That trying to save those people meant trying to save myself. But if he was this much of a mess over the mere idea of it, then burdening him with reality in order to make my point would do more damage than good. I needed to get through to him some other way.

But for right now, in this one moment, all I wanted was to forget. To feel like I was still alive, like I wasn't already dead, walking around waiting for my body to finally be put in the ground. And no one made me feel more alive than Abram.

I leaned into him, kissing him hard on the mouth. His scent and heat overtook me, as it always did. His grip as he wrapped his arms around my waist and lifted me off the floor felt like home. I didn't agree with what he said. We almost never agreed. But the idea that he loved me that much, that he would throw the rest of the world into the incinerator if need be, spoke to a place inside of me that I couldn't help but relent to.

"But you are losing me." I breathed against his lips. "This is who I am. If I can't help these people, then I'm gone. Don't you get that?"

"You're not gone," he said, ripping at my shirt. "You're here." He kissed my collar bone. "And here," he said, moving down toward my breast. "You're right in front of me." He threw me on the bed, and my cheeks burned as the sight of him hovering above me came clear into view. "And that's exactly where you're going to stay."

He did nothing to hide his animalistic nature as he climbed on top of me. The weight of him pressing against my quivering body sent shivers down my spine.

We were wrong to think magic didn't work inside this place, because damn if I wasn't feeling it right now. He pulled at what was left of my shirt, freeing me of its possession and exposing my bare chest to the lantern light that illuminated the room.

I moaned as he traveled farther down my chest, encapsulating my breast in his mouth and flicking at my nipple with his tongue.

"Be loud for me," he said, coming up for air just long enough to give me a command.

"Give me a reason," I responded breathlessly. "Please."

His gaze flashed up at me wordlessly, and I knew where this was going. "I give the orders here, Ms. Bellamy," he said without a hint of a smile in his voice. "Now. Be. Loud."

In a flash that was almost too quick for me to register, he had ripped the rest of my clothes off and was working his way down my body. With the skill of a sculptor, he drove two fingers deep inside of me, sending shockwaves all the way down to my toes.

I wasn't sure whether it was because of the intense pleasure I now felt with his fingers roaming deeper within me than any man had ever been or because I was starting to get off on him giving me orders, but I did as he asked.

A sharp, loud moan escaped my lips. A satisfied smile draped his face as he licked from my naval all the way down to my mound.

A dark thought entered my mind just about the same time as Abram's tongue flickered over my sweet spot.

This was finite. These were the last days I would ever have. And this pleasure, it could be the last time he ever gave it to me. On impulse, I grabbed his head on either side, clenching against him tightly as he pleasured me.

"No," he said. "That won't do." He stopped what he was doing and pinned my hands above my head. "These hands are mine. They do what I say, and nothing else."

He kept my hands steady as he thrust his cock into me. I moaned again, even louder this time. He seemed to get off on it as his thrust grew quicker and deeper with each of my moans.

He squeezed my wrists. "Whose hands are these?"

"Yours," I moaned, back arched in ecstasy.

"What do they do?" he asked, teeth gritted, sweat dripping off his face.

"What you tell them to," I said, writhing into him as he thrust again.

"And what else?"

"Nothing." I moaned so loudly I was sure the entire island would hear. "Nothing else."

His continued thrusts heightened every sensation in my body while driving away every unwanted emotion, unwanted thought, until finally we both came together. He leaned over me, kissing me and biting my lip as he released. A bit of pain to go with the pleasure.

"Damn right," he breathed. "And you better never forget it."

* * *

While cleaning myself up in the bathroom, I couldn't help but notice the woman staring back at me in the mirror. How was it possible to be both the happiest and saddest I had even been in my life at the same time?

I was fulfilled in every way a person could be. I was more in love than perhaps anyone else who had ever lived. At least, that was what it felt like. And yet, it would be gone all too soon. Briar would reappear and send me hurtling to my death. And then Abram, and the love I felt for him, would be as gone as I was.

I splashed water on my face. I couldn't let this get the better of me. I had been through these sorts of dire circumstances before and came out of it stronger than ever. Something would come up. Something *had* to come up.

What if something didn't come up?

Grabbing a hand towel, I made my way back into our bed chambers. Abram sat on the bed, covered at the waist with a sheet and staring intently at something on the television.

As I moved closer, I saw he'd turned on the news. A blonde woman with dark skin spoke at a commentator's desk. My skin chilled as I heard what she was saying.

"Delia Curr, single mother of two, is the latest victim of what authorities and island dwellers alike are calling a case of mass hysteria."

An image of a happy woman and her two sons flashed across the screen, instantly breaking my heart.

"Ms. Curr is the seventeenth suicide victim Grimoult has seen in just under ninety days. A seemingly happy woman, Delia—like the rest of the victims—is said to have been vibrant right up until her death; which begs the question, what is getting into the townspeople here?"

The news anchor on the television shuffled papers.

"Authorities have declared a state of emergency on the island. All consumables are being inspected, with more processed foods being recalled completely in an attempt to get to the bottom of the strange occurrences. What's more, a ban on consuming tap, lake, and spring water has been placed in effect until further notice." An image of the woman and her sons flashed across the screen again. "With no living relatives, Ms. Curr's children will be placed into foster care until a more suitable home can be found. If you or anyone you know is having thoughts of suicide, please call the number on the screen below."

That poor woman. Those poor children. That poor family. I looked over at Abram, filled with horror and pain.

He raised his hand, as though to stop me from saying what I was obviously thinking.

"Fine. You win," he said. "You want to figure out how to use your powers. I'll take you back to that damn mage."

# CHAPTER 20

Turned out the 'damn mage' was even less keen to my idea than Abram was. The instant he saw us on his doorstep, he slammed the door in our faces.

"I just want to talk!" I shouted through the white-painted wood.

Abram's hands balled into his fists at his sides. "Get out of the way. I'll handle it."

"We don't want to draw attention to ourselves, Abram," I said, backing away from the door. "Please don't do anything rash."

"I'm just going to knock again," he said, moving toward it. "Very hard."

He slammed a fist against Ramsey's door. It sounded like thunder as his hand met the wood. The door broke in two as it landed on Ramsey (and Briar's) very expensive-looking carpet. So much for the "respecting people's property" thing he'd been going for on our first visit.

To Ramsey's credit, he didn't look scared. He stood in the hallway, a pistol pointed at Abram's head.

"We both know that's not going to do you any good," Abram said, ushering me through the doorway.

I settled beside him, not as surprised as I should be that—once again—we were embroiled in a gun-fueled standoff.

Life had gotten so weird.

"Put your foolish hand down," Abram said. "You're not scaring anyone."

Ramsey's eyes narrowed. With a flick of the wrist, the gun moved from Abram's head to mine. "How about now?"

My body tightened, though not as much as it had before. Hadn't he proven he *can't* shoot me? But then, what if there was some loophole? Would he if he could? I didn't know Ramsey, not really. And the fact that Briar had basically just told me to go jump off a cliff didn't give me much hope for the merciful capacity of her chosen mate. But there was something about him, a softness around the edges, that told me he didn't want to do this.

"We came here to talk peacefully, Mr. Duldridge," Abram answered, his tone much lighter than I would have anticipated. "And should you decide to conduct yourself in a reasonable manner, that's exactly what we'll do. But if you insist on going down this ill-advised path of aggression by threatening the woman I love, I'll be forced to slit you open and extract the information I need along with a piece of your intestines."

Ramsey's eyes widened. The gun shook in his trembling hand.

"You can't threaten me in my own home," he said.

"It's not a threat, Mr. Duldridge." Abram moved toward him, raising his hand, which had turned into a curved claw—even in broad daylight. "Now put your weapon down, and I'll do the same."

Ramsey lowered the pistol to his side as he backed up against the wall. "Just say what you came to say."

There was a bitterness in his voice that tugged at my heartstrings. It suddenly became very clear to me that I was looking at someone who not only had been threatened by what was likely the most terrifying (if gorgeous) man he had ever laid eyes on, but also someone who was dealing with the aftershocks of basically losing his wife.

I wanted to comfort him, but there was too much at stake right now for me to turn soft. I needed to be strong, not only for myself, but for the people like me who were also in danger.

"Someone else is dead," Abram answered.

My eyes drifted down to his claw, and part of me wondered how hard he was trying to keep the beast at bay right now. Was it dying to come out, to tear this mage from limb to limb and then have its way with me?

Ramsey tipped up his chin. "A lot of people are dead. It's the way of the world."

Abram's mouth tightened. "Someone else has committed suicide. The same cliff, those same words carved into some poor woman's forehead."

"It's a travesty. I know that." Ramsey's face scrunched in a way that made me think he was actually being genuine. "Do you think I like the idea of the woman I love being involved in this? She's my wife, for heaven's sake, not some fairytale character who can be used and thrown away after she's served her purpose."

If there was any doubt Ramsey actually loved Briar, it was gone now. Whether she deserved that love or not was still questionable, though it also wasn't any of my business.

"I know you think I can do something," he said. "That I can help you rid the island of this Conduit who's wreaking havoc on so many people's lives. But I don't have that sort of power. We're not Conduits. My people...we're only the keepers of the secrets, the wardens of history. We know how the sausage is made, but that doesn't mean we make it."

"That's a horrific metaphor," Abram said, his face twisted in disgust. "And it's also patently untrue. You might think you know everything, but the truth is, you never even scratched the surface of what's going on here." Abram lifted his hand again. "I don't trust you."

"I wouldn't trust me, either," Ramsey admitted, eyeing Abram's sharp claws.

Abram scowled. "I need you to know that, should you repeat anything I'm about to tell you or use it in any way to profit somehow—"

"Let me guess. You'll take a chunk of my liver? Or perhaps my appendix?" Ramsey said, the snark seeping back into his tone. "Don't worry. Consider me sufficiently terrified. Now what's going on?"

I stepped forward, placing what I hoped was a calming hand on Abram's arm. "The people jumping to their deaths...they're all Supplicants."

Ramsey tilted his head. "How do you know?"

"That's not important," Abram said with a growl. "Just know that it's true. Whoever the Conduit responsible is, they're luring Supplicants to this island, then using *your* wife and the hex cast on her to coerce them into killing themselves, and then somehow harvesting their blood."

"Well, that doesn't bode well for your girlfriend, does it?" Ramsey asked, looking over at me again. "Seeing as how her blood type is AB witch bait."

"*I'll* take care of Charisse," Abram said testily.

*My love, if only you could.*

Abram closed his eyes for a moment. "The point is, we have to find the Conduit before they gather enough mystical energy to do whatever it is they're planning." Abram's gaze leveled off. "If we accomplish that, there's a good chance we can save your girl in the process."

*And yours*, I thought, looking over to Abram. Of course, I didn't say it out loud.

"And if I could help you, I would," Ramsey said, spreading his hands. "This isn't some dickheaded power play. There's honestly nothing I could do. To cast the sort of spell needed to find a

Conduit who has cloaked themselves with this much power, I'd need a potent Supplicant and a Conduit who knew how to channel that power. I'd probably need at least two scotches as well. And while I have a stocked liquor cabinet and your girlfriend here is, in fact, a Supplicant, I'm going to have to disagree with Meatloaf on this occasion and say that two out of three just isn't going to cut it."

"How about three out of three?" Abram asked, leaning forward.

"A-Abram?" I stammered, suddenly uneasy about laying my secret at Ramsey's feet.

"You're the one who wanted to go down this road," he whispered harshly. "Besides, Mr. Duldridge and I have an understanding about secrets, don't we?"

"Consider me a vault," he said, a slight tremble to his voice.

"I'm a Conduit," I said quickly, blurting it out before I lost my nerve.

"You meant to say Supplicant," Ramsey corrected. "And not a very good one if you don't even have that straight by now."

"She's both," Abram said, shooting daggers at Ramsey with his eyes. "And she's one of the best."

I bit back a laugh. How can one be the best Supplicant? Was I an awesome bleeder? He certainly couldn't have meant the best Conduit, though. I was completely useless for that. Even with the clock ticking down the minutes to my death—not even a full two days left until my demise—it was hard not to find Abram's sentiment amusing.

Ramsey looked back and forth between us, as though he was expecting Ashton Kutcher to jump out from behind the bookshelf and tell him it was all a joke.

"You're not serious," he finally said.

"Do I seem like the 'not serious' type?" Abram asked.

"My God," Ramsey said, staring at me.

He walked over, his hand stretched out in front of him. He

reached for my face, as if to inspect it for some sort of barcode or instruction manual.

Abram grabbed Ramsey's palm and flung him backward. "Hands off!"

"I knew there was something about you. I could feel it. I could sense it somehow," Ramsey said. "Do you have any idea what this means?" He was actually flush now, hands shaking as if he had the jitters. "You're practically solar-powered! You're an unending loop of power and potential—the infinity symbol brought to glorious life." He blinked hard. "We can find the Conduit. With you, we can do damn near anything."

"No, we can't," I said, my tone heavy with reality. "I don't know anything about my powers. I don't even know what they mean, let alone how to use them."

A maddened look twirled in his gaze, complementing the smile that now danced across his lips, really completing the whole 'mad scientist' vibe he had going on.

"But you can learn, you beautiful creature." He nodded at me. "And before you leave this house today, you will." He clapped his hands together loudly. "Now let's go save an island."

And at that moment, I felt hope. A horrible, terribly, awful *false* hope.

# CHAPTER 21

The obvious excitement on Ramsey's face calmed me. If he thought this—the fact that I was a weird Conduit/Supplicant hybrid—was exciting and worthy of hope, then maybe we had a chance. Maybe the itch to cling onto Abram and say goodbye was nothing more than a knee-jerk reaction to something I wouldn't have to consider much longer.

No. I couldn't let myself think that way. Hope like that had a tendency to make people lazy. And I couldn't afford to be anything but focused right now. I would do well to not let the possibility of what I wanted so badly screw with my mind.

Abram took another intimidating step forward, and Ramsey held his hands up as though to imply his innocent intentions.

"With her, we have a chance," he said. "We actually have a chance!" He slid his eager gaze toward me and indicated me with his hand. "Well, come on. Show us what we're starting with."

"I can't," I muttered. "I've been trying, and it's like—"

"Trying to grab soup with two hands?" Ramsey grinned. "It can be difficult at first, especially without having someone there to guide you. But if you're open to it, I think I can help."

Hesitation flooded me. This was what I wanted. It was *my* idea, for God's sake. So why was I so wary about it now that it was in front of me?

"I don't know," I murmured.

As I backed away, Abram turned to face me, eyeing me worriedly.

"Have you—" I cleared my throat. "Have you ever done this before? Helped someone like me, I mean."

"There is no one like you, Charisse," Ramsey said. "But I've guided many Conduits through their transitions. It's part of the training we receive as mages." His gaze flickered to the floor. "And, as I told you, I guided your former friend Dalton as well." He looked back at me. "Not that he was anything like you."

"Right. Dalton," I said, my heart in my throat. Not exactly my former friend. More like more former stalker/serial-killer.

Ramsey had been involved with Dalton, the absolute worst person I had ever known. How could I consider having anything to do with this mage after learning that?

That woman's face—the single mother from the news—flashed through my mind. She was gone now. Gone forever. Her children would never have her in their lives again. And very soon, Abram wouldn't have me.

I needed to make this happen for her *and* for me and all the victims to come. For those children and for Abram. Hell, maybe even a tiny bit for Ramsey and Briar, too. And we didn't exactly have time to find a different mage. We had one and a half days. That was it. Ramsey was all we had.

"What do I do?" I asked, inching forward. From the corner of my eye, I saw Abram's shoulder's ease, though he remained close enough that he could intervene if necessary. I needed to do this, but I still didn't know what *this* was. "I've already tried clearing my mind, getting my meditation on. It didn't work."

"And it won't," Ramsey said, taking a seat in a high-backed chair in an adjacent room. "Come, sit."

Abram and I followed and sat on the loveseat across from him.

"You're doing the opposite of what you need to." Ramsey splayed his hands. "Being a Conduit is a beautiful thing. It affords you control over what is and what could be. The entire universe and all it is capable of is stretched out in front of you. But only if you accept it."

As he leaned forward in his seat and reached for my face, I flinched. There was nothing threatening about the action, but come on. Personal space, please.

Instead of touching me, though, he just waved his hand in front of my eyes. "Clearing your mind, pushing all that you feel away from you, is effectively killing your connection to the magic." He dropped his hand away and leaned back in his chair again, bending up his leg to rest one ankle on the opposite knee. "What you feel, what you think, who you are—it's all vital to the process," he said with a wave of his hand. "You weren't made a Conduit by accident, Charisse. The magic chose you, and it did so for a reason."

My head was spinning now. He talked about magic as though it were an entity. Some being with cognizant thought, some greater plan. He talked about magic as if magic was...God.

I'd gone from terrified to just plain uncomfortable in Ramsey's presence. How did I tell him to get on with it, without sounding rude? I didn't have a whole lot of time.

"Okay, then," I said carefully. "So what do I do?"

"You need to connect with what you're feeling. All of it. You need to let it wash over you. You need to allow yourself to revel in it. That's what will spark the magic. Can you do that, Charisse?"

I looked over at Abram, and a million different feelings lit up inside of me. Could I do that? This mage had no idea just how well I could do that.

I gave a slow nod, and he nodded back. Abram and Ramsey

both looked at me in silence. Right, so they wanted me to try this now. No pressure or anything…

I closed my eyes and let it all flood back to me. At first, it filtered in like a trickle. The way I felt about Abram, the complicated feelings I still had for my father, the rift that had formed between Lulu and I as a result of dating the man she believed killed her brother, the fear I had in regards to everything I had been through. Losing my mother…

Something shifted. I felt as if I was being swept up in a wave, moved and thrown about by the intensity of these feelings. These were emotions I would usually escape, but this time, I let myself be pliant to them. Let them rock me. Throw me. Collide into me.

The fact I was still mourning my mother, the fear and sorrow that came with knowing I would very likely be dead in a matter of days, the bitterness I felt toward fate.

"Channel it," Ramsey whispered from somewhere in front of me. "Whatever you're feeling, whatever is pushing you forward, channel it into doing what you feel like you have to."

And what was that exactly? What did I *have* to do? Save myself? That seemed a bit one-note given the immense power everyone kept telling me I had. No. This was bigger than me. Satina had said there was a plan for me, that I was important somehow, that there were trials I needed to face before my destiny would show itself.

I hadn't really thought about it then. Before the last little bit, my destiny had always taken the detour toward wherever the best sales were. Now it seemed I was being called to do more. To *be* more.

I was going to have to become this thing. I would have to be the Conduit they all needed me to be.

Something like a hundred baby bee stings pricked at my skin. The stingers turned into finger nails, scraping me from the inside, hands pulling at me from under my flesh.

"What is this?" I whimpered, unable to keep the fear from my voice. I felt like the sensation might carry me away.

"It's called the awakening," Ramsey said. His voice sounded both close and distant, like an underwater scream. "All Conduits go through it. Albeit, usually at a much younger age."

"Ouch," I murmured. I wasn't old or anything, but I *had* just found my first gray hair the other day, so thinking about how far behind I was with all of this didn't sit too well with me.

Still, I had emotions to let loose. I had things to feel. I had powers to tap into. I had—

"Charisse..." Abram's voice fell like tin against my eardrums.

I opened my eyes to see him beneath me. But not just him. Ramsey was under me too, and they were both standing on the ground...the far off ground.

But what was *I* standing on?

"Sweet Jesus," I stammered once I realized what was going on. "I-I'm flying."

"Levitating," Ramsey corrected, which was sort of like telling me my poncho was actually a sleeveless raincoat. A distinction without a difference. "And you need to focus."

Warmth, thick and flowing, ran down my cheek.

"That's enough!" Abram shouted, grabbing Ramsey by the collar. "She's bleeding. Stop this now!"

My hand went to my nose and came away bloodied.

"She's so close," Ramsey whispered. "It's only the change. It can be trying, but she has to push through it."

"The hell she does," Abram said, throwing Ramsey back. Ramsey stumbled back, hit hard against the wall, and slid to the floor.

Abram leapt onto the wall, muscles flexing as he made his way toward me. But it was too late. I could feel myself tipping over some internal ledge. A surge of energy rose up in me. Light, bright and blinding, poured out of me, knocking Abram back and taking away the rest of the world.

When it subsided, I was on the floor again. Abram lay at my feet, chest heaving with shallow breathes.

"Are you okay?" he asked breathlessly, even though I should have been the one asking him that.

But the thing was, I *was* okay. I was better than okay. I felt as though a piece of myself had come to life, as though a veil had been lifted from my eyes and I could see the world for what it really was. And best of all, I had come away with one very important piece of information.

I leveled my gaze at him. "I know, Abram. I know where we can find the Conduit."

# CHAPTER 22

*T*his was not the way I wanted to end up at the beach. Ideally, Abram and I would have been sprawled across a towel, soaking up the sun (along with a bit of each other). But things didn't go that way. Our vacation was now a mysterious manhunt with a 'do it or die' clock running in the background.

The last twenty minutes of the afternoon were a blur that had somehow led me here. I didn't know where I was going, and yet I did. It was surreal. Right at the end of my 'awakening,' a feeling had unfurled around me—a sense of something. Maybe the same something Satina had felt but not been able to find. It was a dark energy, and it wasn't pulling me toward it so much as repelling me. I knew if I followed my discomfort, I would find the talisman, and when I did, I would be that much closer to finding the Conduit.

Ramsey said what I felt might be a shield the Conduit had put up for protection. Or, he said, it just as easily could be a ritual tool, or simply an item the Conduit valued. Regardless, I was following that energy, and that energy had led me here.

And the most unnerving part was I knew this place all too

well. This was the end. This was the foot of the cliff where all the Supplicants before me had died.

"Are you sure you can do this right now?" Abram asked, looking me over with that worried expression he had worn ever since my nose had turned into a blood geyser.

"I'm fine," I said, shaking off his concern. "You heard Ramsey. He said it was draining at first, that it was just something I have to tough out."

"Right." Abram plowed across the warm sand as we walked the beach—looking for what, exactly, I wasn't sure. "It shouldn't surprise you to learn I still don't trust Ramsey. And I'm not very excited at the prospect of my girlfriend toughing anything out, regardless of whose life is at stake."

*Even if that life is my own,* I thought, biting my lip.

The truth was, I was more than a little physically spent. Tapping into my Conduit side for the first time had shaken me to my core. While it felt as if I had opened a new side to myself, it also felt as if I had been hit by an eighteen wheeler. So, in a perfect world, I would've ran to some four star hotel, taken a hot bubble bath, and spent the night cuddling with my monster man. But the world was not perfect, and this damn island barely had a seaside inn, let alone a Hyatt. And, thanks to my nighttime rendezvous with Briar, I didn't have an extra day to spare.

"Look. I'm fine," I said, taking his hand and looking him right in the eyes. "I promise."

I hated lying to him almost more than anything. But I did it out of love and concern. That made it okay, right?

He huffed, either believing me too noble for my own good or hating the situation even more than I did. "You better be," he said, squeezing my hand. "I'm not above ripping a mage in half."

"Good to know." I gave him a quick peck on the cheek. The kiss lit me up, but also tinged my mind with hurt. Our kisses were finite now…and our days together were almost up.

I shook my head and turned away from him. I would not let

despair steal this from me. If I was to die, then I would go out fighting, kissing, and doing other things that I'd come to enjoy with Abram lately. And besides, I wasn't dead yet. I still had a day and a half, a suit of powers I didn't have yesterday, and the most powerful man I had ever known standing beside me. This wasn't over yet.

Since awakening my Conduit side, I had come to find a strange connection with things. The world seemed intent on whispering in my ear. It was strange, low, and indecipherable. But something told me that would come with time.

Abram placed his hand on my shoulder. "Are you all right, Charisse?"

"I just need to focus," I said.

Ramsey had told me that. He'd said that, while letting my emotions run free, I needed to narrow my mind so that all my thoughts were on what or who I was looking for.

That, of course, was easier said than done.

I started off again, and Abram strode beside me. Like every time he was in my presence, my thoughts started to wander to him. It took all I could not to settle on his smell, the way his arms felt around me, the sound of his voice in my ear.

Instead, I focused on much less pleasant things. There was a Conduit out here—one who wanted me dead. There had been bodies right where were we now walked—Supplicant victims who deserved justice. I only hoped I was enough to give it to them.

"Anything?" Abram asked. He seemed on edge, as though he thought the Conduit might pop up from behind a rock at any moment.

I paused, trying to feel something. Now that we were closer to the location, the sense of being repelled was strong *everywhere*. I didn't think it could get any stronger than it was, which made it impossible to tell if I we were closer or farther from where we needed to be.

"It's harder than it looks," I said finally, my shoulders slumping along with my hope.

"Really?" he muttered. "Because it looks damn near impossible."

"I can feel it." I closed my eyes in frustration. "I can feel the magic swirling around out here. But it's muddled, like I'm searching for it underwater or something, amidst an under-current."

Abram growled beside me. His body was tense and hard, his stance rigid. "I hate magic."

I knew him well enough to know what was going on. It was the energy on this island. Even now, in the bright sunlight of mid-afternoon, it was zapping all of his energy to stop the beast from taking over.

No wonder he hated magic.

"Can you tell anything, or is it just white noise?" he asked, teeth ground together.

"White noise?" I mused. It was strange which turns of phrase Abram did and didn't pick up on. He couldn't tell you what a podcast was to save his life, but he knew the words to every Springsteen song I could think of and had spent more than one night telling me about his favorite Twilight Zone episodes.

Maybe he was like any other person. There were things that he did and did not gravitate towards, and the reality that he was over a century and a half old only accentuated that fact. But no. I had held his hand, kissed his lips, and felt his heart beat against mine. He was absolutely, one hundred percent *not* like any other person. And I was thrilled about that.

"Charisse?" he asked, breaking me out of my contemplative state. "Can you give me anything to go on? This place reeks of death."

Oh, right. His heightened sense of smell was probably more of a burden than a gift here, where so many people had met their demise.

"It seems like it might be strongest at the foot of the cliff... where all of the bodies landed," I answered, gulping hard. "But it's hard to tell."

I had never been the type of girl who was comfortable around blood, guts, and the like. I had never even been the type to watch Law and Order. Chalk outlines and this girl—they did not go well together.

So how did I end up here, at the epicenter of mystical death and destruction? The world was truly a crazy place.

"Of course it's hard to tell," he muttered. He turned back the way we had just come. "Let's go back that way then and get this over with."

I followed a few steps behind. "I don't know what I'm doing here, and I'm not even sure the information I'm giving you is accurate."

"You're trying," he said, without breaking stride. "That's more than you're obligated to do. And it means something. Don't think it doesn't."

A wry smile spread across my face, though it was ruined by the sadness that came with knowing my personal clock was ticking down quickly toward a violent and splat-filled death at the exact spot where we now stood.

It felt strange to settle at the foot of the cliff. So many people had died here. Supplicants, like me. And the numbers would only increase unless I got my shit together. Soon.

"This is just sand," I said, sweeping my hand at the ground by our feet. "It's dirt. There's nothing special about it."

I would be here, lying on this dirt with Abram standing over me. I would never feel his touch again, or the sunlight bounce across my skin. I would never taste ice cream or have grandchildren or grow old beside an ageless man with a tight ass and a barb-wired heart of gold. It would be taken from me—all of it.

"I just..." I started, but my breaths were coming short now. "I can't do this anymore, Abram. It's too much. We're looking so hard, and fighting so hard, and it's too much. It doesn't mean anything. It doesn't matter. What if it never mattered? What if we *all* end up down here, broken and defeated, and dead? And for no reason, Abram! And there's nothing we can do! And there's—"

He collided into me, pulling me up hard into his arms and pressing his lips against mine in a hungry and soothing balm of heat and desire. I melted into him, letting the emotions and feelings loose inside my mind and heart. I pulled into him and felt his steady, stalwart chest beneath my own.

And the rest of it went away. Suddenly, the world was okay. I was his, and he was mine. And no Conduit in this or any other world could challenge that. Right then, as my mind reduced to pinpricks of pleasure and satisfaction, the answer descended on me like a gift from above.

"Behind you," I murmured, achingly pulling my lips from his. "It's behind you."

Abram turned slowly, his eyes widening. I knew what he saw, because I saw it, too. I'd seen it first. A small opening sat at the base of the cliff, carved into the rock. It was a sliver of a cave—it looked more like a crack in the earth, rather than any kind of real entrance—but it was something. It wasn't hard to see how other people would have missed it, if they had even been able to get past the magical diversion barriers to see it, but I had a sort of knowing about it now that I was looking at it.

"I guess I'm good inspiration," he said, giving me another peck on the lips and setting me back on the ground. I could tell by the way Abram gazed at cave's small entrance that he was impressed.

"That's it," I said. "It has to be. That's why the magic led me here."

Abram moved toward the cave's opening, holding a hand back behind him. "Why don't you stay out here? I'll see what's going on inside."

"No!" I said, much too loudly. I didn't want to be out here—where my fellow Suplicants had fallen—for a moment longer than I had to. Of course, I couldn't exactly tell him why. "What I mean is, what if there's something in there that you can't see... something magical?"

Abram spied me up and down. "Stay close. The instant I get even a whiff of trouble, we're out of there. Do you understand?"

"Completely." I grabbed his hand and stepped in closer to his body, following right behind him.

The way the entrance was designed, we had to snake our way inside, coming in the entrance sideways, and turning a corner before it opened up to us. The opening was so small that I couldn't imagine there would be much illumination. Surprisingly though, when we moved through the opening, I found myself able to see pretty easily.

Not that that was a good thing.

The cave was covered—absolutely slathered—in what looked like blood. It stretched out across the walls, circling and weaving to create the sort of strange symbols that I had come to relate with Conduits ever since my connection to the mystical world forced me to consider that type of stuff.

"This is the least romantic thing ever," I said, trying my damnedest to control my gag reflex.

The entire thing made me sick. The blood in this cave was undoubtedly Supplicant blood, and if we didn't stop the Conduit, mine might very well cover these walls in a day and a half's time as well.

Abram's nostrils flared. "This is inexcusable!"

I squeezed his hand gently. "Supplicant blood," I whispered. "It has to be."

"It's the blood of someone's daughter, someone's father, or someone's loved one. That's what matters." He looked back at me. "I'm going to do it, Charisse. Whoever is responsible for this— whoever is hunting these people like cattle and spreading their blood over these walls like some sick, magical trophy—I'm going to kill them."

"Good," I said, my voice cracking.

Abram turned toward the cave. "Let's see if we can find something that indicates who this person is."

Before we could separate, a loud boom thundered through the corridor.

My body tensed, but before I could react in any other way, it appeared.

Shimmering as if out of thin air, a huge monster took shape in the darkness. It was tall—taller than Abram even, with broad shoulders, ripped muscles, dark fur and...and the head of a wolf. Fangs jutted out of its mouth, a long snout huffed hot breath, and, as my eyes neared the ground, I saw it had massive paws where its feet should be.I gulped, nudging Abram as I took the thing in. "How many of you are there?"

"A lot more than I figured." Abram growled, pushing me backward and crouching. "Get out of here."

A loud howl ripped from his throat, and as his body morphed and changed, I realized he wasn't trying to hold back the beast anymore. He was cutting loose entirely.

"Run!" he screamed at me, more a bark than an actual command.

"No," the wolf-man huffed. "The girl is who she wants. The master can make use of her."

Oh, God. This wasn't the Conduit. This was just some lackey—a big ass, scary-as-hell lackey, but a lackey nonetheless.

"Good luck with that," Abram said, darting through the air and swiping toward the beast. Abram struck hard against the monster, but his claws, as razor-sharp as they were, did nothing to pierce the fur-covered hide.

Once on the ground, Abram went after him again, but the beast reared back and kicked him hard, sending him flying into the cave's stone wall.

I ran toward Abram, finding blood splattered across his fur. Was that the Supplicant blood now covering him, or his own? His flesh didn't seem to be burning, so it must have been his, which worried me more.

"Go!" he growled at me.

But it was too late. The monster was atop us now. With a huge hand, it picked Abram off the ground.

"You should take your own advice." It huffed, fangs glistening in the ambient light. With that, the beast heaved Abram through the air again. HE slammed against the snaked entrance of the cave, an in the blink of an eye, the beast descended on him to remove him from the cave entirely.

Crap. Now I was alone with the monster.

My eyes widened as I scrambled to my feet and darted toward the opening. But the wolf clapped its paw-like hands, making the blood on the wall shimmer and glow. Just as I was about to reach the cave's opening, it sealed shut.

The wolf-man advanced on me. His claws pounded on the ground, and the light in the room dissipated.

"She wants you," he said. "And she will have what she wants."

# CHAPTER 23

$\mathcal{T}$he darkness in the cave was broken only by the monster's bright red eyes.

My heart pounded as I watched those eyes dart around. In another world, they would have been Abram's eyes. They certainly looked the part—at least when Abram was in beast form. But Abram was trapped outside, certainly clawing at the rocks and mounds that had somehow closed off behind him. Magic probably sealed the entrance and, as strong as he was, Abram couldn't fight through that. And even if he could, he probably wouldn't get to me before this monster tore me into tiny (if quite fashionable) pieces.

No. If I was going to get out of here, it would be up to me.

I stood shakily, grabbing at the jagged rocks that made up the cave wall for support. I had to be careful. They were slick with blood—Supplicant blood, to be exact—which was somehow still fresh and wet. How was the Conduit doing *that*? Supplicant blood had a very short shelf life, but clearly the witch bitch of this island had found a way around that.

"You better let me out of here," I said, trying to keep my voice steady, trying to keep my mind steady. "I'm not like the others, you know."

The red eyes flickered, more and more terrible as they neared. "You're exactly like them." The monster growled. "That's why she marked you. Why she used the beauty to number your days. And, like the others, you will die. And she will be made glorious because of it."

His voice lulled up and down, moving from frantic to slow in a way that made me think he was grappling with pain. Did it hurt to be in this condition? Did it hurt Abram, too?

"What do you mean, she'll be made glorious?" I asked, tensing as the red eyes drew even closer.

"You will see." The monster huffed. "Right before the end, you will see."

I felt its breath against me now. Could it see in the dark? Probably. That *would* be my luck.

Grappling scraped from the outside. Abram's hands were likely bloodied and broken by now. But he wouldn't stop. Not ever. Would they kill him next? Would they torture him for trying to help me or, worse, would this Conduit bitch turn him into the sort of whimpering slave thing like the beast that stood before me now?

Anger flashed through me, white-hot and blistering. Taking me was one thing, stealing every day from tomorrow until my natural last was bad enough. But I would be damned if I was going to let whoever this person was hurt the man I loved.

Thinking about what Ramsey said, I let go of my emotions. It was easier this time. Perhaps because I was literally staring down death, perhaps because I had done it before, or maybe because I wanted it so much this time—but the power flew threw me with ease.

It lit me up, and not just metaphorically. A bright light shone through my pores. The light broke through the darkness, causing the monster to stumble backward, illuminated everything, including the rips that Abram had put along the monster's flesh.

The light grew brighter, pulsating as it seared through my clothes. "I told you," I said, swallowing hard, unsure of what would happen next. "I told you I wasn't like the rest." The light pulsated again into a blinding explosion of pure white.

When it subsided, I was left standing stark naked in the cave with an unconscious monster at my feet.

The rocks fell away, and like a bullet shooting out of a gun, Abram darted in toward me.

He pounced atop the monster, not even taking the time to assess the situation, to see that the wolf-man was already thoroughly beaten. His paw reared back, razor sharp claws ready to tear deep into the monster and end him.

"Wait!" I screamed.

Abram turned to me, his eyes widening as they slid the length of my body. "Where are your clothes?" he asked, his hands shaking. "What did this thing do to you?"

I shook my head. "It was me. It was the magic. Listen," I said, using my arms to cover my bare chest. "This isn't the Conduit. This is just one of her servants. We don't have to kill him."

"Of course we do." Abram's beast-face scrunched. "He'll never stop. If anything happens to you—"

"He's just a person, Abram. I can feel it. He's as much a victim in this as you and me. And if we kill him all because he *might* be troublesome in the future, then what does that make us? What has she turned us into then?"

Abram's body and face shifted back to its human form. He stared at the monster on the cave floor and then back at me.

"What do you suggest we do with him?" Abram asked. "We can't leave him here."

"There's a chain over there," I said, motioning to the far end and using my best 'please' voice. "Maybe you can tie him up until we come up with a more permanent solution."

CONNER KRESSLEY & REBECCA HAMILTON

"You're lucky you're pretty," he said, marching over to the chain. "While I'm doing this, look around and see if you can find any clues. And here." He picked up the shirt he had discarded when he transformed. "Put this on. It's not that I don't appreciate the view, but we have no idea what we're going to find in here. And if we need to act quickly—"

"You'd rather I not flash the entire island on the way out. I get it." I grabbed the shirt and pulled it over my head, slipping my arms through the holes at nearly the same time. No one can get dressed faster than a clothing model. The shirt billowed around my curves like an ill-fitting dress, but at least it smelled like Abram, which was always a plus

The cave's new opening allowed ambient light to pout into the cave and light the area. Sure, not as brightly as when I had momentarily turned into a human flashlight, but I had already burned through one set of clothes, and doing it again didn't seem like the best idea.

As I moved through the cave, I was careful to stay away from the walls. A desk sat in the far corner, which was almost as absurd as the rest of what we'd been faced with today.

I walked toward it, the chain rattling behind me as Abram secured the monster. The first thing I saw on the desk was a folded piece of paper with a smudge of lipstick in the shape of puckered lips across it.

Opening it, I read the contents.

*Keep this kiss until we meet again.*

*It's never enough, my love. It'll never be enough.*

*- Yours Now and Forever*

It was a love letter. This murderous bitch was hoarding a love letter? I had to admit, I didn't see that coming.

I refolded the note, kiss side up, and placed it back on the table. I should have torn it up. The people she killed, the single mom she forced off that cliff, would never get another love letter. Why should she? But that seemed petty in the scheme of things.

Besides, if I was going to save myself, I was going to need to find an actual clue.

I felt around the top of the counter, coming up empty save for a pressed feather and what I was pretty sure was a hollowed-out animal skull. Pulling open a drawer, I found another letter. It took all of a second and a half for me to know who it came from. I recognized the opening line immediately.

Dear Valued Customer,

It has been brought to our attention that you've been dabbling with powers that exceed the recommended usage outlined in our guidelines for ethical use of magic and energy. While it not our desire to police you in this matter, nor is it our policy to insert ourselves within the conflicts of those practicing on your plane, we must inform you that any further complaints and accusations will be addressed as violations of our code.

And, should you need a reminder of the consequences of violating our code, we ask you to look no farther than the poor residents of Camelot, now reduced to nothing more than the nearly forgotten tales of those with overactive imaginations.

Of course, should your adversary in this matter meet an unfortunate end and thus is rendered unable to issue further complaints, we'll be left with no choice but to forget it in its entirety.

Best regards, and to the victors go the spoils,

The Company

I swallowed hard. What was a blur on the last letter was more than clear on this one. The Company…King Archibald had mentioned them to Huntsman, but we still didn't know who they were. Not that it mattered. They were pitting this Conduit against King Archibald and—because we had the best luck in the whole wide world—Abram and I were stuck in the middle.

"Abram," I said, realizing I hadn't heard the chains rattling in quite some time. "I think I found something. Maybe if we keep digging there will be some clue as to who she is under all this magic and mystery."

I turned around to find Abram lifted off the ground. His hands were around his throat, and his feet were dangling helplessly, thrashing as he worked to free himself from whatever was doing this.

"Abram!" I yelled, rushing toward him.

As I neared, the Conduit seemed to materialize out of nowhere. I stopped in my tracks as I took her in, feeling the power pouring off her in waves, radiating as it literally pushed me away. But I still couldn't tell who this person was. Her body had been transformed, but not into the usual monster form I'd grown accustomed to. Instead of a human-looking woman, and instead of a wolf-like beast, she was a creature unlike anything I had ever seen before.

Horns jutted from her head, long and curving. Her grotesque face stretched out into a snout, and her jaw squared. She looked every bit of a bull. Her arms were deformed, and her torso blended into an animal's body, her muscular goat-like legs running out into hooves.

"You're one of mine, aren't you?" the Conduit asked in a gravelly voice, though her monstrous mouth never moved. It was more like she was speaking directly into my mind. "And he is yours. Which makes him mine as well, I suppose."

"Let him go," I said through gritted teeth.

"Charisse," Abram said, much calmer than I would have ever been if our positions were switched. "Do you see it? Can you see the thing that's attacking me?"

He was looking right at her, and yet somehow he still couldn't see her? How powerful was this chick?

I shot Abram a look, and then turned my attention back to the Conduit. "I'm warning you one more time. Let him go. *Now.*"

"Oh, I'll let him go," she answered in an almost nonchalant voice. "Right after I show him what trespassers get for breaking into my home." Her bullish face turned to him. "They get to die, wolf."

Her long arm flinched, and Abram's entire form contorted. He let out a guttural, feral howl that twisted my stomach so terribly it nearly brought me to my knees.

And then, when I thought it couldn't get any worse, I listened as every single bone in Abram's body broke.

# CHAPTER 24

"No!" I yelled, my throat dry and scratchy as my feet carried me toward Abram faster than I ever thought myself capable of.

The Conduit, all monstrous features and bull horns, stood over us as I knelt toward my love. But I couldn't will myself to pay her any attention, not with Abram on the ground like this.

He was broken. God help him, he was so broken. His body—his beautiful body—contorted in inhuman shapes, and his lips trembled as though to muffle the screams.

"It's okay," I whispered, unable to keep the tears from rolling down my face. "I'll fix it, I promise. I can fix it. I have to fix it."

"Who are you trying to convince?" the Conduit asked from over me, once again not moving her grotesque bull mouth.

"Shut up!" I snapped. The whole world went red, and my eyes burned as though someone had lit a match in my brain.

"Look at you," the Conduit said, gliding eerily closer. "All dressed up in your big girl clothes."

The world got even redder, and a line of fire appeared at her ugly hooves. That was me. The world was red because my eyes were red, because power was literally pouring out of me.

"That's impressive." The Conduit flicked her elongated hand and snuffed out my flames. "Not impressive enough, but impressive."

Abram quivered under me, and I nearly wretched. He was such a strong man, such a force. And she had turned him into this.

"I wondered when you would come. I knew if I looked long enough, if I drew you all here, then it would only be a matter of time until you graced my fine doorstep."

"Me?" I asked, my voice shaking. Briar's perpetual sleep, all those people who had been murdered by this bitch, was because of me? Oh, hell no.

"Of course it was because of you," she said slyly, practically reading my mind. Or maybe she was literally reading my mind. Who knew what her power set was? "When you came into your own back in the States, you sent out a magical pulse. It was practically a song. You might as well have been singing to me." She splayed her disgusting fingers in front of her. "A Supplicant who was also a Conduit. A creature whose magic is charged by her own blood and whose blood is, in return, supercharged by her own propensity for the magnificent. And that was when I knew."

"Knew what?" I asked, glowering at her. I was so ready to kill this bitch, but not without answers first.

I moved my hand to Abram's jerking body once more, touching him skin to skin. I winced at the sudden pain—*his* pain. It was unbearable, and it invaded every cell of my being. But I couldn't move to react to it. I couldn't snap my hand away. I couldn't scream.

I couldn't do anything.

And then it started to subside. With a jolt, I realized what was going on. The pain was subsiding because Abram's bones were setting. We were connected, he and I. Connected by touch and, with that touch, I was healing him.

"That," the Conduit said, waving her mutated hand toward me. "That is what I knew. That you were enough. That with your

SLEEPING WITH THE BEAST

power, I wouldn't need the rest of them. That you could do all I would ever need, forever."

"And what's that?" I asked, stalling her. I didn't really give a damn. As soon as Abram was up and running, he would take her head off, and the only plan that would matter then would have to do with funeral arrangements. "What do you want from me?"

"You'll be harvested well before you need to worry about that. What is it, Charisse—a day and a half now?"

I shuddered. Not only did this…*thing*…know my name, but she knew my biggest secret. I looked down at Abram. He was still in pain, still writhing. Had he heard what she said? Did he now know about the ticking clock looming over me? Or had the pain dulled the sound or made her words irrelevant? Somehow, though, that prospect worried me more than the rest of it.

And it pissed me the hell off.

"Maybe *you* shouldn't worry about it. Because if my power is what you need to run your little mystery machine, you're going to be sorely disappointed. You're not getting a damn drop of my blood."

"They all say that," the Conduit said. "*All of them.* And now look. Their blood covers my walls. It gives me power. It gives me him."

"Him?"

"But you're different, right?" She practically chuckled, the sound strange coming from inside her bull head. "Because you have your beast?" She waved her hand. "What a joke. You may as well halt that pathetic little healing ritual you're doing. He won't do any good against me."

She waved again, and the motion sent me flying across the room. My grasp ripped away from Abram, breaking our connection.

I hit hard against the floor, but the pain that hurt worst was the one I was sure Abram was feeling now.

Not that you could have told by looking at him.

181

He stumbled to his feet, still bloody and a little broken.

"Stay down," I mumbled as the metallic tang of my own blood filled my mouth.

But, hardheaded as he was, he didn't listen. The stubborn bastard got to his feet, undoubtedly aching with every step he took toward the creature.

For her part, the Conduit simply stood there, taking Abram in with appraising eyes.

He swung...way too far away from her, and it occurred to me that he somehow still couldn't see her. I'd never heard of a Conduit able to do magic like that before, but this world was still new to me. At least maybe he couldn't hear her, either, which would mean my unwanted secret was still safe.

"You see, Charisse," the Conduit said, not even moving as Abram swung at the air around her. "A beast, a creature like the one you've taken league with, is simply a reflection of the Conduit who created it. As for your boy toy here—" Abram swung again. He was closer this time, but still no luck. Part of me wanted to scream to him, to give him directions. But if he hit her, she would only hurt him again. No, I was going to have to do this on my own. "—he's a magical extension of the pauper girl who brought him into existence." The Conduit's bullish head tilted. "And while that little thing was full of righteousness and rage, she's no match for someone like me. And thus, neither is your beast."

She flicked her hand again, and Abram went flying. He hit hard against the wall and slid down beside me.

"If it makes you feel better, I'll let him live until you're dead. That way, you won't have to watch him die. And—because you've been such an unexpected treat for me—I'll send him to the afterlife to meet you right after you go tumbling to your demise." The Conduit moved closer to us. "And you don't even have to thank me."

Bile rose in my throat, and my entire body started to tingle. Apparently Abram was no match for her, as ridiculous as that sounded. Abram was the most capable man I had ever known. He could move a mountain with his bare hands, and likely would if that mountain was keeping him from me. But he was also writhing on the floor, pained in a way I had never seen him before.

He had saved my life so many times. He had given me joy, satisfaction, and meaning in ways I never thought possible. And now it was him who needed me. I would be damned if I was going to let him down. Not now. Not ever.

"You," I ground out as the emotions within me bubbled over the top. The power spilled out around me, coloring every inch of my sight, every inch of my being. "You messed with the wrong woman, *Conduit*."

I wasn't sure what I was going to do. God knew that if I did, I probably wouldn't be able to do whatever it was. All I knew was that I wanted her to stop hurting him. I wanted her powerless and weak, the way she had made us powerless and weak. I wanted her to feel the way I felt anytime I thought about the likelihood I was going to die. I wanted to reduce her to the sniveling, groveling, shadow of a person she really was. And I wanted to do it now.

I slammed my fist against the ground, not because it was part of an incantation or anything, but because I was as mad as hell and I wanted to hit something that couldn't hit back.

The world spun under my fist. The magic in the room cascaded outward, and in that instant, I knew how to stop her.

I had barely even let the idea grace my mind when it happened. The blood on the walls, the stolen Supplicant power that coursed through this room and charged the Conduit's batteries began to glow—all of it—and then it just…vanished.

She threw her hands out, probably to toss Abram and me around like ragdolls again, but nothing happened. I had stolen her mojo. But she couldn't steal mine.

"Let's see who doesn't have a chance now," I said through gritted teeth.

I struck the ground again, and it wretched out under her. The cave shook, knocking her to her knees. Then a stray rock flew across the room, striking her in that grotesque helmet she called a head.

Abram breathed heavily next to me. "I can see her."

"Good," I answered. "Watch this."

Another rock flew across the room, striking her. And then another. They came fast and heavy until she was on her back.

I stood, red coloring my eyes and hate filling my heart. I wanted to kill her. I should have killed her. But where would that leave me? Like she said, I was hers now. I had already been cursed. I needed to know how to break this curse, how to break all the curses.

Like one of those unkillable sociopaths from a slasher movie, she jumped up, tearing at me with her claws.

Abram darted toward her, but it was too late. She drew her claws back, covered in blood.

*My* blood. The absolute best source for a creature like her to do the absolute worst things.

# CHAPTER 25

"*T*ime's up!" She snarled. "I'm done playing games with you. No more poetic justice, no waiting for you to jump. This ends now!"

But then, like a gift from the heavens, she started to convulse. She screamed as she crumpled onto the floor and, looking past her, I saw the culprit.

Ramsey Duldridge stood in the entrance of the cave, taser in hand. It ran all the way into the Conduit's back.

"*You* end now," he said, sneering.

"Ramsey," I breathed. "What the hell are you doing here?"

"The same thing you are," he said. "We're finally getting somewhere, Charisse. I'm going to show you how to make this bitch give us some answers."

Electricity jolted through the Conduit's body. She jerked and pulled, but I didn't show her even the slightest bit of compassion. She had caused too much pain for too many people. She deserved this. She deserved worse. Besides, I had more important business to deal with.

"You tasered her…"

"Oh, that," he said, dropping the weapon to the floor. "As it turns out, when it comes to my wife, I've decided I rather be a fighter than a mage."

"But—"

"No buts," he said. "Don't worry. The words from my books will be erased for breaking code, and I won't be able to assist in any rituals, but they can't take away what is in my mind. I still know enough to guide you."

I nodded and took a deep breath. "Okay, then. Keep her down while I take care of Abram."

Abram grunted. "I'm fine."

Always the old-world gentleman, he would never admit to needing anyone. This was me, though—me and *him*. And, whether he asked for help or not, he was going to get it.

"You're not fine," I said, "but you will be."

As I pressed my palm against his arm, the connection between us raged back in full force. His pain was mine again and, with a shift behind my eyes, my healing powers flew into him.

With no pesky Conduit to break us up, I had no trouble putting back together what the Conduit had torn apart. I mended his skin and tissues. I set and knitted his broken bones. And then, when I was done, I gave him a kiss to mend whatever else this horrible day had bruised or ruined.

"You shouldn't have done that," he breathed when I was finished.

"Kissed you?" I asked.

"Healed me," he answered, standing up.

I stood to meet him. "That's not exactly the thank you I was looking for."

Abram shook his head. "The more precision you garner with this sort of thing, the more powerful you become, and the more danger you're going to find yourself in. This makes you a commodity, Charisse. Don't you understand that?"

"*This* makes me a commodity?" I balked. "I'm already more popular than a fifty percent off sale at Nordstrom's. And I don't care what you say, I'm not about to let you suffer through something like that just because you want to keep me safe."

"I *need* to keep you safe," he muttered. "And what I do or do not suffer through is my choice, not yours."

"I have to protect you, too," I shot back. "Not for you, but for me. Because if anything happened to you—" I swallowed hard, my eyes darting away from him. "So no. I don't think it's your choice."

"While all this is very touching," Ramsey chimed in from behind me, "we still have the business of an unconscious Conduit to deal with."

Turning, I glared at the Conduit still on the floor. She had stopped shaking. She had stopped moving altogether.

"Is she…"

"Dead?" Ramsey provided. "Hardly. It'll take more than a couple hundred volts of electricity to put an end to someone with her kind of power. Besides, we can't kill her yet."

"And why's that?" Abram asked, brandishing beastly claws.

"Because she's still connected to people," Ramsey said. "Briar, the Supplicants who are currently under her spell. If you kill her, then they all likely die with her."

*Me included*, I thought.

"So what do we do?" I asked, glancing at her massive frame on the floor. She looked almost peaceful there, her deformed chest rising and falling in shallow breathes.

"Something that's going to hurt," he answered.

"Hurt who?" I asked. The way he looked at me, deep and apologetic, left no room for misunderstanding.

Abram grabbed my arm and pulled me closer to him. "I will not put her through any more pain. I suggest you get that idea firmly planted in that thick skull of yours."

I eased Abram's hand from my arm and caressed his shoulder. "Abram, calm down. I can do this. I was *meant* for this."

His nostrils flared. "You don't even know what 'this' is. There's no way you can possibly know if you can handle it." He pulled me close, my face inches from his own, and tipped his forehead against mine. "I told you I didn't want you involved in this. I've been around enough to know that magic always comes at a cost. I won't have you paying it."

I closed my eyes as I answered—afraid that if I didn't, tears might spill down my cheeks.

"I'm already involved," I said quietly.

He shook his head. "Not yet you're not, and damned if I'll let that change."

"There's no other way," Ramsey said. "If we're going to have any chance of stopping whatever this wench has in store, then we need to inform ourselves of her motivation, her history, and her weaknesses. To do that, we need to get into her mind. But it takes a Conduit to get into another Conduit's mind. So unless you think we have time enough to scour the Earth for another one—one willing to help us, I might add—I suggest we use Charisse. Especially considering she's her own power source, which means we won't have to track down another Supplicant, too."

A low growl came from Abram's throat. His eyes opened and slid over to Ramsey, glowing red.

"It's okay," I said, taking his head in my hands. "I can do this. Just trust me, okay?"

He stared at me for a long moment before finally answering. "The instant I think it's too much for you, I'm putting a stop to it."

"Okay," I agreed, even though I knew I wouldn't let him. I turned toward Ramsey. "What do I need to do?"

"First? I wouldn't be opposed to you telling me why the both of you are half naked."

I looked down. I had almost forgotten. I stood in Abram's shirt while he was bare chested in a pair of pants so battle-worn they were barely hanging on.

"There was a magic incident," I explained.

"Silk," Ramsey nodded. "Wear silk. Magic doesn't burn through it. Don't ask me why." He rested his elbow in his opposite hand and tapped his finger against his chin. "Though that is just one of many helpful little tidbits having a mage on your side affords you."

"Ex-mage," I reminded. I moved toward him, one eye on the Conduit as I settled next to Ramsey. "Can we please just get this over with?"

"A Conduit's mind has natural protections like an onion has layers. Walls and walls of energy block anyone and anything from piercing her mind and stealing her secrets or invading her consciousness. Because you're a Conduit, you can peel away those layers." He swallowed, belying his confidence as his jaw gave a small tremble. "But it won't be easy."

"When is it ever?" I asked, rolling my eyes. "Though, for the sake of argument, just how 'not easy' is it going to be?"

"Peeling back the layers of protection is a high level act of magic. It's going to be very intensive for a newer Conduit like yourself and as painful as a surgery for her," Ramsey said, looking down at the witch.

"I'm not exactly a surgeon," I answered hesitantly.

"You're the closest we've got," Ramsey said. "Let your emotions overtake you again and focus on connecting with the Conduit, on opening her thoughts to you. You can touch her if you think it would make it easier."

I shook my head, remembering the innocent blood that, just minutes ago, covered these walls. "Not for a million dollars."

"Fair enough." Ramsey didn't look as though he blamed me all that much. "Just focus, and get ready for some pain."

"You know, as long as it means I can make her hurt, too, I'm surprisingly okay with that," I said.

I knelt down, shuddering as I neared the Conduit. Her body was horrific, stretched and changed by magic. There was hardly a piece of a woman in there. Whoever she had been was likely a million miles away by now, but there was only one way to find out for sure.

I stretched my hands over her horned head and instantly felt her energy intensify. It was darker than Abram's, and full of a vengeful heat that threatened to burn my palms. Closing my eyes, I pushed through it. Was this the pain Ramsey had spoken about? If so, he was sorely underestimating me. I could deal with this.

A hard jerk pulled at my insides, lighting my gut on fire and causing me to wretch forward. My eyes flew open wide.

Okay. *This* was the pain. But no matter. I had to do this—for Abram, for myself, and for everyone who had already fallen to this monster.

"Open up, bitch," I murmured through clenched teeth.

I let go of my previous decision not to touch her and grasped her horns hard, needing something to hold onto as the pain pulsed through my body.

Light filled my mind and my vision, and suddenly, I wasn't in the cave anymore. I was in the woods at night. A young couple stood before me, crying and grasping at each other.

"Please, Luca. Let's just leave," said a young girl. Her dark hair stuck wet to her head, and her eyes welled with tears. "We can get new names, new lives. A new land would be kind to us. We can be together."

The boy, tall and lanky, but somehow familiar, shook his head. "And what sort of life would we have together, Ameena?" His eyes flickered to the ground. "You know I am not as a man should be. I am weak. I am sickly. Your father is right. How could I care for you? The Lord you were promised to is a much better fit—for you, for your family."

She opened her mouth, but he lifted a finger to silence her.

"He is a king, Ameena. He'll give you the world. "

"I do not wish for the world," she said. "I wish for you."

Ameena clamored for the boy again, but he brushed her away.

"He has a daughter, Luca," she said. "A daughter who is nearly my own age. You cannot leave me with him. I will not survive it."

"I'm sorry," Luca said, and he darted off into the forest.

Ameena crumpled teary-eyed to the ground.

And then I was gone.

I was in a castle now, watching from above as the woman from the woods married King Archibald. Only he *wasn't* King Archibald —at least not then. He was Jacob Navaar. And this was the Conduit from the original Sleeping Beauty tale.

My God. This Conduit *was* the Conduit from back then. How old was she? How powerful?

I left that scene as quickly as I came to it. Now I was in a darkened room. Ameena sat with energy crackling around her. I could feel her emotions. She was afraid. This was the first time she was coming into her powers, and it was freaking her out.

I was gone again. Reappearing in the same room. Time had passed, enough time for Ameena to become the badass Conduit from lore. Luca was at the window.

"I knew you couldn't stay away." She cooed, marched over to the window with energy swirling around her, and kissed him.

I was in the woods again. Things were moving faster now, too fast for me to keep up. A hand ripped Luca from Ameena's arms. It was Huntsman. His hair was longer, and the ax across his back didn't glow. But it was him nonetheless.

"You must leave her. She has bewitched you, brother," Huntsman said, his voice heavy with apology. "Look at what you have become."

The world whipped around, and I was gone again. I stood at the edge of a long cliff...of the cliff that all the Supplicants had thrown themselves from.

"Please!" Ameena cried. King Archibald stood next to her. They both looked out at a beast—a beast I knew in my mind to be Luca.

"He won't die." She turned to the king, as though she was trying to convince him of something. She must have been the one to make him a beast, perhaps as a way to stop King Archibald

CONNER KRESSLEY & REBECCA HAMILTON

from killing him. "Throw him off that cliff a thousand times, and he won't die. I won't allow it."

"I don't doubt that, my love," King Archibald said. "But he will hurt. And should he come to you a thousand times, then yes, he will be compelled to throw himself from this cliff a thousand times. And I promise you, my love, eventually he will stop coming."

He had put a curse on Luca. No, that couldn't be it. He wasn't a Conduit. That meant he'd convinced someone else to do it.

The world melted away, and I was at the bedside of a beautiful sleeping woman. I didn't need to guess as to who it was. It was the original Sleeping Beauty. Ameena—the Conduit who intended to kill me—had been her stepmother and the wife of the man we now knew as King Archibald

"Fine," King Archibald said, kneeling beside her. "You've made your point—you will have your way. Curse me instead of my daughter, and I will let you have him. Let me take her place, and you can have your lover."

Ameena appeared from the thin air, fiercer than before. "An eternity," she said coldly. "An eternity in this castle in exchange for the eternity you stole from me. Agree and promise never to break your word, and I will release your daughter."

Luca appeared beside her. He was the beast we now had chained to the cave floor. God, it all made sense. But something about him seemed...off... He was different from how he had been in the visions. Had Ameena bewitched him, as Huntsman had suggested, or had something else been stolen from his mind?

"Fine," King Archibald said, and a flash of lightning seemed to seal the deal.

Another clap of magic, and I saw Briar dancing in a nightclub. Ameena sidled beside her, dressed to the nines and grinding against her. She kissed Briar flush on the lips and then they disappeared into a backroom.

She was seducing her. She was using Briar for the charm

Ramsey had placed on her. I knew it in my bones. And, as if to confirm my suspicion, Ameena's voice vibrated through my ears.

"I need you, Briar. You're very special."

Pain shot through my body, and when I opened my eyes, I was back in the cave. Ameena was being pulled away from me, breaking our bond. Her beast, Luca, had her hoisted over his shoulder. And her hand was spotted in blood...my blood.

"How?" I murmured, but my hand traveled to my face to answer the question. My nose was pouring blood, probably from the strain caused by the magic I was performing.

Abram leapt toward the fleeing pair, but Ameena clapped her hands, and a wave of energy nearly froze us all where we stood (or, in my case, sat).

Energy returned to my body, but every movement was so slow...as though weighted beneath quicksand. Apparently that was something my blood could do—if only it was me who had done it instead of Ameena.

"Damn it," Ramsey said, only his lips moving at first, but his body and Abram's soon "woke up" as well.

"He's not just any beast," I said, my mind flickering back to the memories I had just witnessed. "He's her one true love. And I think he's how we stop her."

# CHAPTER 26

*A*bram and I walked back to the castle, almost literally licking our wounds. While he wasn't physically injured anymore thanks to my weird Conduit abilities, we still had a lot to mend.

Though we had come across more than a piece of information about who the Conduit was, we had just been through what anyone would see as an incontestable defeat.

Abram walked along the beach beside me, the low hanging sun casting dark shadows along his jaw. We didn't have much time left before he lost ability to control the beast inside of him, and yet neither of us hurried our steps to get back.

He huffed as we headed up the beach's incline, away from the ocean and toward the high path to the castle.

"She's powerful," he said, his nostril's flaring.

"That's an understatement," I mumbled, as ready as he was to rehash what we'd learned. Bad news always took more than one go around to really sink in. "She's old—so old that she makes you look like a newborn. And her power is unlike anything I've ever seen. I felt it, and it was enough to burn my eyeballs out."

"Not the greatest visual," he said, cutting his gaze toward me.

"She was married to King Archibald back in the day," I said, ignoring his glare. "She's the one who put his daughter—the original Sleeping Beauty—into a trance and used the energy to rebuke a spell King Archibald enacted to keep her away from her true love. As long as Sleeping Beauty slept, then Ameena could nullify the spell and be with Luca, who she turned into a beast in order to give him eternal life, big muscles, and that sexy musk thing you guys have got going on."

Abram growled. "So it's not just me?"

I stopped, and he spun toward me, his eyebrows pulled together. I spread my hands. "I'm serious, Abram."

"Then what's your point?" He turned to hike back up the incline again. We'd reached the road now, and he waved one arm out to the side, as though indicating the path ahead. "That the king is the victim here? Should we feel bad for him? He's still pretty villainous, if you ask me."

Now *he thinks the king is a villain, and* I'm *the one defending him? Could my life get any weirder?*

I came to Abram's side and placed my hand on his arm. His muscles were tense. A vein bulged in his arm under my fingertips. "But Archibald sacrificed himself in order to save his daughter. That's why he's stuck in the castle." I shook my head. "At least I thought he was. Once his daughter was safe and long gone from this world, the Company began helping him break the curse, and that risked Ameena's lover being away from her again."

"Luca," Abram mumbled as we crossed the street and headed toward the castle's path. "Ameena and Luca; the Conduit and her lover-turned-beast. God, I can't believe this is all about love."

I'd already tried skimming over the details for him once, but it was hard to summarize it all, and here we were—Abram hadn't taken much but their names from the first go around, maybe because I'd been talking a mile a minute.

"I think she sensed her slipping hold on the king and sort of went crazy, if you can believe it," I added, rolling my eyes. "And got all hell bent on finding a way to re-enact the curse. Remember, if she doesn't keep someone trapped, they can't be together."

"Looks like she found her way," Abram muttered.

"But that's not all. I think the Company helped her with it. I just don't understand *why*. In the letter they wrote the king, it sounded as though they were trying to help him."

"I'm not so sure," Abram said. "The magic is not the same. She's using Briar this time, not a Supplicant."

"The letter made it sound like she was manipulating magic in ways she shouldn't."

Abram rubbed the back of his neck and blew out a tired breath. "It also made it sound like maybe that's what they wanted her to do."

"Which brings us back to why."

Abram shook his head. "Let's forget the Company for a minute. What *do* we know? Ameena is using Briar, who's already gifted with a persuasion spell, to draw Supplicants to the island and control them through their dreams. And she's using the blood of those Supplicants to feed the curse that keeps the king trapped."

"Right. And I already considered maybe using her own magic against her, but even if Briar could choose the victims herself, she can't turn on Ameena—"

"Because Conduits don't sleep," Abram continued. "Not even mutt beasts like myself."

I bit my lip. That part wasn't entirely true. Somehow, my Supplicant nature had nulled that aspect in myself. That, or I hadn't awakened that side of myself soon enough. If only we'd met Ramsey sooner...if only we'd done the awakening ritual before Briar had visited. Would my life not be on the line if we had?

"We also have the issue of how she's storing this Supplicant blood to begin with."

"So I've noticed," Abram said. "It makes her impossible to contend with, at least until we find out how she's doing that. It's as though she's mutated her magic beyond the natural way of things."

"That's not the only thing about her that's mutated," I mumbled with a shudder, remembering her bull-head and satyr-like body.

"We're missing something," Abram said. "If the king is trapped, why is she still doing this?"

"Briar might have special abilities, but she's not a Supplicant, and she doesn't have the makings of one. For all of his crappy-ass ethics, Archibald's daughter was an honest-to-God Supplicant. Since Ameena can't curse him directly, I'm guessing Sleeping Beauty got those Supplicant traits from her mother. But Briar—"

"Doesn't," Abram finished. "That's why Ameena needs a constant supply of Supplicant blood."

"Right," I said. "But that's—"

"But that's not all, I know," Abram said, heaving a sigh. "What else?"

"I think the Company that's writing those letters has something to do with that, too. The storing the blood part, I mean."

"Char—"

"No, Abram. This is important. I can feel it. Something else is going on here. Something big. Both Archibald and Ameena got letters from that company, and I get the feeling neither of them knows the other is getting assistance from the same people."

"That's not unheard of in this world, though, Char. We don't have time to go chasing down some company."

"But the Company is the one pitting these people against each other, and the feud between Ameena and Archibald is the core reason Supplicants are being killed. This company is playing both sides, and there *has* to be a reason for it."

"And what reason would that be?" Abram asked, though I got the feeling he didn't expect me to have the answer.

"I'm sure whatever it is, it's not good."

"It's also not something we can worry about right now," he said as we crossed through the large fence that told us we were back within the grounds of the castle. "I mean it, Char. Leave it alone. One mountain at a time."

"This was supposed to be a vacation," I said, a saddened smile breaking across my face.

"We'll have a lifetime together for vacations, I promise you."

I winced, but I bit my tongue. The sun was about to set on the day *before* the day I die. The thought started a ticker in my head: *Tomorrow night I die. Tomorrow night I die. Tomorrow night I die.*

"We need to get inside," I mumbled, motioning toward the horizon and trying to keep my voice from cracking.

Abram took my hand, and we ascended the steps that led to the front door of the castle.

"Oh," I said as something else entered my mind. "But that's not—"

"Don't say it," Abram warned.

*But that's not all.*

I forced a smile to keep back the words. "Luca is Huntsman's brother. I saw it inside Ameena's head."

Abram's hand slipped down to the small of my back as he guided me toward the castle's gates. "This little web couldn't get any denser," he murmured.

"Let's hope not," I said. "Unless you're going to tell me that Ameena is actually your long lost sister or something."

"Don't be ridiculous. My sister isn't lost."

I was about to ask what he meant by that when the door of the castle flung open. Archibald stood, dressed ridiculously in a purple suit studded with bird feathers. A pipe hung from his mouth, making him even more disgusting than usual, and he was flanked by his usual bevy of armed guards.

"Good of you to finally join us," he said to Abram. As was customary between the two of us, Archibald didn't bother making eye contact with me. "I was afraid you would miss dinner. We're having stuffed quail. I shot the bird myself. Well, Charleston did," he said, patting the guard beside him on the back. "But he did it with *my* permission. Isn't that right, Charleston?"

"Yes, Your Majesty," Charleston answered, seeming more than a little tired of the question.

"You must be positively enamored of yourself," Abram said as Archibald moved aside and allowed us to enter.

"Usually." Archibald grinned as we made our way into the main hall. "Normally, I would instruct you to make yourself presentable for dinner, but I'm too excited."

"Excited?" Abram asked with raised eyebrows.

"Yes. I got you a present, and I simply can't wait to see what you think of it."

Immediately, I was on guard. Archibald wanted us dead. I had heard that much with my own ears. Whatever this present was, I was sure we didn't want it.

As the main doors to the dining hall were pushed open for us, I braced myself, half-expecting to see Huntsman on the other side, all glowing ax and fervor.

Instead, one of the most beautiful women I'd ever laid eyes on lounged in a chair near the foot of the table. Her skin was dark caramel, and her hair was raven feather and glistening. She wore a red dress I would've killed for and filled it out in a way that made me bite my lip in envy.

"This?" I murmured, before I could stop myself. "This is the present?"

"Well, you've had the same companion since you got here." Archibald nudged Abram, typically ignoring what I had to say. "I figured you could use a little spice. I got her from Bolivia. She's rumored to be very good at what she does."

"Of course she is," I muttered under my breath, knowing full-well that Abram's sensitive hearing would pick up on my frustration.

"Besides," Archibald continued, throwing a disgusted glance in my direction. "I imagine you've worn a groove into that one by now."

A low groan escaped my lips. Today had been rough. Was it too much to ask not be met at the door with rhetoric so sexist that Don Draper would have considered it outdated?

"Don't be jealous," King Archibald said, looking over to me. "I'm sure I can find some way to keep you busy while your companion is otherwise occupied."

My stomach churned. I turned a pleading gaze toward Abram, but he wasn't even looking at me.

"That won't be necessary," Abram said, holding his hand in front of him. "While I appreciate the thoughtful gift, I'm afraid I won't be able to indulge in it."

*It?* I didn't like this place, and I didn't like the person Abram had to pretend to be while we were here.

"Is she not to your liking? I'm nearly certain there's a German redhead in here somewhere."

"No," Abram said, an edge in his voice. "It's only that I'm perfectly comfortable with my current traveling companion."

Archibald narrowed his eyes. "Oh, come now. Every man prefers the feel of variety. It's the way we're born. It's in our genes."

My eyes drifted over to the dark-skinned woman. God, she was beautiful. Would Abram actually prefer her? Could I blame him if he did?

"Perhaps," Abram said. "But my companion's been quite mouthy to me as of late, and I had hopes of teaching her a lesson tonight." A smile spread across his face. "The hard way."

A matching smile graced King Archibald's smug mug. "In that case, by all means." His eyes slid over toward me, and I instantly longed for a shower. "Bad girls get what's coming to them."

It took all I could do to stifle a shudder from running through my entire body. I could not stand this bastard. And if I was anywhere else on the planet, I would drill my heel into his privileged ass and teach him a lesson. But there was too much at stake, so I held my tongue and my temper.

"My apologies, madam." Abram nodded to the achingly beautiful woman. "Perhaps another time."

I knew he wasn't serious. With any luck, we would be away from this place in a few days, never to return. Or, Abram would be at least.

I shook my head. I couldn't think about that right now. I couldn't think about any of it. My body was exhausted. My mind was completely wiped. I needed sleep. I needed to be in Abram's arms, pressed against his heart. If this was going to be my last night, then that was how I wanted to spend it.

As if he could read my mind, Abram motioned to King Archibald. "I hope your chef won't be too offended, but—"

"There are more pressing matters than hunger pangs." Archibald nudged him in the stomach. "Do enjoy yourself. I'll see that our Bolivian treasure is treated well."

I winced, looking over at the woman. She was prettier than me, which meant I instinctively hated her, but she didn't deserve to be subjected to this.

"My prince," I said, taking Abram's hand. "Perhaps she can be of assistance for us later. After you are finished with me."

He narrowed his eyes for a long moment, reading my meaning within them.

"Good thinking," he answered. "Keep her on hold for me, King Archibald. I'll likely be back for her later." To me, he added, "Don't think that curries you any favor with me."

Noticeable relief flashed across the woman's eyes—surely if she was to be subjected, she would prefer Abram to King Archibald, and I couldn't blame her. With that, Abram and I made our way to our room.

As soon as the door closed behind us, he turned toward me and slipped his hands down to my hips. "That was uniformly horrific."

"It's been one of those days," I said, pulling away and plopping down on the bed, then tossed my shoes off, letting my feet rest for the first time all day.

Closing my eyes, I felt Abram's heat next to me.

"I'm sorry," he said flatly.

"What?" I asked, opening my eyes. "What on Earth could you have to be sorry for?"

My feet were in his capable hands now. He deftly massaged them, pressing against a hundred pleasure points I had no idea even existed.

"All of this," he said. "I promised I would keep you safe. I promised I would make you happy. And now everything is spinning."

"I *am* happy," I said, running my hand against his shaped arm. "I'm happier than I ever thought I could be. And I have no doubt you'll keep me safe."

*As long as you can, anyway.*

"Let's take tomorrow off," he said, kissing me on the cheek. "This was, after all, supposed to be our vacation. I know things haven't gone to plan, but that doesn't mean we still can't enjoy our time here." He took my hand and squeezed it. "How would you like to spend tomorrow laying around on the beach? We'll get drunk and become one of those couples who are way too handsy with each other in public." He brought my palm up to his lips and kissed it. "And then, I'll cook you dinner. I'll tell you how beautiful you are, and then I'll find a way to show you." This time his lips grazed across my knuckles. "We can worry about all this other stuff later."

A shot of pain ran through me so strong that I had to jump off the bed.

"What?" Abram asked, leaning forward with a furrowed brow. "What's wrong?"

"Nothing," I said, facing the window and trying to bite back the tears that were ridiculously bubbling up in my eyes. "I'm fine. That sounds—that sounds like the best day ever."

And it really did. If I could pick a way to spend my last day on this planet, it would be what Abram just described, word for word.

But the thing was, I didn't want it to be my last day. I wanted this one, the next one, and a hundred thousand more after that. And the fact that I wasn't going to get that was just truly dawning on me.

"Don't lie to me, Charisse. We've been through too much for that."

He was right. He'd been there for me ever since the moment he first laid eyes on me, barreling down that staircase, heels over head—almost quite literally. I was lying to him. I was stealing away what little time he would have with me, and I was doing it so I didn't have to face this.

It wasn't fair to him, and I wasn't going to do it anymore.

"I'm dying, Abram," I said without turning to him. "I saw Briar two nights ago in a dream." I swallowed hard. "Tomorrow's my last day, babe. Tomorrow is the day I die."

# CHAPTER 27

When I finally turned back to Abram, the look on his face was unreadable. I expected to see pain or horror—to watch him melt into a pile of worry and anguish. Instead, his expression was as smooth and unaffected as stone.

"It was just a dream," he said, tilting up his chin. "She was on your mind. That particular sequence of events was on your mind, too. Of course you'd dream about it. It's only natural."

"It was on your mind, too, and you didn't dream it," I said in a small voice.

"I don't dream." A bit of curtness had snuck into his voice. "But you humans dream every night about all sorts of things. The only thing that dream meant was that you were worried. Nothing else."

I sighed. I didn't expect this. I figured that, faced with the truth, Abram would get laser focused. I imagined him scouring heaven and Earth, looking for a way to stop the unstoppable. But this—denial in its purest form—it just seemed so...well, so *human.*

"I know it's hard to process, but it's happening," I said, moving toward him. "I saw Briar twice, just like all the other Supplicants did. And the Conduit and her Beast both confirmed it."

Abram shrugged. "You've unlocked your Conduit side now. You won't dream tonight, anyway. It's a moot point."

"I don't think it works that way," I said, half-wishing he was right, and half-knowing I couldn't count on it. "It's happening, Abram, and we can't stop it."

"The hell it is!" Grabbing a ceramic egg that looked equal parts old and expensive, he flung it against the wall. I flinched as it shattered into a thousand shards and spilled in tiny pieces on the floor.

"Abram, I—"

"It's not happening, Charisse." He turned back to me, and the panic in his eyes that he'd been hiding before burst through clear as day. "And do you know why it's not happening? It's not happening because, if it did, that would mean you've been lying to me for two days. And you wouldn't do that, Charisse, would you? Not after all we've been through. You wouldn't look at me and *not* see the man who you could tell anything to. You wouldn't *not* see hands that would move continents to spare you the smallest hint of pain. You wouldn't look at me and not see me, Charisse. Not you. So no, that is why this is not happening."

"I was afraid," I whispered, looking down at my fidgeting hands and finally ready to come clean to myself about the reasons I had kept the whole thing under my hat. It wasn't to spare Abram, and it wasn't to keep him focused in the way he needed to be. No, the reasons I lied about this were much more obvious. Much more human. "I thought if I didn't tell you, then it wouldn't be real. I thought that, if we could just get through this, then I'd never have to think about it again. We could be us—just us—and we could be happy...and alive." I blinked back tears and searched his dark eyes that had become the closest thing I had to a home since my mom died. "And we'd have all the time in the world."

He stared at me for a long moment, his panicked eyes relaxing, his tense body regaining its normal composure.

After taking in and releasing a deep breath, Abram said, "We do have all the time in the world, Charisse." He stepped toward me, his knuckles brushing some stray hairs from my face. "You have me. We have us. And as sure as the sun will rise tomorrow, I will not allow you to leave this world even one second before your time. No Conduit is going to take you away from me. *No one* is."

His palm, rugged and large, moved across my cheek now. I turned into it, kissing the calloused skin of his hand.

"I'm going to make it right, Charisse," he said, wrapping my back with his arm and pulling me tight against him. "Do you believe me?"

I wanted to say yes. I needed to say yes. God knew I believed it. I had to. But I couldn't. I had made peace with this. To open myself up to the possibility that Abram might be able to undo this for me might have been too much for me to take.

"Do you believe me?" he asked again.

Slowly, he turned me around and laid me onto the bed. He rested over me, pushing me against the mattress with the weight of his body.

I closed my eyes and ran my hands through his hair. The heat of him lay against me, lighting me up inside. But still, I didn't answer. Opening my eyes, I pulled at his shirt, ripping it open and working it past his shoulders and off his back. Then, as quickly as I could, I pulled at my own shirt, fire rising from my core.

"Slow down there, tiger," he whispered, slowing pulling my shirt over my head and laying it beside us on the bed. "I promise you, we've got all the time in the world." His fingers grazed my cheek, drawing soothing circles around my lips. "We've got tomorrow." He moved his lips toward my neck, kissing it gently. "And the next day." He trailed along my collarbone and then to my breast. "We have the day after that," he continued, cupping me in his hands. "And the one after that, too."

My hands searched his back, but slower this time, more gently. Before, I wanted to scour every inch of him, to make sure I had revealed everything there was to know about him while I still had time to do so. But, for whatever reason, he had quieted that demon within me, at least for now.

As he slid off the rest of my clothes, exposing me to him in a way I hadn't been in days—with all of my body and all my secrets laid out on the table—a wave of peace washed over me.

Maybe he was right. Maybe we did have the rest of our lives. Maybe we had the rest of eternity. Maybe tonight was just an overture for a symphony that would stretch out into forever.

Abram seemed intent on driving that point home. It felt like hours that he laid beside me, half propped up on one arm, leaning down to kiss me while his fingers played over my nipples, slow, teasing, testing, making me squirm. His mouth never left mine, reducing me to beg him only with soft, pleading moans. God, I'd never felt so close to orgasm just from nipple play, but Abram had a way about him, always knowing when to pull back with his touch and leave me aching for more.

When it became too much and my whimpers became too insistent, he smiled against my mouth.

"Shh, my love. There's no rush."

I growled. "If I said I believe you, would just…you know."

"Hmm," he said, kissing me again and murmuring against my mouth. "I don't know."

"Please, Abram," I begged.

He pulled back and stared down into my eyes. "Ms. Bellamy, you should know by now I require more convincing than that. Why don't you tell me exactly what it is you want?"

"You already know," I said, but I barely got out the last word as his hand slipped between my thighs, eliciting a gasp from me and making me squirm beneath his touch. "*Abram…*"

As he slid a finger between my folds, my hips bucked involuntarily. He paused for a few heartbeats before slowly working his finger into me. His intense gaze made me feel both hyperaware and like a Goddess at the same time. He started to press in another finger from his large hand, stretching me while nearly sending me to the brink at the same time. That was Abram— always pushing me to my limits both physically and emotionally, making me uncomfortable and aroused all at once.

My mind was swimming in a pool of desperation. I couldn't think straight, and I suppose that was the best gift Abram could give me right now. All we had was this moment, this thumping desire.

Abram's skilled hands drove me to the edge, over and over, creating that eternity I wanted within just this one night. The tension building from my core made my eyes roll back, but every moan was stifled by his lips playing over my own. At any moment, I would explode. I squirmed beneath him, certain that at some point, he would not pull back fast enough, and I would shatter—I would explode into a million glorious pieces. If not, the need building inside me might kill me before tomorrow could get to me.

When he slowed his touch again, he lifted his mouth from mine to stare into my eyes once more, his thumb still grazing over my clit while his fingers teased between my legs.

"Tell me you know this isn't the end. Tell me you believe I can save you."

"I do," I said, sliding my hand up to his neck. "I do believe you."

He didn't reply—just smiled and kissed me square on the mouth. At some point, without my noticing, his pants had found their way to the floor, and he pushed apart my thighs to get between my legs. The head of his cock rested just at my entrance, hard and unmoving, exhibiting Abram's centuries of practiced self-control that I could not match. My body rocked eagerly to try to get more of him, to get him inside of me, but he was using every movement, every kiss, every touch, to prove that we were not running out of time. That we would never run out of time.

I wrapped my arms around his neck, as slowly, achingly, he pushed into me inch by inch, the pressure building up in me so

CONNER KRESSLEY & REBECCA HAMILTON

hard and fast I was certain I would be done before he even got all of himself into me.

"Abram, please," I begged. "I really can't anymore."

"Always," he whispered, driving the rest of the way into me. "Always, Ms. Bellamy."

And finally I had all of him, his thick shaft filling me in a way that made me feel complete in every way imaginable, that made me feel impossibly full, that made me combust.

My body shuddered and my nails dug into his shoulders and my body rocked with orgasm.

"You belong to me," he said, grunting as he ground deeper into me, and impossibly I disintegrated all over again, my orgasm squeezing over his own.

When he finished, he rolled off of me and stared up at the ceiling. "You belong to me," he said again. "And no one is going to take what's mine."

\* \* \*

I should have expected the dream. I should have known that, Abram's pleas and expertise aside, what was real wouldn't stop just because I begged it to.

I was at the edge of the cliff now, looking out onto the ocean and peering down at the rocky shore below.

It was different than it had been in reality, though. A hundred corpses littered the ground, one twisted and rotting body piled onto the next. It was like a mountain of death, and I was about to join it.

"They never leave here," Briar said from beside me. I turned to find her wearing the same elaborate dress. Her hair swung up in curls, and a studded tiara graced her head. "Not really. They sort of just lay there. I think they're just...just like me."

"Just like us," I answered.

She looked down, and I followed her gaze to my hand. In its grasp was a shard of a broken mirror. My knuckles were covered in blood.

210

"What...?"

My confusion was soon placed with understanding as something dripped into my eye, clouding my vision in red. I lifted my fingertip to my forehead and gently prodded what had once been Cover Girl smooth skin. Not anymore.

"She sleeps," I whispered, my gaze moving back to Briar.

"At least you'll have people to talk to," she said, shaking her head. "All I get is an endless parade of one crying face after the next. Do you have any idea how sick I am of consoling people? All I do is listen to their problems, hear about why they don't want to die, how they don't deserve it."

"Is that so hard to believe?" I asked. As I went to take a step to approach her, I realized my feet were stuck. I wasn't able to move back from the edge.

"It happens quickly for them," she said, not looking at me. "If it took longer—if they stayed here as long as I have—they would welcome death."

Her voice cracked at the end, and I found myself feeling bad for this woman who I had hated so much for reasons that seemed so silly now.

"I saw your husband again today," I said.

"Ramsey?" Her gaze cut over to me. "Isn't he a dish? How is he?"

"Sad," I said. "He wants you back."

"He never knew what was good for him." She grinned. "I'm going to tell you something I never would have if I thought either of us was going to survive this, Charisse. I'm not a good person."

"I know," I said, smiling.

She chuckled. "No, not like that. What happened between me and you was business. You were good at what you did. So was I. Just friendly competition."

"Didn't seem so friendly to me," I said. "You slept with my boyfriend."

"Charlie Prince." She smiled, looking up and to the side as if having a fond memory of her time with him. Another day, I would have liked to smack her for that—but this was not another day. "Can you blame me? He had an ass that didn't quit. Besides," she said, her voice getting darker, "I seem to have a bad habit of doing that."

My mind flashed back to what I had seen in Ameena's mind, to the Conduit seducing Briar and leading her down this horrible path.

Of course, she felt guilty. She felt responsible.

"Have you ever been in love, Charisse? Because I'm not sure I have."

"Yeah," I said, thinking of Abram.

"Ramsey loves me. God knows he does. But I never—" She stared down at the mountain of death. "He deserves better. I hope he gets better once he has the good sense to move on."

"It's not too late," I said, though honestly, I had no idea what I meant by that.

The crash of the waves below seemed to get louder, the wind picking up sharper and whipping my hair in my face so that it tangled between my lips. It was as though nature was trying to rebuke my statement.

"I've seen too much for that," she said, her whole essence eerily still in what felt like a storm brewing around us. But her voice was louder, as though she needed to shout over the waves. "But at least I can make this much right." She turned to me. "I'm sorry about Charlie Prince, and I'm sorry about spreading that rumor about you sleeping with Andy Dick."

"You did what?" I asked.

"Look, I don't particularly like you, but you deserve better than what you're about to get. And you damn sure deserve to go into it with your eyes open." She took my hand. "The next time you see me, you won't be dreaming. It'll look like you are. It'll feel like you are. But you'll be moving. And when you jump off this cliff, make no mistake, it *will* be the last thing you ever do."

I looked back at her, but this time there was a huge darkened castle behind her. I shuddered, but she tightened her hold on my hand.

"Tell Ramsey I'm sorry, will you? Tell him I'm setting him free. That I want him to be happy." Tears rolled down Briar's cheeks. "And tell your guy that you love him, while you still can."

And like that, she was gone. The dream was gone, hurtling me back to reality and shooting me awake in a cold sweat. I turned to Abram's side of the bed, looking for a bit of comfort.

But he wasn't there.

# CHAPTER 28

The bed was empty. Where Abram once lay—where he *always* lied—was now a naked space. I glanced around the room, and when I didn't see him, I ran to our bathroom and threw open the door and flipped on the light.

Empty. Empty for all but my reflection in the mirror staring back at me. The words "She sleeps" carved crudely into my forehead. My legs buckled beneath me, and I stumbled over to the vanity to hold myself up while I puked into the bathroom sink.

*No.* Tears burned hot down my cheeks, and my head spun, my vision blurred. There was no denying it. There was not even so much as a *thread* of hope. My dreams had been real. And if Abram had seen this, there was no doubt he now knew the truth with no uncertainty.

After some not-so-steadying breaths, I splashed my face with cool water and tried to keep it together while I used my own blood to tend my wounds. The magic seemed to stitch my skin back together and mend the scars, but there was nothing my Conduit abilities could to do heal my heart.

Even with the words gone, I couldn't look at myself in the

CONNER KRESSLEY & REBECCA HAMILTON

mirror another second. I spun around, my back to the vanity, looking out the bathroom door and into the bed chambers.

*Abram, where are you?*

On shaky legs, I made my way to the bed, trying to make sense of it. He wouldn't have left me, not with everything I just told him. He would want to be here with me, to soak up every minute we had left in each other's arms, or try to brainstorm with me some way to stop this.

Why would he bolt away and waste what little time we had left?

Maybe it was too much for him. Maybe the truth had sent him running for the hills. He had, back in the day, been something of a Lothario. And he told me himself he wasn't good at goodbyes. What if this—leaving me here in the dead of night like some walking, talking memory—was his way of avoiding a goodbye?

I shook my head hard. That wasn't him. Not anymore. My imagination was getting the better of me. He was probably just around the castle somewhere, getting me breakfast in bed or some equally chivalrous thing that guys of my generation wouldn't even think to do.

But then another thought hit me that sent my heart hurtling into my gut. He wasn't the old Abram. He was *my* Abram. And what would my Abram do? He would fight tooth and nail for me, and he would relish every second of it. He told me as much, and he had done just that in the past.

What if that was where he was now? Thundering toward the Conduit's lair to face her alone. As strong as he was, he couldn't take her on alone. Their last altercation was proof enough of that.

I had to find him.

I scrambled to get ready, trying my best not to think about the fact that today was very likely my last day on this planet. What time was it, anyway? The sun hung sort of low in the sky, so we couldn't have been far into morning.

This was very likely my last spin around the globe, and instead of savoring every second, every sensation, I would be chasing down my boyfriend to make sure he didn't get killed, too.

With any luck, maybe I could save my own life in the process. Unfortunately, I didn't exactly have much luck to speak of.

After throwing on my favorite red dress and matching flats—the ones I'd been saving for a special occasion—I scrambled out the door and into the hall.

Was this how my mother felt as the cancer marched her toward her own unavoidable cliff?

"I wish you would have told me," I muttered, closing my eyes. "I wish you would have said it felt like this."

God, I was terrified. It would have been better to die a sudden and unexpected death. But to see it coming...to know death would soon wrap you in its long talons and steal away everything that was beautiful...it was too much. I couldn't let myself think about it, and yet, I couldn't stop myself from thinking about it.

Abram said this wasn't the end for me, and maybe he was right. But if it was—if I was going to meet my Maker and stand judgment for all I had done or didn't do—then at least I could stand tall.

I paused at a mirror, forcing myself to look at myself once more. Not as the woman who was dying, but as the woman who was going to fight. The women who would, at the very least, save the love of her life before she did.

Confidence bubbled up inside of me, and I continued in a rush down the hall. I turned a corner and right into King Archibald's path. His presence caused me to shudder. He wore a suit with medals I was sure he hadn't earned studding his right breast and striped across his left shoulder. The minute his gaze met mine, I knew he wasn't going to let me pass by him easily.

"Dressed up for me today, I see," he said as an oil slick smile disfigured his face.

"Not for you," I said, feeling oddly free of the constraints that

CONNER KRESSLEY & REBECCA HAMILTON

had stopped me from putting this pig of a man in his place before today. "You know, I doubt anyone has ever dressed up for you."

"I love it when you play hard to get, you little spitfire," he said. And then he took his disgusting hand and slapped me on the ass.

*Nope. That was just about enough, thank you very much.*

Not one more minute of my day, not one more minute of my life, would I deal with that man and his nonsense.

Rearing back, I slapped him hard across the face. His eyes went wide, and his mouth dropped.

"You know something?" I said, relishing the shock that seemed to freeze him in place. "You've got a lot of nerve. But what you don't have is a lot of brains. Because, if you did, you'd be able to see the obvious. We're here to help you. You've got an island full of murder victims, a Conduit who's kept you impotent and trapped in this castle like some fish in a tank for hundreds of years, and a plan so ridiculous that Vegas wouldn't book your chances of surviving this, let alone winning."

"You—How did you—"

"Shut up. It's my turn to talk now," I said, pointing a silencing finger at him. "If I were you—and really, thank God I'm not—but if I was, I'd shut the hell up, tell your stud muffin hitman with the enchanted ax to stand down, and take the help that fate and fortune has dictated is in my best interest to give you. Because certainly, you don't deserve it."

As I walked off, over my shoulder I added, "And tell Huntsman that if he really wants a chance at getting his brother back, he needs to strongly reconsider whose side he's on."

\* \* \*

Moving through the castle, I found Abram was nowhere in sight. I strode faster and faster as room after room turned out to be empty of the one person I was looking for, further confirming the suspicion I so desperately wanted to believe was wrong.

Something was off, though. He wouldn't have run off without at least leaving me a note.

I burst through the double doors of the castle and found Satina standing on the grounds like some sort of grim confirmation of all the fears that were swirling within me. She wore a huge purple sun hat and matching bathing suit, but her face was free of its usual careless tint.

"Abram..." I murmured, terror plain in my voice.

"He's been kidnapped." She moved toward me faster than I had ever seen her go.

"What?" I asked, feeling as though the entire world had been ripped out from underfoot. "That's not possible. How can you be sure?"

"He's my creation, Charisse. I'm connected to him. I can feel him." She looked up at the castle. She grabbed my arm and started leading me away, down the castle path. "Of course, this magical cock block of a building muddied the sensation. But the instant he was pulled out of it, I could feel him. He wasn't afraid, at least not for himself, but he *was* fighting."

I thought about Abram, about him being taken away in the dead of night, ripped away from me while I slept beside him like some useless, snoring moron.

"I would have felt it. I would have heard it. God knows I would have. I was sleeping right next to him," I stammered, trying to punch holes into Satina's theory.

"Unless whoever did this—and I think we both know who it was—cloaked the room with magic."

"What magic?" I asked. "This place is supposed to be a stronghold."

"A stronghold that Ameena made," Satina reminded me.

"But that bitch hasn't killed a Supplicant in days." *Three days, to be exact.* "How did she get the magic to spell the room?"

"From your blood, genius," Satina spat. "If I'm not mistaken, the Conduit was pulled out of that cave with a fistful of your blood for her troubles."

My stomach tightened. This was my fault.

"And let me tell you something," Satina continued. "This Ameena chick is potent. No sooner had I zeroed in on Abram's plight than she blocked me again, knocked me right on my ass."

"So you don't know where she took him?" I said, the both of us walking too briskly down the hillside to seem at all normal.

"Not precisely, no. But it doesn't matter. This Conduit has world-shaking powers. Going up against her would be a death wish."

I raised by eyebrows. "Your point?"

Satina spun toward me, and I had to stop short myself to keep from crashing into her.

She glared at me. "You'd have to be insane to even consider it." Her eyes narrowed. "This is a trap, Charisse. She's using Abram to draw you out."

"That doesn't make sense. She already has me. I already saw Briar. I'm a sitting duck. All she'd have to do is wait. Why would she throw kidnapping into the mix?"

"She's tasted your blood." Satina traced her tongue along her teeth. "She must think you have the power to undo what she's done, to save yourself and everyone else. That's the only explanation."

"Then I hope she's right," I said, and I started walking toward the gates that led out to the island's main grounds.

"And where in ten hells do you think you're going?" Satina called from behind me.

"Abram wouldn't hesitate if it was me, and I'm not going to hesitate for him, either. If Ameena wants a fight, it'll be a fight to the death."

CHAPTER 29

*I* fervently marched along the beach with Satina shuffling close behind.

"I don't know what you're expecting to accomplish," she yelled. Then, stubbing her toe on an errant seashell, she cursed me for my "unimaginably hard head."

"I'm doing what I have to," I answered without breaking stride. "I wouldn't expect you to understand."

"I'm going to ignore that, as it had the tone and inclination of an insult. But I am going to reiterate how mind-bogglingly bad this idea is." She moved in front of me and stopped short, staring at me through a dead girl's eyes and shaking her head disapprovingly. "You're going to get yourself killed. You have no idea what you're doing out there. Magic is complicated. It's difficult."

"I've been practicing," I answered, sidestepping her and continuing on my way.

"With your mage?" She scoffed.

*How much of what we do can Satina see?*

"If you think an afternoon lesson is all you need to go up against a Conduit as powerful as the one we face now, you're delusional. Charisse, that woman is even more powerful than me."

"And she's afraid of *me*. That ought to tell you something," I spit out, undeterred.

Satina sighed. "Yes, it tells me that you're even more foolish than I thought."

Off in the distance, I could see a spot of a man. I wanted it to be Abram. Maybe he had gotten out somehow and was walking toward me the same way I was walking to him. We would meet in the middle, and it would be very Pride and Prejudice and whatnot.

But that didn't make sense. If Abram got out, then Satina would have felt him. She would've pulled me to a stop, and I would've been happy to oblige.

As I neared in on the figure, it became more and more obvious this man wasn't Abram. He lacked Abram's muscle, his dark good looks. But he was still familiar.

"What the hell is going on?" the man asked as I came upon him. Ramsey Duldrige stood on the sand, arms folded and eyes narrowed.

"What are you doing here?" I asked, and then I kept going right on past him before he could answer.

"I-I got a message," he said, keeping pace with Satina and me. "On the mirror in my bathroom. The steam wrote out that if I didn't come to this place at this time, the entire world would end." He looked over to Satina. "Who is she?"

"I imagine she's the source of your messaging mirror," I said, rolling my eyes. She'd probably invited him to get in my way, but I wasn't about to let anything slow me down. "Ramsey, New Age mage, meet Satina, decidedly *not* New Age Conduit."

Satina gave him a pert nod.

"Another goddamn Conduit?" Ramsey sighed. "How many of them are on this troublesome island anyway?"

"One too many," Satina answered. "Though I'm doing my best to remedy that." She gave me a pointed look.

"So am I," I said, balling my fists. "Why did you bring Ramsey here?"

Ramsey cut his gaze to Satina. "I was about to ask the same question."

"I figured I'd have trouble talking sense into you," Satina said from my side. "Backup is never a bad thing."

"Uh," Ramsey said, a clear hesitation in his voice. "What sort of sense?"

"Ameena kidnapped Abram." I picked up my pace. "She's trying to cut me off at the knees, stop me from ruining that death spell she put on me."

"You saw Briar?" Ramsey seemed more stunned than I figured. "Was she—was she okay?"

My mind flashed back to the way she pleaded with me to tell Ramsey to move on. I was supposed to give him the strength he needed to live a happy life, to let Briar go. But that was before all of this. That was before Ameena took the one thing in the world I cared about.

For that, I was changing everything. I had been ready to accept death. I had made my peace with my imminent end. But no more. That bitch went too far. I wasn't dying today, not for her and not for anybody. And neither was Briar.

"She was fine," I lied. "She said you better find a way to get her out of there. She's pissed it's taking you so long, and said she's missed one too many of her favorite annual sales."

"That's my girl," he said, a smile crinkling his face. "So what do we do?"

"I know where Ameena took him. So we go there." I turned to Ramsey. "We get Abram back, and we make that Conduit regret she ever screwed with any of us."

Ramsey's pace picked up a little so that he was by my side instead of walking behind me. "I'm good with that."

"What!" Satina shrieked, appearing in front of us again. But we just walked around her and kept going. "You're not serious," she said from behind us. "You're not actually encouraging her, are you? She's going to get us all killed, some of us for the second time."

"Then we die," Ramsey said. "At least my wife will know I went down fighting for her."

Okay. That impressed me. If Briar could inspire that sort of devotion, maybe she wasn't the evil ice queen I always imagined her to be.

*No, she probably still is. But that doesn't mean she deserves this.*

"And you think that matters?" Satina jumped in front of us again. She waved her fingers, and suddenly we were both stuck in place.

"When did you get my blood?" I growled.

"Castle bathroom, before it the enchantment kicked me out again," she said offhandedly. "And you know how that stuff has an expiration date, so believe me, I hate to see it go to waste."

I scowled at her, but I couldn't do much more than that.

"You're being selfish, the both of you," she continued. Then she pointed at me. "I told you that you have a destiny."

"You said *we* have a destiny," I corrected.

"Technicalities." She dropped her arms to her side. "You and he did have a destiny, but it was the same way a mosquito has a destiny with a windshield. I know about cars now," she added, giving me a rueful wink. "The point is, all of this is about you. Yes, your road would be easier traveled if he was by your side, but at the end of the day, what matters is that you're around to travel it. The fate of so much is on your shoulders. The entire world—everything that is, was, and will be—it's on you, and you need to keep that in mind."

*Geesh. No pressure, right?*

"And what *you* need to understand," I said, "is this road of yours doesn't interest me, not without him. I don't know what you think you know about me, but I'm here to tell you that, without him, there is no me. I can't do this without Abram, and I won't. So you either come with me or you let me go. Either way, I'm doing this."

"If you knew what was at stake—"

"I don't *care* what's at stake!" I said. "But if *you* care so much, you can help me save the man that gives me a reason to care." Fire rushed through me, and a pulse of energy flew from my body, freeing both Ramsey and I from Satina's hold.

"Good Lord," Satina said, rearing back from the force of my magic.

"You listen to me," I said, sticking my finger in her face. "This conversation is over. The most important person in my life is waiting for me to come get him, and I'm not about to let him down, not even if it means the whole damn world falls down around me."

"That's incredibly selfish," Satina muttered, glowering at me. "And probably exactly what will happen."

"Uh-huh," I said. "Maybe it is. Or maybe it's selfish of everyone else to think I should sacrifice someone I love to save someone they love. Ever think of that?"

She opened her mouth, then closed it again. I was sure she had a valid point on hand, but my guess was she was starting to realize it was a losing battle.

"And I'll have you know," I continued on, feeling angrier and more powerful by the moment, "I could die tonight anyway. So maybe that'll change your view on hunting this bitch down!" I stuck out my chin. "Either get on board or run back to that castle and cower beside King Douchebag and Huntsman. But you *will* stay out of my way."

"You don't have to get so testy," Satina said, looking me up and down. "I'll help you. But I'm warning you—if you ruin this body I've borrowed, I'm going to ruin every spare moment you get with Abram from now until eternity."

"Whatever," I said, and I sped off again toward our destination.

Satina moved along with us, kicking dirt as she made her way.

"Can we at least come up with a plan more complex than walk in and fight?"

"Sure, if you can think up something before we get there."

"I'm sorry," Ramsey said, stepping between us again. "Did you say that Huntsman was here?"

"King Archibald hired him to kill us...among other things. Have you heard of him?"

"Only since I was a child," Ramsey said, eyes going wide. "He's fabled. His ax was gifted to him by some pretty badass mystics. It's rumored to have the power to cut through anything in a single stroke."

"So he's a formidable assassin. Doesn't mean I have to like him."

"No. That isn't right. Assassin isn't the right word. He's more of a vigilante."

"He's being paid to murder, and we aren't exactly the bad guys," I said. "Sounds like an assassin to me."

"That doesn't make any sense. All the stories—"

"If I've learned one thing from all this," I said, "it's that you can rarely trust 'the stories.' But it doesn't matter. Magic ax aside, I don't think he'll be a problem for us. Turns out Ameena's beast is actually his brother. He wants to free him of the curse so, at the very least, he'll stay out of our way."

"Or maybe he'll help us!" Satina said. "I can think of less useful things than a muscleman with a deadly weapon on our side." Her whole borrowed face lit up. "I think a plan might be forming after all."

"No," I said, still walking. "I don't trust Huntsman, and even if I did, I don't have time to scour the island for him. We do this on our own, and we do it now."

"How, though?" Ramsey asked. "We don't even know where to find the Conduit."

"You don't. But I do." I spun around, more than a little agitated at these two distrusting my capability. "And you can thank your wife for that." I pointed to the top of the cliff—the same cliff I was destined to die on. "There," I said. "That's where we'll find them."

"Are you daft?" Satina asked, her face all twisted up. "There's nothing up there. It's a cliff, a plateau almost. The one you're worried about throwing yourself off of, I'll remind you. What the hell do you think you're going to find up there?"

"The castle," I muttered, looking up at the admittedly empty space of the cliff.

"*That* castle?" Ramsey asked, pointing in the direction of the very visible castle I had just left.

I shook my head. "The original castle. The one where it all went down."

"That is the original castle, Charisse," Ramsey said. "The royal family had it moved brick by brick after Sleeping Beauty woke up. The king thought better placement would lead to better fortune. Or so the stories say."

"The stories are wrong, Ramsey," I said, as sure of this as I had ever been about anything. "Ameena just wants people to think the castle was moved. She didn't want anyone looking for her. And she wanted to give Archibald a prison away from the home he had helped build."

"There are documents, Charisse. I've read them." Ramsey waved his hand toward King Archibald's current home. "There are paintings depicting the great move."

The logical part of my mind questioned if this was the same logic that sent every victim storming up this mountain. Were they as sure as I was that they were heading toward a chance to rescue themselves, when really, they were heading toward their deaths? But it wasn't my mind driving me right now. It was a *knowing*, a gut feeling, and I trusted myself. At least on this one thing.

"Do you know what I saw?" I asked. "I saw the original castle standing on that cliff with your wife in front of it. It's there. I can feel it." I turned to Satina. "I just need your help to unmask it."

"Ugh. Figures." She held her hand out to me. "What do I need to do?"

"Guide me," I said, grasping her fingers. "Imagine if your power was greater than hers, then you'd already be able to see past Ameena's illusion. I could, though. With your help, I could make it so all of us could see it."

She squinted and rubbed her temples with her free hand. "You're energy is amazing. Disorienting, but utterly amazing."

She probably meant that as a compliment, but it wasn't anything I could take credit for. It was a product of my birth, like having bright eyes or full hips. It was just who I was.

I funneled my energy, which had lit up like a candlewick the instant Satina grabbed my hand. I pushed all of my energy out into her and then flinched as she poured it back into me, as focused as a pinprick. Our magic cycled together might just be enough to overcome whatever this witch bitch had going on.

The air crackled around me as my Conduit magic, fueled by my Supplicant blood, swirled like a fog, thickening and settling into a cloud over the cliff.

And then, when it dissipated, the castle—the original castle—sat dark and looming on the cusp of where so many Supplicants had died.

"My God," Satina said, looking up at the monstrosity. "You were right."

"Can everyone see it?" I asked.

"No," Satina answered. "Just the three of us."

"Are you sure?"

Satina cut a glare my way, and I decided to leave it at that. If anyone knew what other people could or couldn't see, it was her.

I looked over at Ramsey. He was so white, he wouldn't be allowed out of the house after Labor Day. Except he wasn't looking at the castle. He wasn't looking upward at all.

"Ramsey, what—"

"I didn't tell you everything," he said. "The message in the mirror wasn't the only reason I came here today."

A chill ran up my spine just from the tone of his voice alone. I dreaded whatever his next words would be, and yet, he couldn't get them out fast enough.

"I got a call from the hospital earlier. They couldn't find her. They said it was like Briar just woke up and walked out of there. And now..." He coughed. "And now..."

I followed his gaze. Briar stood there, dressed in a hospital gown with her eyes closed. She turned and began walking up the path toward the cliff.

"It's not really her," I said. "It's an illusion. She told me as much in the dream last night."

Satina slowed her steps and shook her head. "I'm not so sure. I think it *is* her. Sleepwalking. The Conduit must think...she must think you're the last."

I swallowed around the tension building in my throat. "Well, real or imagined, she's leading us to the castle."

"Like lambs to the slaughter," Ramsey muttered.

"Not necessarily," Satina said, her finger pressed to her lip. "I've got an idea." She looked over at me. "But I need your help."

# CHAPTER 30

We followed Briar as she sleepwalked her way toward the once long-hidden castle. I cut my gaze toward Satina, who was keeping pace at my side.

"Are you sure this is going to work?" I asked.

She laughed bitterly. "Of course not. We're in uncharted territory here, Supplicant. But if it doesn't work, I *am* sure we're all going to die today. So I'm trying to keep up my optimism."

Her hand grasped mine, energy cycling through us, but in a different way than before—even more tiring this time. And the spell she was trying to cast using my Conduit/Supplicant hybrid powers was even trickier than when we unveiled the castle.

"Keep up with us!" Satina snapped at Ramsey who, for the second time since we began our trek behind Briar to the top of the cliff, was lagging behind. "It's important we're all in a line when I complete the spell. We won't get a second chance."

He sped up, but his eyes had glazed over since the moment he saw he wife up and moving about. It was as though there was something about seeing her here and unable to control what she was doing that made all of this more real for him. Or maybe I was just projecting my own feelings…

Ramsey let out a sigh. "What are we going to *do?*"

Satina stopped short, cringing, and spun in a slow circle to face him. "If you weren't so busy pitying yourself, you would know the answer to that!"

"Well, I don't," he said, sneering. "Sorry I can't be as focused as you, Miss Ice Queen, but some of us are worried about people we *love*. Not that I would expect you to understand that."

She flinched. "Ouch..." Her expression softened, and her shoulders relaxed. "You know, some people handle their feelings a little differently. Doesn't mean they don't have them."

I gave Satina's hand a gentle squeeze and locked my gaze on Ramsey with what I hoped was a sympathetic stare. "Briar's going to be okay. But we do need you to focus. Like Satina said, we only get one chance at this."

"I know," he said quietly. "I'm sorry. You have my undivided attention."

Satina gave a firm nod. "What *we're* doing is basically a bastardization of the illusion spell that still surrounds this place. I'm using Char's ability to create mirror images of us. Then I'll direct them to follow Briar wherever Ameena is commanding her to go. Then I'll make us invisible. Hopefully that'll give us enough time get Abram out before Ameena realizes what's going on. But we have to be in a straight line. The spell reaches horizontally, and I'll only be able to do it once," she said, looking from Ramsey to me and back again. "You ready?"

Ramsey swallowed, then nodded.

"Do it," I said, my mind filling with images of Abram.

Sooner than I expected, energy surged between us and then flowed out of me like a wave. But as the wave spread, Ramsey jumped out of line, shaking his head and waving his hands.

"What the hell did you do?" Satina yelled as a mirror image of both her and I appeared behind Briar, following her mindlessly. "You're not there, you moron! You think she won't notice that? She'll send that beast of hers looking for you, and he'll find us!"

"No, he won't. I'll be with them," Ramsey said, pointing to the mirror images.

Satina scoffed. "Why the hell would you do something as foolish and dangerous as that?"

"Because Briar's with them," I muttered, reading his face.

"She's my wife, and I won't leave her—not while I'm still able to follow."

Satina's jaw clenched. "If Ameena finds you out, she'll kill both of you."

"Then the last thing my wife will see in this life is me fighting for her," he said evenly. It was as though his strength had throttled back into him. "We've been through too much. We promised each other our lives, and while things haven't been perfect, I'm not willing to give up on that promise yet." He turned to me with tears in his eyes. "You understand that, don't you?"

"I do." I stepped forward and hugged him. "She loves you a lot, you know."

"I know," he said, hugging me back and then stepping away again. "And you'd better believe I'm going to make her say it after all of this is over."

"Be careful," I muttered as he moved in line with the mirror images.

"You, too," he said. "See you on the other side."

"One way or another," I said under my breath, and watched as they disappeared up the cliff. Then I turned to Satina. "What now?"

She raised her eyebrows. "Now we go find your boyfriend."

I followed Satina as she circled halfway around the castle. I walked hesitantly, as though there might be some sort of magical landmine I needed to avoid. More realistically, I was afraid Ameena or Luca might see us and wonder why the us that was walking toward them with Briar wasn't...well, us. With Ramsey there, though, she was more likely to think they were the real us, and that made me worry for him. Surely Ameena knew he would want to save his wife as much as I wanted to save Abram—this had probably been a trap for *both* of us.

"Don't be so prudish about your movements," Satina said, grabbing my arm and yanking me forward. "This woman has been hiding in plain sight for over a thousand years. I promise you, she's gotten out of the habit of standing guard."

She might have been right, because as we made our way toward what looked like the opening of a cave at the back of the castle, no one seemed to be the wiser.

"This opening will lead us into the castle," Satina said, sauntering toward it with all the aplomb of a woman bouncing into a sale at Barney's.

"How do you know that?" I asked, right behind her.

"What, you thought I spent my entire afterlife following the likes of you around all the time? You'd be surprised what I know."

"I don't doubt that," I muttered.

The interior of the cave got cooler and darker the farther we trekked into it. Unlike the cave at the base of the cliff, this one did not look lived-in at all. In fact, Satina and I were clearly the only people to set foot inside it in a very long time.

"Light us up," Satina said from in front of me.

"What?" I asked, scrunching my nose and jogging to keep up with her insanely quick pace.

"Haven't you figured out that glowing thing yet? It's pretty standard Conduit fare."

"Right," I mumbled and, letting my emotions go again, I emitted a soft light from my pores. As we ventured deeper into the cave, I was like a walking, talking glow worm.

After a while, the magic seemed mundane. The light I produced made our path visible, and it was easy to see just how empty this place was. Not even vermin existed in here, which worried me more than it should have.

I thought I heard footsteps behind me once as we walked, but

Satina didn't so much as hesitate, so I figured it was my imagination.

Just as I was about to ask her how much longer we were going to have to walk, we came upon a huge door. It was wooden and held carvings similar to the images I had seen back in the club Abram and I renovated.

God, that seemed like forever ago now.

"We gotta get through *that*?" I asked.

"Look at how smart she's getting." Satina grinned. "Would you like to do the honors, or do you want to gash your hand against one of those rocks and let me have a little fun?"

"I like my palms intact, thank you," I said, rubbing them together and placing them against the huge door. Then I mumbled under my breath, "Besides, I don't have much time left to practice."

A bright strike, like lightning, flew from the door, knocking me backward through the air. I collided with the cave wall and swore as I slid to the floor.

"It's protected," Satina said, looking it over.

"I sort of gathered that." I grunted, clambering back to my feet before marching back toward the stupid thing. "Let's see how much juice it's got."

"You're even crazier than I thought," Satina said, grabbing my arm. "Do you not value your own life near as much as I do? Absorbing the shock of any more energy from that door would cook you like pig on a spit fire."

"What?" I asked, pulling my hand away.

"Are there more efficient ways to do that now?" she asked, then shook her head. "Never mind that. There's an anti-magic barrier surrounding that door. More magic would just feed it. You'd power the stupid thing until it was potent enough to kill us both."

"Or I'd overpower it," I answered. "I'm stronger than you think."

CONNER KRESSLEY & REBECCA HAMILTON

"You're certainly more cocksure than I think, especially for a maiden. But it won't save your life. We need to find another way in."

"The barrier protecting this door will be protecting all of them," I said. "You know that as well as I do. The only other way in is the way Briar is going. And if Ameena finds out that we're not actually with her before we can get Abram out, then he's as good as dead. And I won't have that. We go through this door—"

A bright object whizzed past my face, cutting off my sentence (and very nearly my nose). It spun until it struck the door, shattering the barrier into thousands of pieces. Looking down where the object now lay, I saw it was an ax.

*Huntsman's axe.*

# CHAPTER 31

"Or go through another?" Huntsman finished for me, stepping into view.

"I knew I heard footsteps," I hissed. "Satina! You said no one else could see this place."

"Oops," she said with a sly smile and a shrug.

"You did this on purpose," I said, remembering how she'd wanted him here. Ugh! I could kill her! I spun toward our uninvited company. "What the hell are you doing?"

"Helping you," he said. "And *not* receiving a thank you, I might add."

He was even more handsome up close, the lines of his face symmetrical and perfect. But I needed to get to Abram with as little difficulty as possible, and Huntsman was nothing if not a ripped and rippling hunk of steaming hot trouble.

"Am I going to have to deal with you?" I asked. My nostrils flared. Power surged through me, and my light pulsated brighter.

"I suppose that depends on how smart you are," he said with an easy grin. "From where I see it, we have a common goal. We both want to save someone we love. Your lover and my—"

"Brother," I finished, ignoring the implied 'ew' factor I always got when anyone described Abram as my 'lover.'

"You got in that wench's head," Huntsman answered. "That bodes well for your chances." He stepped forward. "I bode well for your chances, too."

He lifted his left hand, and his glowing ax flew back toward him. He snatched it out of the air and fastened it behind his back. "Or you could value stubbornness and conviction over the life of your loved one. Either way, the door is open now, and I'm stepping through it."

He brushed past me, knocking my shoulder with his own and stepping into the castle.

"We could take him out of the equation," Satina said, watching him from behind. "I could teach you a spell that would paralyze him for at least half a day."

"No," I said, shaking my head. "Whatever else he is, he's obviously powerful. He couldn't hurt our chances."

"Better hope you're right," she said as we followed him into the castle.

"He was *your* idea," I muttered through my teeth the back of her head as I followed her.

Huntsman held out his ax before him like a lantern. Its brightness dwarfed my own. The room we now stood in was expansive, filled with file cabinet after file cabinet.

"What is this place?" I asked, stepping into a fresh puddle.

"A storage room," Huntsman answered. "Filled with what is most likely records of every heinous thing this monster of a woman has been responsible for in her far too-long life."

"You're one to talk." Satina leveled a stare at him. "You're every bit as old as her."

"I made a promise," he said gruffly. "My life and the state of it is nothing more than a way to keep that promise."

"To your brother?" I asked.

Huntsman blinked hard. "I wish it was that simple. Luca is

only a piece of my puzzle. Though I assume your lover could be described as the majority of yours. So, unless you'd like to stand here and get to know each other a bit more, I suggest we move."

He scoffed, turned from Satina and me, and headed for a door at the far end of the room.

Not exactly Mr. Congeniality.

As I headed toward the door, one of the file cabinets I was passing flew open. A file sat just a touch higher than the others.

Satina shot me a look. She knew magic, and I knew her. This was meant for me.

I hesitated, though, looking after Huntsman instead. "Why does she keep these records?" I asked. "That's just so...weird."

Huntsman paused but didn't turn around. "Trophies, perhaps. Or contracts she needs to protect." Finally, he spun toward us. "Really, what does it matter? Look at what she does," he said, waving his arm around. "Why does she do any of it?"

He had a point, but it still all seemed a little too...convenient. What if she wanted me to see this file? What if it was a trick of some sort?

Then again, what if fate, or something like it, was telling me I needed to see this file, that it was important I understand the contents?

As much as I knew I had to save Abram, I also knew we couldn't ignore this. It was going to be a setback or a clue, but either could give us more knowledge about the situation that might help.

I snatched up the file. The cabinet slammed shut, and I opened the manila folder. Huntsman continued onward, and I walked a short distance behind, Satina at my side.

It was another letter, one from the same damn company.

*Dear Valued Customer,*

*It has come to our attention that you are displeased with the current nature of your physical shell. While we understand and certainly sympathize with your plight, we regret to inform you that the contract you signed is both binding and completely transparent.*

*You were made aware that sacrifices would have to be made if you wanted to transcend to the level at which you now enjoy. To claim ignorance on your part would be both dishonest and insulting to those who have worked tirelessly to help you achieve your goals, i.e., us!*

*We, of course, are aware you have no desire to insult us or attempt to backtrack on the deal you made with us. A fruitless attempt that would be, we are sure you realize.*

*We hope you will find it within yourself to come to terms with your new body, and cease and desist these foolish attempts to wriggle out of the promises you made.*

*Might we suggest horn sanders?*

*The Company*

"That confirms it. They're definitely helping her." I shook my head. "Why are they pitting them against each other? Who is The Company?"

"Those are not questions for today," Satina said, grabbing my arm and ushering me to quicken my step. "Today is for saving...if we can."

The file slipped from my hands, but Satina didn't loosen her grip or slow down to let me retrieve it. Ahead of us, Huntsman slowly opened the door. After sticking his head out into the well-lit hall and stealing a glance in both directions, he stepped out with us following close behind.

All the walls were black and free of both mirrors and pictures. This woman really did hate the way she looked now, and who could blame her? Had she really turned herself into a bull-monster just to have the power to keep the man she loved?

Would I be capable of something like that?

Huntsman took his ax again. Pressing it to his forehead, he whispered, "Show me where."

Fluidly, he threw the ax into the air. It spun and stuck blade first into the floor, standing straight up.

"Why—"

"Watch," he said, pointing to the ax.

The hilt spun around although the blade remained still, the ax moving like the needle of a compass. It turned far to the left, settling in front of a long hallway.

"There," Huntsman said. "Your lover is that way."

"That's cool," I muttered. "I mean, it's sort of weird that you keep calling him my 'lover,' but it's still cool." Why couldn't I have a magical ax?

He plucked the ax from the ground and fastened it across his back again.

"Your lover is strong," he said. "If it makes you feel better, he put up a valiant fight before he was finally overtaken; he took a chunk out of Luca that he won't soon forget." After a pause, he added, "Don't worry, I do not hold it against him. My brother, at present, is dangerous. I would have done the same if I had to."

"Wait, you were there? You watched Abram get kidnapped, and you didn't do anything to stop it?"

"I needed to get into this place, and to do that, I needed to find it," he said. "You were my best chance. I apologize if you disagree with my methods, but I do not regret them. This is a dark world we live in, Charisse Bellamy. No one leaves it the way they came in."

He knew my name? Great. What else did he know?

"Just get me to Abram," I said, scowling. "Before we get found out."

We walked through the barren hallways, turning right and then left. Each time, the ax on Huntsman's back twitched, indicating the direction we needed to go.

"There are no guards here," he said. "Luca and his witch are alone. So long as your trickery keeps them otherwise engaged, we'll have no problem getting your lover out of here. And then, when you've made your exit, I'll do what I came for."

"And what's that?" Satina asked.

"I'm going to split that witch in half and free my brother," Huntsman said, settling in front of another room. "The ax has settled. He's inside."

I grabbed the door handle, and to my surprise, it opened.

I gasped as my gaze settled on a form I didn't want to accept was his. Abram was beaten and broken. Blood caked his hair and skin, and he was chained up, hanging from a rafter in the ceiling, his toes barely grazing the ground beneath him. His eyes were swollen shut and long gashes cut deep into his bare chest. I didn't think things could get any worse than that day back in New Haven, but this—this proved me wrong. Gut-wrenchingly wrong.

"My God," I shrieked, shaking away the terror and bolting toward him.

"No, wait!" Huntsman said, but it was too late.

I felt it as I moved through it; a magical barrier, an alarm system no doubt meant to alert of our presence.

The lights went out instantly, and a low, deafening groan sounded through the whole of the castle.

"Now she knows," Satina said in a broken voice. "The Conduit's coming."

# CHAPTER 32

*I* rushed over to Abram, still glowing enough to light a path through the now darkened room. The siren of the unholy alarm hung in the air, signaling Ameena's impending arrival.

But screw that. I had been through too much, faced too many demons, and come too far to back down now.

I might still die today, but Abram wouldn't. Not if I could help it.

"Are you okay?" I asked, wrapping his body in a hug.

I should have went right for the chains. We didn't have much time, after all. But I couldn't wait even one more second to touch him. I needed him in my arms—needed to know he was okay.

He answered me with an inaudible groan. Oh God, how hurt was he?

"Just stay with me," I said, wiping a bit of stray blood from his cheek. "I'll heal you as soon as I can, the way I did back in the cave. But we have to move now, okay? There's not much time."

Hesitantly, I pulled my hands off of him. I wanted nothing more than to be in constant contact with him for every moment of what was left of my very likely to be much-shortened life. But there were more important matters to deal with at the moment. And all of my attention needed to be on freeing the man I love.

I couldn't let my emotions overtake me this time. They were already going haywire. So I looked down at the chains, splayed my fingers wide, and let go.

A bright blue spark shot from my fingertips. But when it reached the chains, it bounced back at me, searing my skin and knocking me backward as it landed.

Satina rushed to my side and assisted me back to my feet. "The chains have been shielded."

"Then help me unshield them," I said, blinking away spots of light and readying myself to try again.

"I could, if we had hours to figure this out." Satina dusted dirt from my shoulders, as though preparing me to go back out onto some battlefield runway. "As it is, I'm afraid we're going to have to leave him."

I pushed her hands off of me. "Do what you want, Satina, but I'm not going anywhere without Abram."

"We can come back when—"

"Not an option!" I said, walking back over to him and reassessing the chains. "Ameena already knows we're here. She got what she wanted out of Abram—I'm here. She has no incentive to keep him alive anymore. We're going to have to think of a different way." I spun to Huntsman, the only other asset we had at the moment. "You've got a big axe."

"Kind of you to notice," he said, his eyes trained on me. "But I'm afraid it won't prove very useful to you at this given moment. It works as a current. It *will* shatter the chains, but it will also destroy anything touching them, namely your love—"

"I get it." I sighed and walked back over to Abram, studying his face for a short moment as though I might find the answers there. But I didn't. "There's only one thing left to do," I whispered, turning to Satina and Huntsman. "Leave."

"What?" Satina's eyes narrowed. "You can't be serious."

"I'm dead serious," I said. "Ameena will be here any second. I'm the one she wants. You two can still make it out. I doubt she'd even follow you."

"You know that's not what this is about," Satina growled. "I'm doing all of this for you."

"And I'm doing all of it for him!" I said, tears welling in my eyes. "There is nothing in heaven or hell that will get me to leave this place without him. And you don't have the power to make me. So unless you're a glutton for punishment, I suggest you get out while you can."

"I lived my life already," Satina said, straightening. "This was bonus time...bonus time, and a chance to do something that mattered." She cracked her knuckles. "I got nothing to lose, and I'm going for broke."

To think, we were here now because Ameena was afraid I could break the curse. She wanted me dead sooner than later, thought I was a risk to her and her plans. And yet, none of us could think of a way to stop her.

I tipped my chin toward Huntsman. "What about you?"

He stared at me, an incredulous look narrowing his eyes. "A man does not run, Charisse Bellamy. Especially not when he has people willing to stand beside him." He pulled the axe from its place on his back. "I've courted this moment for longer than you've been alive. What sort of man would leave without at least showing what they were capable of?" He spun the axe in his hand. It whistled as it cut through the air. "She could not come soon enough for me."

Abram squeezed at my hand. Again, he mumbled something inaudible.

"What, babe?" I asked, leaning closer.

"The Baltics," he said.

"What?" I asked, confused.

"In '67 I ran across a Conduit." The words came out warbled and around short bursts of coughing. "A special one." He coughed again, and this time blood splattered on his dry, cracked lips. "She could pull the magic from anything." He licked his lips and swallowed. "Just pull it…out."

"Well, I wish she was here," I mumbled, an ache tearing through my chest at the sheer state of him. As he glared at me with swollen eyes, I realized what he was getting at. "I can do that?" I asked. As confidence built inside of me, I nodded. "I can do that!"

I grabbed the chains, braving the way they burned and crackled against my palms. The siren's groan grew louder, which probably meant the Conduit was getting closer. Or angrier. Or something not good for us. But I could feel the power surging into me. It was happening so quickly, as though I was hooked up to a car battery with the engine revving.

I began to glow brighter, and the chains followed suit. Soon, I started to take them over. I could feel the integrity of them begin to weaken. I was doing it. What Satina assured me would take hours, I was doing in seconds. But would it be fast enough?

As the magic poured into me, every cell in my body burned. I tried to bite back the pain, but it became too great. Tears sprang to my eyes, and my whole being begged me to let go. A scream ripped from my lips, but I held on, my whole body trembling from the pain. My glow become blinding—a beacon in the dark— and the chains shattered.

And Abram did not shatter with them.

I stumbled back, gasping for breath. Abram was free, though a bloody and battered mess crumbled on the stone floor. Time to get the hell out of this place.

"Help me get him up," I said, turning to Huntsman. "Maybe we can get out of here before that bitch finds us."

I went to step closer to Abram, but my legs gave out beneath me. I could feel an inordinate amount of power surging through my body, and yet every limb felt so fatigued I could barely move. Tears streamed down my cheeks, and I choked out a sob.

All I could do was slump hopelessly on the floor, reeling at Abram's injuries. He'd been taken hours ago, but he looked as though his torture had gone on for weeks. Magic was to blame— as always. Even now that he wasn't chained anymore, his beastly healing abilities still hadn't kicked in, telling me all I needed to know. Something wasn't right here.

This place, this castle—it was stopping him from getting better. If we didn't get him out of here quickly, he would die. And love him as much as I did, I didn't want his company for that.

Satina and Huntsman rushed to my side, tugging at my arms as though they were going to help me. No one could help me now. I swatted their hands away and glared up at them.

"Get him out of here!" I hollered. "Go!"

Huntsman backed off with a short, solemn nod and hurried to Abram's side. He scooped Abram's arm over his shoulder and lifted the large man easily. I had little doubt he could have picked him up and carried him all by himself, but there must have been some unspoken man-code about that, because he didn't help Abram any more than he absolutely had to.

Satina was still at my side. "Get up," she ordered. "Or are you going to leave Abram's fate to a stranger?"

"I thought you would help him," I said, glowering at her.

"I am, by helping you. Now get up."

"Don't you think I would if I could? My body literally does not work right now."

She grabbed my arm and started to pull me up. "God, you are simple, aren't you? Use the damn magic!"

Huntsman was leading Abram toward the door, but Abram resisted, pulling him toward me.

"Char, come on," he said, wincing. "I'm not leaving without you. You can do this."

The groaning siren increased to the point my ears ached, and my mind started to shut down. "We don't have time. You need to go *now!*"

Abram ripped from Huntsman's support and fell to his knees in front of me. He cupped my face in his hands, tears dampening his face. "Don't do that to me, Char. Don't save me just so I can live a life dead on the inside."

My throat constricted. I could barely get out the words. "I can't. There's no time to figure this out."

"Damn it, Char!" he rasped. "The only thing we don't have time for is your self-doubt! We all know you can do this. Hell, Ameena knows it, too. That's why you're here *now*, when you had hours left."

Usually I hated when he was right, but this time, it felt good. A new determination swept through me, and I wiped my face with back of my wrist and nodded.

Huntsman returned to Abram's side to help him back up, and Satina nudged me with her foot.

"Done feeling bad for yourself?" she asked.

"Shut up and tell me what to do."

"I already did," she said, rolling her eyes. I'd almost forgotten this life-and-death situation wasn't as pressing to her as it was to the rest of us. "Think magic, not muscle. I'll help you do the rest."

With that, she pulled me up, holding my weight against her with my arm draped over her neck. My legs were still dead weight, though, and we needed Huntsman to help Abram.

"*Magic*, Charisse," she scolded, and I closed my eyes and tried to will the magic coursing through me to do something.

I envisioned the magic as sort-of helium in my limbs, taking place where my muscles would normally function. I could nearly stand now, but I would probably tip over sideways or back if Satina let go.

"Come on," she said, moving toward the door. "Let's get some fire under our feet."

"Interesting choice of words for a witch," Huntsman said, carrying the brunt of Abram's weight.

"Be that as it may, if we don't get out of here, unintended puns will be the least of our problems." Satina pulled the door open, and we were all immediately hit with a gust of icy and very unearthly wind.

Ameena was here. She was in the wind. She was in the air. And soon enough, she would be in the room.

We were too late.

## CHAPTER 33

"*H*urry!" Satina screamed over a howling wind, her eyes growing wide. "We have to move faster!"

She must have felt it, too—the magic permeating every inch of this place like an encroaching shadow falling over everything, over all of us.

Satina's body twisted. Her face went white and lost expression, and she lifted off the floor, leaving me nearly floating and wobbling in place like a lost balloon.

"Go," she said, gasping for breath as the wind crashed into her. "Get Charisse out of here. It all depends on—"

Before she could finish, she flew out of the room, disappearing into the darkness as if pulled by some unseen hand. The door slammed shut behind her and, perhaps to replace the light made by both me and Huntsman's axe, a bright red illuminated the room.

I nearly fell trying to get my limbs to move in a way that made sense, inching closer to Abram and Huntsman and using Huntsman's shoulder to support myself as things got eerily quiet.

"Is Ameena *here*?" I whispered.

Huntsman shook his head. "I believe she took Satina and left."

My whole body trembled with uncertainty. "That doesn't make sense. I thought I was the one she wanted."

Abram mumbled something. He must have used all of his strength earlier to convince me to try to leave with them, because his words were nearly inaudible again.

I focused on getting my body to move to the other side of Huntsman, so that I could be closer to Abram. "What are you saying?"

"Divide...and...conquer," he choked out.

Huntsman nodded. "She's toying with us. She didn't expect all of us here, so she's picking us apart piece by piece. She still wants you—she just wants you *alone*."

Abram's hand came up to my arm, drawing my attention back to him, to his battered and bloody body that twisted me up inside. "She's still...here."

As if to prove him right, the room began to spin. Ameena had placed us onto the head of a top and given it a twirl. The walls started to melt away and all that was left was a blur and the sick spinning. I held onto Abram, my anchor in a troublesome sea. If I lost everything else—if I lost the rest of the world in total—I could keep hold of his hand and be content.

But the spinning didn't slow, and my body was already out of sorts from being supported by nothing but magic. I sank to my knees, using the entirety of my magic to hold tight to Abram. His body acted as little more than a frayed tether to Huntsman—the only person here functioning in their normal capacity...aside from Ameena.

The red flashed brighter, and the room jerked faster. In the sudden shift, I lost sense of my footing and, in a moment horror, my hand slipped from the man I loved.

I was alone, spinning and lost. I turned, hoping to see him, hoping to see Huntsman or anything at all. But all I could see was red.

And then the pain started.

It ran into my gut first, like a hot knife searing into my flesh. I would have fallen from the pain, except I had no idea which way the floor was.

The agony intensified, sloshing waves of fire through my insides. Between the spinning and the hurt, roiling nausea became the undercurrent to everything I felt.

My mind flashed back to New Haven's country fair and a ride called The Gravitron. It did the same thing, spinning us around and around until we couldn't think straight. I hated it then, too. But Lulu always told me that all I had to do was lean back.

"Keep your head against the wall, Charisse. Close your eyes, take a deep breath, and think of home. And then you'll be there." That was what she said.

So, with Lulu's words roaming through my head, I pretended we were back at the New Haven County Fair.

"Keep your head against the wall," I muttered, leaning back… though it took me a while to actually reach a wall. "Close your eyes. Take a deep breath." In through the nose, out through the mouth. "And think of home."

Mom. Abram. Lulu. Dad. New Haven. New York. Myself.

A pulse rushed through me and, when I opened my eyes, the world was still again.

Abram was lying on the floor beside me, and Huntsman stood half-dazed with his axe in hand.

Ameena, every bit the bull-monster she had been back in the cave, stood before us. Luca, the beast from before, crouched in front of her in a protective stance.

But there was something in the air. A deeper red shimmered against the crimson illumination. And it was floating toward Ameena.

I looked down and saw that it was coming from me. The pain from before had been real. It came from a gash in my side, a gash that was now bleeding. Ameena was feeding off me, and her power was growing by the instant.

"Before you die, let's try something new" she said, mouth unmoving. Her voice was a demon-like whisper ebbing through the room. "Imagine how many more of your kind I can lure here with your blood tonight. Imagine if I made *you* the new Sleeping Beauty."

"No…"

"It wasn't a question." She tilted her head. "You still think you can stop me."

"I can," I said, but the tremble in my voice belied my confidence.

"No," she said, a smile in her voice despite the bull-head's consistently expressionless face. "You're out of time. Your powers are better suited for a real Conduit, where your abilities won't go unrealized and wasted."

I didn't want to think about what she could do with what magic I had figured out, let alone all the abilities of mine that were still untapped.

I stepped toward her, but with a flick of her wrist, she contorted Abram's body into an angle that was just short of breaking him in two. "Freeze, mutt."

During the course of our conversation, Huntsman had made his way around the room and was now standing behind her. The bull-headed Conduit laughed bitterly. With another wave of her hand, fire burst from the floor in a circle around him.

This bitch was impossible. She strolled forward, her pet beast-boyfriend at her side. The gap between us shrunk. Abram's body twisted more. Chills plucked the fine hairs on my skin all the way up my spine, and my body ached with desperation.

A stream of my blood still floated between us like a ribbon, and her power was now swirling around the room and sparking at her fingertips.

I looked from her to Luca and back again. "Does he even really love you?" I asked. "Do you ever wonder if he would love you without your magic binding him to you?"

She froze for a moment, then charged at me. I managed to dodge her horns, but one still grazed my side, creating another wound for her to feed from. I slammed into the wall with such impact that we bounced forward again. I shoved her off of me with unexpected force. The push did little more than send her stumbling back.

With a low growl, she thrust her hand out toward Abram and began to lift his body from the ground. "You thought your friends would help you? That's why you are a failure as a Conduit! All you've done is get your friends killed, and your boyfriend is next!"

I choked on the air. That couldn't be true.

Except, it could be. It could be the truest thing ever, and certainly the most likely. Had she killed Ramsey? Surely she hadn't killed Briar. She needed Briar. Not that I was starting to consider Briar a friend. Was I? If Ameena had killed Satina, had she found a way to make the death permanent?

The truth was, we had no idea what this Conduit was capable of. With the alterations on her magic granted to her by The Company, no one had any way to prepare me for what I was up against.

"You're running out of time," Ameena said through a growl. "But before you go, I'd like you to experience what I did when I lost the man I loved."

Fear shuddered through me, but it was quickly replaced by an anger so severe that, with a flash, it switched the deep red of the room to a hot white.

"No!" Using nothing but magic to move my limbs, I flung my hand up, breaking the connection between us. The remaining stream of blood dissolved into a puff of smoke. "You are done taking what's mine, you loathsome bitch!"

She huffed at me, lowering her bull-head. I remembered the horns, the way they'd pierced Abram's flesh. That wouldn't happen again, not while breath was still in my body.

Abram's body plummeted toward the ground, but I was able to

slow his body to decrease impact. With Abram safe for the time being, I sent out my magic to create a film-like barrier that I doubted would keep her trapped very long. But if it was long enough to save Abram, then it would have to do.

Huntsman appeared in front of me, his clothes seared from the fire. "Your lover—can he stand?"

"I don't think so," I admitted, taking in the way his body lied crumbled on the floor.

"Then he'd better fly," Huntsman said.

With that, he struck the floor with his axe. A small crack appeared and quickly spread until the floor was crumbling pieces. It shattered beneath us, and we went sailing through the air.

I tensed my body, but then I remembered what Huntsman said.

"Fly," I murmured. I'd seen Abram do it before in New Haven —well, more a really high jump—but he couldn't in the condition he was in now, and it was still new to me. But then again, nothing more than magic was keeping my body upright at this point anyway.

I willed the magic to hold my body the same way I had used it to lower Abram's body back in the red room, and the magic obeyed. I stopped in midair and, with a flick of both my finger and my heart, Abram did, too. I held him there, above the carnage of long-ago fallen bodies and raining debris.

We were literally falling toward her own little hell, toward a pile of discarded supplicant bodies. This was Huntsman's great idea for an escape?

Although we had magic on our side, gravity was a solid contender. Abram and I hit the ground with more force than desired, just feet away from the pile of death. Huntsman tucked and rolled, getting to his feet, all in one swift motion.

Ameena lied to one side of the room, impaled by a pole that stuck from the ground.

Huntsman rushed her, glowing axe in hand. Could this be it?

Could he just strike her and cut her in half like he wanted? Would it be that easy?

As he reared back, ready to strike, Luca jumped in front of him, crouched and growling. He was ready to take the hit, ready to die for the awful creature he still somehow loved. Or thought he loved. Or whatever was going on there.

Huntsman stopped short, jerking the axe up inches before it hit his brother.

"Luca! Let me end this!"

Luca growled and swiped at his brother, and Huntsman pulled away.

"I will not let her destroy you, brother," Huntsman said. "If I have to die to save you from this, I will do so gladly. But this witch's hold on our family ends today. It ends now."

Huntsman rolled past his brother and readied to strike Ameena again, but Luca clawed his back and yanked him away.

Our magical-axe-wielding comrade flew through the air and slammed against the wall. From the corner of my eye, I saw Ameena totwitch back to consciousness. God, she was going to get back up from that?

"What are you waiting for?" Huntsman screamed at me. "Be gone!"

I blinked hard, my heart breaking for what was happening in front of me. A family was being destroyed forever, and there wasn't anything I could do about it.

"Good luck," I whispered under my breath as I contorted the magic.

As Abram and I flew upward and then back through the door, I tried telling myself Huntsman would have done the same thing. We all had our own battles to fight today, and he'd only been at our side to arrive at his own.

I guided us through the hallway, but Abram became too heavy and, after a few minutes, I couldn't hold him anymore. The Conduit must have siphoned more magic than I realized, and that blast back there took away what was left. My body was destroyed from breaking the chains earlier, and Abram still hadn't healed.

We both fell, and I hoisted his body up against my shoulder. We had nothing left. Nothing but a thin thread of hope that Huntsman was ending things right now.

The room was dark again, and with my power depleted, I could only emit enough light to break slightly through the darkness.

After a few deep breaths, I used what physical energy I could to try to start dragging myself and Abram away from this hell. I stumbled around for what felt like an eternity, and with each moment that passed without Huntsman returning to our side, I became more and more convinced we wouldn't make it out of here alive. She'd killed him, and she was coming for us next.

God, this *was* how it ended.

I pulled Abram close to me, resting against the darkened wall. If I was going to die here, I wanted it to be with him. He seemed worse now, and I was starting to think this castle was messing with all of us in more ways than one.

"Abram?" I whispered.

His hand crawled to mine and gave it a gentle squeeze.

I smoothed my thumb over his knuckles. "I love you."

"Don't," he rasped. "No goodbyes. I want to spend the rest of my life with you."

I smiled sadly, thinking how he would probably get at least that much. "Me, too," I said quietly, resting back against the wall. "Me, too."

And then we fell hard, tumbling in a downward spiral.

We hit grass and dirt. Moonlight shone against my skin, and a cool dry breeze danced across my skin.

It had been a door. I had leaned against a door, and now Abram and I had fallen ass backward into salvation.

*Thank heaven for unintentional favors.*

"Abram," I said, both startled and relieved. "We need to go. We can make it. We can actually—"

"I'm sorry," came a woman's voice I knew all too well. Standing before me was Briar...or her spirit, anyway. Her face was sullen and sad. Her eyes were repentant. "I know you might not believe me, Char, but really I am."

The moment hit me like a nightmare. A very familiar nightmare. I spun in a slow circle, though the world around me seemed to spin much faster, and my mind whirled even faster than that.

*Oh God.* We were at the cliff—the cliff where I would die.

# CHAPTER 34

This was it. The time had come. Briar was about to guide me off the edge.

I felt it immediately—the pull Briar had over me. It was strange. When we were younger, back in our modeling days, I absolutely hated this woman. Nothing in the world could have gotten me to sit in the same room with her for even an hour. And now I found myself drawn to her, unable to stop my feet from moving toward her, toward the edge of the cliff.

To my death.

Odd that she'd never tried to kill me before, but I hated her less now than ever. This time, she was as much a victim as me.

"I didn't want this to happen," Briar said, not quite making eye contact with me. "My body is here, isn't it? It's weird, but I think I can feel it. It's sort of calling to me." She shook her head. "At least...at least I think you're the last one she needs. I can tell because I'm dying. I can feel my heart giving out, and there's no way she'd let that happen if you weren't the last. There's some solace in that, isn't there? That the killing will finally stop?"

"It will," I whispered. "But it can't stop like this, Briar. *We* have to stop it."

But even as I said that, I knew it was too late. My feet inched closer against all my protests.

Tears freckled her cheeks; her eyes were hollow, no longer vibrant and full of life. "Did you tell him? Did you tell Ramsey what I said?"

I felt pressure against my ankle. Looking down, I saw Abram clasping my leg. He was still beaten, but his wounds were in the early stages of healing. No matter, though. He would never heal quick enough to stop this, and I didn't have time to heal him—not as I was literally marching toward my death.

My body kept moving, pulling Abram across the damp night ground behind me. I'd felt his body on mine enough times to know this should be impossible—that I wasn't strong enough to lug his weight—but I didn't even feel it now. His efforts didn't slow me down. Damn Ameena and whatever magic she was using.

"Char," Briar said sharply, snapping my attention back to her. Her hands balled into fists at her sides. "Did you tell him what I said?"

It was a question, but she said it like a demand.

"I sure as hell didn't," I said, a stony edge to my voice. "You can tell him yourself, once we get out of this."

With me moving closer to the edge of the cliff, that seemed pretty unlikely, but if we had any chance now, it was Briar breaking the curse for herself.

"Nice thought, Char, but we both know that's not going to happen."

Abram's hand tightened around my leg. His other hand, morphing into a claw, dragged against the ground, creating deep valleys in the soil. But it still didn't slow me. My body continued to betray me, and there was nothing I, Briar, or Abram could do about it.

My heart raced, and my blood boiled. This could not be happening. But it was. After everything we had been through, after all the ways I had tried to fight this, I was going to come up short. I was going to die here, and the man I loved was going to watch it happen.

Knowing Abram, he wouldn't let go. He would go right over this cliff with me. And if that didn't kill him, he would be killing himself on the inside from every day here forward.

In the end, I wouldn't even be able to save the one person I wanted to save the most.

I shot Briar a pleading look. "Please, Briar. You have to try."

"Do you remember when we were in New York, Char?" she asked, speaking around my question as though it'd gone unspoken. There was something odd in her voice, a complete and total lack of pretense. For the first time ever, she was just talking to me plainly. "We were just kids then, but we thought we knew everything." A weak smile slipped across her face. "What do you think we'd have said back then, if we knew it was going to end like this?"

"I'd have probably said that I'd rather hammer nails into my eyeballs than be anywhere near you."

"Me, too," she said. "But we were kids. World's a bit bigger than we thought, isn't it?"

"It shouldn't have happened this way," I said, the terror rising in my throat. It wasn't the fall I was afraid of. It wasn't even death that scared me anymore. I just didn't want to give up, and I was afraid I had already done just that.

"I'm sorry about Charlie Prince," Briar said, shaking her head. "I know it doesn't matter anymore. Maybe it never did, given the man who's literally worshiping the ground you walk on as we speak." She looked down to where Abram was still clinging to my leg and being pulled across the ground. "But I figure that if this is the end, I should go ahead and say that. I'm sorry, Char. I'm sorry about a lot of things."

"Don't you dare!" I screamed. "Don't you give up on either one of us! We're the baddest bitches New York City ever saw. Where's the girl who made my life a living hell? Where's her fire?

We have to get out of this. We have too much to live for. Both of us."

The cliff loomed closer with each passing second. It wouldn't be long now. I searched my mind. I had to be overlooking something. There had to be something I could do to put an end to this. This was not going to be how I died. Not if I could help it.

"Not for long," she mumbled. She wasn't even walking. She was just floating there, moving alongside me like some ghostly apparition, as if she had already died or something. "None of them will last much longer, Ramsey included."

My blood ran cold. I hadn't even thought about the others, the people that *I* brought here with my stubbornness, the ones who believed in me enough to put it all on the line.

"Where are they, Briar? Where are the others?"

She sighed, as much as a ghost could sigh, I imagined. "Where all the people she can't use go. They're lost in that place." She pointed to the castle, now nearly a hundred yards behind me. "In those endless rooms, trapped in nightmares."

Something flashed through my eyes, and suddenly I saw them. They were all in different places, but I saw the three of them at the same time somehow.

Ramsey was on the floor of a stone room. His eyes were red, puffed, and tired. Briar's body weighed down in his arms. She was pale and cold-looking. If she was breathing, it was barely. She was right. She *was* dying. Maybe she would always be dying, and that would be their nightmare—stuck in some endless goodbye.

Satina fell through a dark well. She wasn't herself anymore...at least not the 'her' I had come to know. She was back in her old body, stained with the blood that must have been a result of the way she died.

"I didn't mean it, Father," she said over and over again. "I didn't mean it."

She would fall forever. She would live in this regret until her heart stopped, or maybe until she lost her mind.

Finally, Huntsman stood in a room with a large coffin in the middle of it. Flowers lay around the box, aged with time. And statues of the Titans stood stalwart, as if to guard whoever was inside the box.

Unlike the others, though, Huntsman didn't look distraught. Much to the contrary, he held his axe over his head, waiting for something.

"You're mistaken if you think this will break me, witch!"

No sooner did the words leave his mouth, but the statues popped to life. They headed not for him, but for the coffin. He did a somersault through the air, landing between the monsters and the casket. He swung his axe, and the statues shattered. But just as quickly, they reassembled.

This would go on forever, too, most likely powered by my blood. And no matter how strong he was, he *would* eventually break.

With a shake of my head, the images disappeared, and when the world reappeared, I found the edge of the cliff looming under-foot. Waves crashed against the rocky shore, and the sea breeze whipped at my hair. Here I was, at the edge, at my final moment.

"You have to let go of me, Abram," I said, panic flickering across my mind. "You have to let go!"

"No!" He growled and pulled against me tighter. I couldn't control my own movements, which meant I couldn't even attempt to kick him off. Not that it would have done any good.

"Abram, please. I'm begging you. You'll go over with me if you don't listen. We'll both die!"

"Then we'll die together." His voice was still a bit mangled, still more than a little hoarse. But he was sturdy, and I knew nothing was going to change his mind.

But that didn't mean I couldn't keep trying. "What good would that do?" I asked, tears burning down my cheeks. "I can't die knowing you're going to end up like this."

"And I won't live if you're not around to do it with me," he said. It was poetic, but unrealistic. He would survive the fall. If I wasn't part Supplicant, I could, too. If only there was a way to rid myself of that.

"I can't be the one who pulls you over this cliff," I said, my voice more pleading than before. "Please, Abram, do not make me kill you."

His gaze turned up to me, and I could read a million thoughts in those eyes. He couldn't let me die without feeling he'd tried everything to save me. But he also didn't want me to die knowing I'd brought his body over the cliff with me. Despite that visible torment, he clung tighter. Maybe somewhere inside, he still had that hope I had finally given up on.

"You're the greatest man I've ever known," I said, trying to keep my voice even. "Now it's time to let go."

And that's when it happened. As if a piece of grace fell from the sky and an inch of me freed itself.

Magic—all that I could muster—flew from my fingertips. It landed on the ground behind Abram, and a chunk of earth rippled up, knocking me from his grasp and carrying him away from me.

"Don't do this, Charisse!" he screamed as the enchanted earth carried him back toward the castle. "Don't you dare take this decision away from me!"

"I love you," I said quietly. "I love you always."

"Charisse!" He tried to scramble back to me, but vines from the castle walls wove around his arms and held him in place. I was stronger than him—maybe not physically, but definitely magically.

*All monster, no magic.* That's how everyone who knew Abram described his condition. And now it was getting the better of him.

"Charisse! Charisse, I love you," he finally said. "I love you forever. You're a part of me. You're the best part. And you're not alone. Do you hear me? You are not alone!"

"Thank you," I murmured, closing my eyes, wishing it was enough. Wishing this was some fairytale where proclamations of love were enough to break an enchantment. But my life was not so lucky.

"She'll have all she needs after you," Briar said. She was floating in midair off the edge of the cliff. "She says it'll be enough, that all she wants is to keep the curse going. But how long do you think that'll last? She'll want the world before it's over. Not that we'll be around to worry about it."

"Where is she?" I asked, teetering along the edge. "Where's Ameena?"

"Right here," she sang from somewhere inside my mind. "Oh, come on, you don't think I would miss this, do you?"

She appeared in a shimmer of light, standing farther down the cliff, along the edge. Luca crouched beside her. Was it all really for this? For love that maybe was never genuinely returned?

"No!" Abram's howl cut through the night. But it wasn't enough. It wouldn't be nearly enough.

Ameena started toward me, and I almost wished I could go ahead and jump off the cliff already. But my body was hers now, and it wasn't budging one way or another.

"You're wondering why you're still standing there," Ameena said, settling beside me with Luca at her side. "Well, don't. This is a big moment for me. This is when I finally fulfill all my goals."

"What the hell do you want?" I asked. "You already have Archibald. What else do you need?"

"Archibald isn't a permanent solution. No mortal is meant to live for as long as he has. Eventually, their mortal form becomes resistant to the magic. That's why my love had to be transformed into something greater." She reached down and pet Luca's beastly, wolf-like form. "Even now, I can feel that ridiculous king becoming useless to me. I can feel my love pulling away." Closing the gap between us, she lifted her hand and grazed my cheek with her claws. "But with you, my precious little party favor, I'll have all the power I need. My love and I will be together forever. And nothing will be able to stand against us."

"Let go of me, Charisse!" Abram yelled, still bound by enchanted castle vines. "Let me help you!"

"I wouldn't do that," Ameena warned. "Not if you like his head still attached to his body." Her monstrous eyes darted from me to Abram and back again. "Luca is more powerful than him by tenfold, because I am more powerful than the Conduit who created him by as much. You should know that, Charisse. You saw what I did to her."

"You have to release them," I answered. "You can't just keep them there like that. You don't even need them."

"You'll be free soon enough," Ameena said, still unnerving me with the way her bull-head's lips never moved when she spoke. "The moment you go over this cliff, you will be free, and your enchantment will end. Just in time to watch the world rush up to greet you."

"This needs to stop, Ameena. True love does not make people do what you are doing. Let them go, *now!*"

"You're in no position to make demands," she snapped, her tone turning angrier. "Besides, no one leaves the maze of my castle. Eternity melts into a moment within those walls, especially if that moment is torturous. Huntsman, the lesser Conduit, and the cuckold mage will suffer for the rest of their tragic little lives. And it will be because you were brazen enough to think you could defeat me." She patted me on the shoulder. "I'd say that you have to live with that, but...you know."

Her eyes slid down to the open air below, the air I was about to take a header into.

"Charisse!" Abram screamed again, and in a moment that I would regret if I lived to do so, I silenced him. There was nothing he could say, and his screams were ripping at my heart.

"You're a monster," I muttered to Ameena.

"And you're a corpse. I wonder which most people would prefer."

Her hand rested on the small of my back. This was it. I could feel it. For as much as I could move, I turned my head toward Abram. A thousand words passed between us silently as I stared at him, bound and pulling futilely toward me. A million kisses were exchanged, though we never touched. Our hearts melted into one perfect masterpiece of goodbye.

"Don't worry, Charisse," Ameena whispered into my ear. "I'll take good care of him for you."

And then I stepped unwillingly off the cliff.

# CHAPTER 35

*P*anic rushed through my veins. My mind raced a mile a minute in a final desperation to do something. I thought about flying, as I had when Huntsman shattered the floor underfoot. But I was too drained; nothing happened, no matter how badly I wished it to.

As promised, the second my feet left the cliff, the enchantment lifted. An instant too late. My body spun to face them as I fell, and my answer filled my line of sight faster than I could process it.

Instinctively, before my fraction-of-second opportunity passed, I grabbed my one and only chance: I snatched at Luca's beastly hand. I nearly missed, securing only one digit of his claw, the nail cutting into my palm. But I held tight, and the weight of my body falling jerked him forward. I reached up with my other hand and secured a tighter grasp on his arm.

It'd all happened to fast, the collective gasp of everyone came as more of an aftershock. I scowled at Ameena, challenging her to do something to send me the rest of the way over. If I was going to leave this earth, I was taking the thing she loved most with me.

Luca's animalistic eyes went wide, and for a moment, I almost felt bad for him. But if his life was to be nothing more than Ameena's pet, he was as good as dead anyway.

As Luca's body followed mine off the cliff, I braced myself for the fall. Only it didn't happen.

I stopped short, jerking hard and keeping tight with Luca's arm.

Looking up, I spotted what was stopping us. Ameena, cloven hooves dug into the ground at the edge of the cliff, had Luca's other hand in her own.

"What the hell are you doing?" she screamed, her shrill voice bouncing around in my head.

"Exactly what you're doing to me." I braced my dangling feet against the vertical side of the cliff and used the leverage to pull hard at Luca, moving him closer to the fall just as Ameena had done magically to me seconds ago. As she promised, the enchantment was broken now. She couldn't control my movements anymore.

"You're being ridiculous!" Her voice broke at the end. "It won't kill him. He's my creation. He's powerful. You're doing it for nothing."

"No," I answered, shaking my head. "You're too worried, too panicked. There's something about this cliff, isn't there? You spelled it to make sure nothing and no one could survive the fall." I pulled again, and felt Luca (and myself) falter farther through the air. "And it's about to bite you in your bony ass."

"I'll kill your lover!" Ameena shrieked. "If you do this, know that I'll flay him until he's little more than anguished tissue and bone."

I flinched. Saving Abram's life was the only reason I was here. Did I really want to throw that away just to be vengeful?

And then, like clarity provided by some unseen designer, the truth laid itself in front of me. I wasn't doing this for vengeance. I wasn't doing it for me. I wasn't even doing it for Abram.

This woman was about to have my power—a power I still

couldn't even begin to understand, but also a power that Satina swore was strong enough to shape the world.

If a woman as dangerous as Ameena was about to come into control of that, I had to make sure she couldn't hurt people with it. I had to break her. And the most thorough way to break someone was to take away the person they loved most in the world. I knew that from experience.

"Abram's stronger than you think," I answered, my teeth gritted from the effort in which I was using to pull at Luca.

The beast's face turned to me. His snout was scrunched in fury, and his eyes glowed red. I didn't see a person in there. I didn't see the boy Huntsman had waited centuries to save, or the teenager who was so in love with someone that he was willing to forsake not only his family but his entire life and body.

He had to be in there, though, just as the girl Ameena used to be must have been inside of her.

My heart broke a little, and not just for me. This started with love. All of this came because two people couldn't imagine facing a cold world without each other's arms to shield them.

And the thing was, I understood that. I understood it more than I ever could have explained. But that didn't absolve them of their actions, and it didn't change the facts.

"Say your goodbyes," I grunted to Luca, feeling us slipping from Ameena's grasp. "And make sure they're good," I said, thinking of Abram. "She's going to have to live with them for a long time."

Luca's red eyes lightened. They were blue now, like Huntsman's. And they were full of something so primal and human that it had to be either fear or regret.

"I…" His tone was light, almost like a child's, and he turned his face from me to Ameena. "I love you," he said. "And I'm so very sorry, my love."

And then her grip on him proved to just not be enough.

We started to fall again, but then, again, we stopped. Ameena crouched over the side of the cliff. Her hand was wrapped around Luca's leg. Her face held more rage than I had ever seen before.

"You think you can hurt me? You're an ant, an insect on the face of a world you could never hope to understand."

Blood, my blood, began pouring from my nose, eyes, and mouth. It wafted toward her on the air, and she took it in, drawing more and more of my power.

"You are nothing!" she screamed through the unmoving lips of her bull head. "Absolutely nothing! And I'm about to prove that to you."

With newfound strength, she whipped us both forward, sending me flying through the air above her. I tried to keep a hold of Luca, my only bargaining chip. But I lost him in the fray.

From the air, I watched Luca hit hard on the grass of the cliff. He was safe.

But I wasn't.

Ameena caught me, grabbing my throat with her massive and disgusting hand. She hoisted me over the cliff, letting me dangle there.

I was a rag doll she was about to rid herself of. And I couldn't stop her. All I could do was suck in choking gasps around her hand, trying futilely to pry her fingers from my neck. Blood dripped down the front of my face, blurring my vision and running past my lips.

"You thought you could stop me?" She scoffed. "No one can stop me. Death itself must relent in my presence. The Brothers made me immortal. They gave me everything. And, in return— with your powers—I'm going to show them what I'm really capable of." She squeezed hard against my windpipe. Still, I knew she wouldn't choke me to death. She would have to let me fall, let me go, if she wanted the ritual to work. She hissed. "I'm going to enjoy this."

"I'd rethink that," Abram's voice boomed with surprising energy.

Looking past Ameena, I saw Abram had broken free of his confines. He stood behind Luca, who had been pushed to his knees. Abram pulled her pet's head back and held his claws at Luca's exposed neck.

"Drop her off that cliff, and I'll rip out his throat."

"He's stronger than you," she said, voice wavering.

"Not right now he's not." Abram's eyes glowed with a gold I had never seen before. "At this moment, there isn't a thing in the world more powerful than me. So let me make myself clear. You *will* give her back to me."

Ameena glared at me for a long moment, then turned her attention back to Abram. "No."

"I will kill him!" he roared.

"I don't doubt it," she answered. "And when you do, I'll bring him back. Like I've done a hundred times over a thousand years. And, with your girlfriend dead, Luca and I can be together forever. You have no cards to play here, Beast."

Abram's eyes went blank. He looked past Ameena to me, hanging seconds away from death. "I'm so sorry, Char."

"It's okay," I answered hoarsely. "It's okay."

He tilted his chin toward Ameena. "What about me?" he asked, letting go of Luca and walking toward us. "Trap me instead."

I tried to tell him to stop, but Ameena's grip had officially cut off the last of my air. I couldn't push out another word.

"Stop where you stand!" Ameena said, lowering my body enough to let Abram know she wouldn't hesitate to drop me if he came much closer. He froze where he stood, and she continued: "Now tell me—what rubbish are you rambling on about this time?"

"You need someone to be trapped. That's the way you negate the original spell. You trapped the first Sleeping Beauty in a coma. You trapped Archibald in his castle. It's why you put Briar to sleep to draw more Supplicants here, because you felt Archibald breaking free of your grasp and you needed help for your magic to keep him there."

"Get to the point," Ameena warned.

"Charisse is powerful. She's very powerful, but at her core, she's a human. That's what makes her different. You kill her like this, you get the powers and limitations of the form she's in now. And, in case you haven't realized it yet, she's something of a novice. Think of how much more powerful you would be if you waited until her powers were mature, until she had reached her full potential." He shook his head. "You could rule the world. Even the Brotherhood."

"The *Brothers!*" she spit out, an antsy irritation about her tone.

I'd never heard of the Brothers before Ameena mentioned them, and from the sounds of it, neither had Abram.

Abram continued, unmoved by her correction. "No one would be able to stand against you. You would never have to worry about anyone ever again."

"Nice try," Ameena said, lowering my body even more. "But what you're forgetting is that I need the power *now*." Her hand trembled. "So, if you'll excuse me—"

"Right!" Abram said, holding his hands out to let her know he wasn't finished. "You want her power so that you can be with Luca without someone having to be trapped. That's shortsighted, though. Be with Luca *and* grow Charisse's power for the future. You can have it all. All you have to do is trap someone."

"Who?" Ameena asked.

"I already told you," Abram said. "Me."

*No!* My mind screamed, but the words wouldn't come out. I stared at him pleadingly. *Abram, don't you dare.*

The Conduit squeezed my throat tighter, as though to make certain I wouldn't get another word out. "You're a base creature created from a lesser Conduit. It might take millennia for Charisse to fulfill her potential. You won't be able to carry magic like this for that long."

"But you would," he answered.

Ameena's eyes narrowed.

"My curse, the one the lesser Conduit gave me—she didn't just turn me into a beast...she *imprisoned* me as one." Abram stepped closer. "I could give you this curse. I could trap you in your body —in your powerful body that will last for the rest of all time. *You* would be *your own* anchor. As long as you lived, forever and ever, you could be with Luca. And it would afford you more than enough time to let Charisse become powerful enough to fulfill your grander plans."

She looked over at me. Was she actually considering this?

"So I would take your curse, but not your person?"

"That's right," Abram said evenly.

"No," Ameena answered.

"You need someone to be trapped for Luca to be free," Abram continued in a rush. "You yourself would be the one who is trapped. You, in your immortal body. You wouldn't have to trap someone else ever again—you wouldn't have to rely on other, lesser beings. You wouldn't have to fight back against someone trying to undo your enchantment. Surely you see how perfect that is?"

"Perfect, but for one thing," she said. "Once Charisse grows into her power, there's nothing to stop her from destroying me. If she's as potent as she seems, how would I get her to give me her abilities once they outmatch my own?" A smile stretched across her grotesque bull-face. "I'll tell you how." She looked over at me. "With love." Looking back at Abram, she continued. "I will take your curse onto myself, but I will also take you. You will come with me. You will be my prisoner, and serve me for as long as it takes for Charisse to grow in power. Once I deem that power sufficient, she will cede it over to me in return for your freedom. Agree to this, and I will let her live. Do not, and she dies now."

"No!" I choked out, but it sounded more like a gurgle.

"Agreed," Abram said without missing a beat.

She threw me toward Abram, and our bodies collided. He stumbled backward, but he kept standing and didn't hesitate to scoop me into his arms.

"How could you?" I screamed, pounding fists against his chest. "You had no right to agree to that! To just give yourself away!"

"It's all right," he whispered into my ear. "It'll be all right."

"Yes," Ameena said, moving toward us. "After all, it's just a few millennia. It'll fly by." She outstretched her arm. "The curse. I'll take it now."

I squeezed Abram tightly, then he pushed me off and walked toward her.

I winced as he placed his hands in hers.

"You understand that, when transferring one's curse, the recipient has to freely accept it," Abram said.

"Of course I understand. I'm a First Order Conduit."

"You have to say it," he told her. "You have to say the words aloud to initiate the process."

If she could have rolled those bull eyes, I figured she would have as she answered. "I accept this man's curse into myself for now and all time."

With those words spoken, Abram began to glow bright gold. The light moved from him and settled onto Ameena. He breathed heavily as the last of the light left him, then he let go of her hand.

This was it. She was going to take him away. And I wouldn't see him again for—what, two thousand years? The idea seemed unfathomable.

"I can feel it!" Ameena gleamed. "I can feel my own curse being negated from within me. I can feel your curse trapping me!" She looked over at Luca. "I can feel the—Wait, what's happening to you?"

Luca was beginning to transform. The fur, muscles, and fangs of his beastly form dwindled. Slowly, he was turning back into the boy from my vision. But why?

"Luca, what—" Ameena bowled over. She too was changing.

Her hands, long and gangly, were shortening. Her bull's face was morphing into something much more human in shape.

They were...they were changing back.

"What did you do to me?" she asked, and this time, her voice came from her exceedingly human-looking mouth.

"You did it to yourself," Abram said, settling over her. "My curse comes with all its attributes." He looked over at me. "All monster, no magic. Remember?"

"Oh, God..." I murmured. He knew what he was doing the entire time. He gave her the curse to cut her off from her magic. To render her powerless.

Suddenly, the air behind us shimmered. An invisible veil fell from the world and, with a loud pop, the black castle became visible to me (and probably the rest of the island) again. How were they going to explain *that?*

A door from the castle swung open. Huntsman, Satina, and Ramsey strode through it. Huntsman had his axe in hand, Ramsey carried an unconscious Briar, and Satina looked royally pissed. She threw up her hands, immobilizing Ameena.

"You took it all!" the Conduit screamed, now completely human.

"Not yet," Huntsman said through gritted teeth.

He reared back, the head of his axe poised to come down on Ameena's head.

"Go on!" she cried. "You can't kill me! You people might have tricked me out of my magic, but you can't undo what the Brothers did. This body is immortal. You can't kill it!"

"Perhaps," Huntsman answered. "But I imagine I can still cut it into a thousand living pieces."

He began to swing, but Luca stumbled toward him, a skinny boy with shaggy hair and tears streaming down his face. "No, brother, please! Leave her be!"

Huntsman stopped short. Looking to Luca, Huntsman's eyes

widened as hurt flashed through them. It was clear he hadn't seen Luca like this in a very long time.

"She's a monster, Luca. She turned you into a monster. She's killed more people than either of us can count. She deserves to be punished."

"Then so do I," he said, his voice shaking. "You think I'm some victim to all this, that she spelled me and made me do these things? She didn't. These choices were mine. I did what I did because she asked me to, not because she forced me to. I did those things because I love her." He closed his eyes. "So if you must do this to her, then you must do it to me."

Huntsman glared at his brother. "So be it," he said, voice heavy with regret. Then, shockingly, he reared back his axe again.

"Huntsman," I said, darting to his side and taking his arm. "Let's think about this for a moment."

He growled. "There's nothing to think about. Stop making this harder than it has to be."

I called over my shoulder to Abram. "Make sure no one goes anywhere," I said, then I lowered Huntsman's arm, and he didn't resist. "Talk to me." I pulled him a few feet away. "Is everyone okay?"

"They'll be fine," he said gruffly, ticking his gaze toward the others. His attention lingered a moment longer on his brother, still standing guard by a frozen Ameena. "Once I found them, I was able to lead them to safety, but that does not change what I must do, Charisse."

"No, it doesn't. And I don't want it to," I said. "See, that's the sort of person you are, isn't it? You save people. You lead people. But if you do something like this—if you kill someone you used to love—it'll change you." Dalton and Lulu flashed through my mind. "And I, for one, don't think this world can afford to have you change."

"Justice is justice," he answered flatly. "Regardless of my emotions, it must be served."

"And it will," I answered.

His eyes narrowed.

"Just trust me," I said, patting his shoulder and moving away from him.

"You like to trap people," I said, walking toward Ameena. "What is it you said, 'lost for eternity'?"

She glared at me, but could do little else with Satina's hold on her.

"Well, let's see how you like it." I let my emotions—and there were a lot of them—flow through me as I grabbed Satina's hand. "I'm going to need your help with this."

Ameena scoffed. "Oh, what now, you're going to trap us in that castle for the rest of eternity?"

"One of you," I said, motioning toward Luca. "I have another spot picked out for you." I looked toward Archibald's castle.

"You're not serious!" Ameena's body seemed to struggle against Satina's hold now, but it was useless. She wasn't the stronger Conduit anymore. "We-we'd kill each other."

"Oh, sweetie," I answered, as the magic swirled around, doing my will. "Like you said, you can't die. It'll just be one long honeymoon."

As they both vanished, I smiled. "Let's see how that misogynistic asshole likes that."

Abram sidled over to me. "You know, with both Ameena and Archibald trapped forever, we're going to have to find Grimoult a new royal family."

"I may have an answer for that," Satina said, running fingers through her hair. "You see, there was a reason Ameena chose Briar to be the new Sleeping Beauty."

"I know," I said. "Because of the persuasion Ramsey put on her."

"That's barely a spell," Satina said. "The reason it worked so well on her, is because she shares blood with the person it originated from."

"You mean...you mean Briar is related to..." I shook my head, unable to even finish the ludicrous thought.

"She's the original Sleeping Beauty's great granddaughter five times removed," Satina said. "Unfortunately not related enough to have blood that's of any use to me. She's just a human."

"You say that like it's a bad thing," I muttered. "Why didn't you tell us sooner?"

Satina waved her hand dismissively. "I told you what you needed to know, when you needed to know it. You should thank me for not telling you more sooner."

"Well, I would have done fine to never know I made Briar a freaking queen."

"Hey!" Ramsey breathed from the ground. "I think she's waking up!"

Briar's eyes were, in fact, fluttering open. And the thing was, I didn't really hate her anymore.

It was funny how things worked out. I thought about that for a long time, standing on that cliff with people who had—against all odds—become something close to friends.

We talked for hours after that, laughing, reminiscing, and fighting off sleep as—for the first time in months—rain fell over Grimoult.

## EPILOGUE

"*I* can't believe I don't get a castle," Briar said, rolling her eyes. She stood beside me at the airport, with Ramsey holding her hand.

It had been three days since she woke up, three days since I banished Ameena, Luca, and Archibald to their respective prisons, and three days of hearing Briar complain about every little thing.

As one might expect, it had taken her all of two seconds to get used to the idea of being royalty.

"I mean, just because all the castles on the island are being used as magical jails or whatever doesn't mean I shouldn't get my due. Can't they just, like, build another one or something?"

"Honey." Ramsey smiled, a freer look on his face than I would've thought imaginable five days ago. "The country's been through the biggest drought in over five hundred years. I'm not sure now's the best time for massive spending."

"Fine." She sighed, resting her head on Ramsey's shoulder. "But as soon as there's a crop of something, I'm buying diamonds."

I laughed. "Same old Briar."

"Queen Briar to you," she said, but there wasn't any bite in her words.

It was weird. Almost dying actually helped us to move past our differences. Which was a good thing, given how childish they seemed now.

"And who do you have to thank for that, your majesty?" I asked, winking at her.

"Do you really have to go?" she asked, stepping away from Ramsey and taking my hands in her own like we were long lost best friends who hadn't been reunited not nearly long enough.

"I do." I gave her a quick hug and stepped beside Abram, wrapping my arm around his waist. "I want to get out of here, maybe take an actual vacation."

The airport buzzed around us. Well, as much as an airport on some obscure island could. I peered up to Abram and gave him a knowing smile.

"And New York is the best place to do that?" Briar asked. "I don't know about you, but I've had my fill of that city."

"I did have my fill of it," I said. "And I had amazing times there, too. That's the thing. I want Abram to get to know that part of me. I want him to know all of me."

I felt his hand at my back, and felt the rush that came with knowing he was mine forever.

Nothing and no one would change that.

"What about me?" Briar asked, nuzzling up on Ramsey's neck. "You want to know all of me?"

His hand slipped below her waist to give her butt a squeeze. "Ask me again tonight. I'll be sure to remain interested in every piece of you."

"Moron," she answered, kissing his neck.

Ramsey turned to me, and I could see how grateful he was. Somehow, it had taken this—almost losing everything—for the two of them to realize what they had together. And that was a beautiful thing.

"You know I'm always around, Charisse," he said. "If you ever need lessons, or even the answers to questions, I'm here to help. It's what a mage does."

"Given that Satina's disappeared again, I might take you up on that," I said.

Satina had disappeared the day after we took down Ameena. Part of me wondered where she had gone off to. But a bigger piece of me was happier not to know. The last conversation we'd had before she left didn't go over very well. Mostly because knowing Briar was related to the real Sleeping Beauty wasn't the only thing she'd been keeping from us.

As it turned out, Satina knew *all* about the Company. Had since before we ever even stepped foot on the island. In fact, half of the snooping she'd encouraged me to do wasn't to stop the Conduit, but to see what more I could learn about them.

She'd known the Company and the Brothers were one and the same. She knew the Conduit's magic had been contorted by a magical provision granted by the Company. That was how she was able to use stored Supplicant blood, as if the shelf-life rule didn't apply to her. Satina had known from the onset that the Company was putting Ameena and Archibald against each other, and that the provisions they had granted each of them was causing the magic to mutate.

She played it off saying she didn't want us focused on the wrong thing, but Abram and I didn't see it that way. It wasn't her place to decide what information we should base our decisions on, no matter what she thought.

We'd insisted she tell us everything she knew about the Company, but all she would tell us is that they were causing magic to mutate in ways we wouldn't understand—which would explain Ameena's bull-like appearance. People were selling their souls to get help from the Company without realizing the Company was the one fabricating the problems to begin with.

We'd asked Satina why, and she's said, "That's what you need to find out."

And that's about when Abram snapped on her about keeping things from us. She took a hint and stormed off, but unfortunately, I still doubted that would be the last we saw of her.

"Come on," Abram said, giving me a nudge. "They're boarding."

I said goodbye to Ramsey and Briar, looked one last time at this island that very nearly became my final resting place, and headed toward the gate.

As we stepped into line to board, Abram gave me a nudge. "I think he wants to see you."

Following Abram's finger, I spotted Huntsman standing off in the distance. His ax was strapped to his back, and his hands were in his pockets.

"Do we have a minute?" I asked. "I think I need to talk to him."

"Of course." Abram kissed me on the lips. "I'll get our seats settled on the plane. Take all the time you need. And Charisse." He squeezed my hand. "Thank him for me."

I smile as I neared Huntsman and, though he didn't return it, I could tell a cloud had been lifted from him.

"I don't think that's allowed here," I said playfully, pointing to his ax.

He laughed easily. "Oh, come now. Surely you realize no one else here can see it."

I raised my eyebrows, certain I would never get the hang of this whole magic thing. "I'm not sure what I know anymore. Like why you're even here right now. Don't tell me you still plan to off us for the king."

Another laugh, and this time with a lasting smile. He was so handsome it was making me uneasy—I was in love with Abram. Though I supposed it was only human to still notice when someone was hot.

"Not here to end you," he said, dimple peeking out from beneath his shadow on his jaw. "The opposite, in fact. I wanted to make sure you got away unscathed."

"You know I have someone for that," I said. "And a pretty

badass set of super powers of my own. I'll be fine." I stared at him for a few beats. "Why are you really here?"

"My brother," he said quietly, the smile slipping away. "I want to apologize to you for the part he played in all of this. What you and your lover went through was horrific, and if I could have stopped it—"

"Stop it." I shook my head. "You're not your brother, and you didn't do anything wrong. In fact, I think you did most of it right. You're one of the good guys, Huntsman. Don't forget that."

"There's much I won't forget about my time here, Charisse. You among them." He gave me a nod. "You're quite special, quite spectacular."

"Well, you're not so bad yourself." I bit my lip, my eyes flickering to the ground. "You know, I saw you in the castle. I saw what Ameena did to you." I looked back up at him. "Who was in the casket?"

"Someone who shouldn't have been," he said evenly. "I told you, there are many facets to my story, many wrongs I have to right if I have any chance at redemption."

"Where are you gonna go now?"

"To do what good guys do, Charisse Bellamy. To right wrongs. Some of them my own."

"Well, if there ever comes a time when you feel like your brother needs to be freed—"

"I'll find you," he finished. "Until then, be safe."

I gave him a smile and patted him on the shoulder in parting.

"Oh!" I said. "Before I forget—because if I don't ask you, I'm never gonna forgive myself—under that shirt of yours is a pretty righteous set of abs, right?"

"Most definitely," he answered, offering another of those heart-melting smiles.

"Thought so," I said, and I twirled back toward the plane, back toward Abram and *his* righteous set of abs. No one would ever compare.

CONNER KRESSLEY & REBECCA HAMILTON

~

LANDING in New York was a world away from the tropical and airy atmosphere of Grimoult, but I loved it. It felt like coming home. The obscenely crowded streets, the graffiti lining the walls, the way people were way too rude for no reason; I was in my element.

"Are you sure this is the right place?" Abram asked as we walked down 2nd Avenue.

An old woman—the sort you would imagine baking cookies and knitting quilts in her spare time—had just bumped into him and screamed, "Hey, watch where you're going, flat ass!"

"You'll get used to it. It's sort of the flavor of the city. And don't worry," I said, giving him a kiss on the cheek. "It's not flat."

"Where are we headed first?" he asked, a small smirk playing at the corners of his lips.

"There's a pizza place right around the corner. Antonio's. I had a lot of great nights there, and a lot of awesome slices. I figured we could head there, order a pie, and have a good old time."

"Or, we can get it to go, head back to the hotel, and I'll show you what a good old time really is."

"You *are* a beast," I said, giggling.

And the sad part was, he *was* still a beast, and not just in the bedroom. I thought giving his curse away would change that, but apparently he'd done little more than *share* his curse with Ameena. He still had to fight the pull of the moon, and he still had to leave me come midnight. Although, he was happy about that—happy he could still protect me, even though I'd already proven I could do quite a bit of the saving myself.

"We protect each other," he'd said. But I still hated it.

As we made the left toward Antonio's, cars sat deadlocked in traffic, and for the first time in ages, I felt like me...and not the Conduit/Supplicant me. I was the Charisse Bellamy from before.

288

But I was better, because I had Abram at my side. I had returned here complete.

"Took you long enough," came an irritatingly familiar voice ahead of us.

I gulped, knowing who it was before my gaze even set on her. Satina stood in front of the door to Antonio's, a pizza box in her hand, dressed in long coat with mink at the neck and sunglasses even though it was dark out. Of course, she didn't look like the first two Satinas, or her real self, but I knew it was her. "I hope everyone likes mushrooms."

"What the hell are you doing here, Satina?" Abram growled. "Also, you know I hate mushrooms."

"I was waiting for you." She scoffed as though feigning hurt feelings. "You don't think these missions just set themselves up, do you? I've been here for two days now getting the pieces into place."

"Oh, no." Abram shook his head. "No more missions, not right now. We're here to relax. We're here to enjoy each other's company. We're not here to fix something."

"Not something," she answered with a grin. "Someone. And it just so happens he's headed this way right now."

We both turned and, as soon as I saw him, my heart fell.

He looked nearly exactly the same as he had the last time I saw him. The same shaggy hair, the same light eyes, the same crooked smile that had melted my heart and kept me with him for entirely too long.

"Charlie…" I muttered before he got close enough to hear me.

"Charlie?" Abram asked. "Charlie Prince, as in your old boyfriend?"

The second Charlie smiled at me from up the sidewalk, it was as though a spell lifted from my mind, flooding me with memories of him that seemed impossible to have forgotten. And yet, I had. Somehow, the most crushing reality of my relationship with

Charlie came hurtling back into my mind, and I instantly wished I could erase it again—both from my mind and from reality.

"Listen," I said, turning to Abram. "There's something you don't know about him...something that happened here, things that I should have told you about."

Abram's expression fell. "What are you talking about, Charisse?"

"Charlie and I—"

"Well, if it isn't Charisse Bellamy," Charlie said, reaching us. He smiled his crooked smile and batted shaggy hair out of his light eyes. His voice was as deep and free as it had ever been. "As I live and breathe. I didn't know I was coming to meet you."

I couldn't speak. Suddenly plummeting off that cliff didn't seem so bad.

"Charlie Prince?" Abram asked, extending his hand.

"I see my reputation precedes me." He took Abram's hand and gave a firm shake. "I assume you're the guy banging my wife?"

The End

Continue the Conduit Series with Book 3, Charmed by the Beast.

# ABOUT THE AUTHORS

Conner Kressley is a USA TODAY Bestselling Author represented by Rossano Trentin of TZLA. He is an avid reader and all around lover of storytelling. His book "The Breaker's Code" is the first in the epic "Fixed Points" series that pits free will against fate and true love against good intentions and bad situations. You can learn more about Conner and his books below.

Visit His Website: http://connerkressleybooks.weebly.com/

NEW YORK TIMES, USA TODAY, AND WALL STREET JOURNAL bestselling author Rebecca Hamilton lives in Georgia with her husband and five kids, all of whom inspire her writing. Somewhere in between using magic to disappear booboos and sorcery to heal emotional wounds, she takes to her fictional worlds to see what perilous situations her characters will find themselves in next. Represented by Rossano Trentin of TZLA, Rebecca has been published internationally, in three languages.

Visit Her Website: http://www.rebeccahamilton.com/